A False
Sense
of
Well Being

A False Sense of Sense of Well Being

Jeanne Braselton

Ballantine Books • New York

Grateful acknowledgment is made to David Bottoms for permission to reprint
lines from "Coasting Toward Midnight at the Southeastern Fair," from
Armored Hearts: Selected and New Poems, Copper Canyon Press.
Copyright © 1995 by David Bottoms.

The beauty and poetry of the prayers listed in this book can be found in
*The Book of Common Prayer, and Administration of the Sacraments, and Other Rites
and Ceremonies of the Church. Together with The Psalter of Psalms of David,
According to the Use of the Episcopal Church.*
The Seabury Press, New York.

www.ballantinebooks.com

Cataloging-in-Publication Data for this title is available from the Library of Congress

ISBN 0–345–44311–X

Text design by Holly Johnson

Manufactured in the United States of America

First Edition: October 2001

10 9 8 7 6 5 4 3 2 1

For Charles Eldon Ingram

and Al Braselton,

companions

We all want to break our orbits,
float like a satellite gone wild in space,
run the risk of disintegration.
We all want to take our lives in our own hands
and hurl them out among the stars.

DAVID BOTTOMS

FROM "COASTING TOWARD MIDNIGHT

AT THE SOUTHEASTERN FAIR"

ACKNOWLEDGMENTS

Special thanks are due Kaye Gibbons, whose friendship and generosity of spirit give me faith enough to believe in all manner of miracles.

Thanks, also, to those friends and fellow writers who endured my endless chatter about this book and offered encouragement, inspiration, and guidance: Richard Bausch, Sam Camp Berry, Clint Chezem, Stella Connell, George deMan, Jr., Philip F. Deaver, Jon Hershey, Mary Hood, Silas House, Bobby Carroll Johnson, Terry Kay, Sheldon Kelley, Dawn McFadden, Karen Sprague Marsee, Dr. Robert F. Norton, Maureen O'Neal, Padgett Powell, Arthur Smith, Jim Smith, Lee Smith, Janice White, Dr. Barbara C. Wyatt and Dr. C. J. Wyatt; the late James Dickey, whose advice and kindness live on; and the late Calder Willingham, friend and mentor, for whom my own fictional Glenville is a tribute.

A False
Sense
of
Well Being

ONE

Dear friends in Christ,
here in the presence of Almighty God, let us kneel in silence, and with
penitent and obedient hearts confess our sins,
so that we may obtain forgiveness
by his infinite goodness and mercy.

CONFESSION OF SIN

THE BOOK OF COMMON PRAYER

I was married eleven years before I started imagining how different life could be if my husband were dead. Beginning that year,
and not, to my recollection, prompted by any overt unkindness
or sudden disruption of affection, images of random damage, of
events more simple and unpredictable than murder, invaded my
dreams both sleeping and awake. The more I tried not to think
about it, to purge these worrisome ideas out of my head, the louder
my unconscious mind wailed. When I woke in the sheet-twisted

dark and found myself pasted to the body of my very real husband, his whimpering snore as high-pitched as a cat's, it was a bitter comfort. The familiar smell of him on the pillows, a pungent mix of his daily dousings of cologne and hair tonics, seeped into my pores with all the nauseating effects of a virus. I spent my nights, and an embarrassing number of days, picturing how I would react, what plans I would make, when misfortune cast me in a new role: that of grieving widow.

I would see him rounding the curve of the old highway, eyes closing, driving head-on into someone else's headlights. Stumbling into the line of fire during a convenience-store robbery. Stepping off the curb to be dragged under the wheels of a bus. When he fell asleep in front of the television late at night, head tilted backward over his chair, I would see him strangled that way, his breath cut off in mid-snore, a large bubble of exhaled air dancing cartoon-style in front of his face.

Every day I imagined some new way for it to happen. I saw the harmless objects of our ordinary lives turning against him, his body betraying him in one violent, irretrievable moment.

He'd crack his skull on the shower wall while reaching for a towel.

He'd try to light the pilot on the furnace and trigger a freak explosion.

He'd stumble over a child's bicycle in a neighbor's driveway and snap his neck.

Once, when I was turning my key in the kitchen door, my left arm balancing a bag of groceries, I found myself thinking, *He could be dead inside this house, in our bed, and I wouldn't know it.*

Sometimes he would fall as he made the climb toward the sixth hole at Glenville Meadows, his heart squeezing in upon itself with a final cholesterol-clogged pang, his long, rigid body landing like a toppled game piece on the freshly mown fairway. The last thing he'd see is the dimpled ball sailing skyward toward the green, where it rides the hillside on waves of light and dark, hopelessly out of his reach.

T W O

The first time I make my confession I know I'm making a big mistake, as if I've taken the wrong exit off the interstate and am barreling full speed down rain-slick, unlit streets with no on-ramp or telephone booth in sight. It's a Saturday, the day my next-door neighbor Donna Lindsey and I reserve for what we affectionately call our "suicide strolls." At 6 A.M. sharp on most Saturdays, Donna and I meet at the boxwood hedge separating our two lawns—lawns kept green, well-trimmed, and dandelion-free by the Lawn Doctor, not our husbands—and set out along the bicycle paths that wind around the cookie-cutter Georgians and mock Tudors in our thoroughly modern and fitness-friendly subdivision.

Donna and I begin our walk by streetlight and moonlight, leaving our homes bundled in sweat suits and windbreakers, stealthy as teenagers sneaking out past curfew. Much of our route is uphill until we reach the cul-de-sac where, in a mirror version of our own cul-de-sac, Phase Four of the Heritage Knoll development ends, so we usually talk only on the way back to our respective homes, when we can catch our breath.

Donna and I swing our arms purposefully and tell ourselves we aren't getting older but healthier. We wave to the other, younger wives who jog at a faster clip, the cheeks of their aerobicized size-six butts barely jiggling. These women all carry or strap to their arms and legs reflective devices that each weigh five pounds or more, and when they trot past us, graceful as butterflies, pores freshly scrubbed and cucumber-soothed and without the slightest hint of perspiration, one has the distinct impression that they might, at any moment, take flight if they were not weighted down so carefully.

We keep walking, dreaming of the day when we can look just like them, when we can prance into Rich's Department Store and buy identical pairs of red silk running shorts in a size six, completed, of course, by red silk cutoff T-shirts that show off our tanned and liposuctioned midriffs. We tell ourselves we're happy with our own less-than-flawless bodies in case our plan doesn't work, and I'm guessing it probably won't, so until then we resent the presence of these other wives for making us want it so badly.

It is during today's walk, on the return trip down a particularly steep hill, that Donna tells me she's having an affair with a salesman in the department store where she works part time, that it's been going on for two months, and that she needs me to tell her husband David we're going shopping next Tuesday after work. David will never even ask me about it, she points out a little too enthusiastically, so it isn't like I'll actually have to lie for her, but she wants to warn me just in case a lie is necessary. She also hints that it wouldn't be wise for me to be seen in my yard between the hours of 5 and 8 P.M. on Tuesday since, quite obviously, I can't be at the Glenville Meadows Mall with her and trying to resuscitate my ailing geraniums at the same time.

"I'm sleeping with that young guy in menswear."

That's actually how she breaks the news. She says it matter-of-factly, as if she's just told me, "I'm painting my kitchen blue."

I remember that Donna made a point of introducing me to him a week or so earlier when I stopped by the mall to pick her up for lunch. When I arrived, I found him leaning over her jewelry counter, two fingers looped through a display of freshwater pearl bracelets.

His name is Perry Ferguson, and on the day we met he wore stylish burgundy suspenders over a cream-colored button-down broadcloth shirt and a pair of neatly pressed black gabardine trousers, and he had a lock of blond hair that, despite his efforts to slick it into place, kept falling over one of his eyes. He did, I noticed, wear a wedding ring. And he's young. At least ten years younger than Donna is my guess, which means he's maybe fifteen years younger than me. His leaning over her counter, touching those bracelets the way he did, was hardly the innocent gesture it had seemed.

I can't think of a thing to say. This is news I do not want to hear.

As we walk, we pass 1980s-style Victorians and country ranches, houses we've visited with our husbands for impromptu dinner parties and Neighborhood Watch–sponsored backyard barbecues, houses where the owners spend weeks searching antique stores for the perfect armoire and wouldn't dare refinish it. A lawn mower cranks somewhere nearby, a clear violation of the 10-4 rules. The people on this street must mow their own lawns. The Lawn Doctor knows the rules.

"You don't have to look so surprised," she says finally. "You could show a little enthusiasm. C'mon. A little, well, a little something. I mean, we're both married so it's safe, right?"

I'm surprised I don't blurt out, "How could you?" or "What about your children?" Her logic on the other issue leaves me more than a little stunned. Safe how? Safe when?

"You're using condoms? I mean, that's what people do these days, don't they?" I can't believe I'm even asking the question, that the question even needs to be asked. Sheltered suburbanite that I am, safely married in an era when safe-sex commercials no longer shock, my fear of any wayward step outside monogamy is all wrapped up in latex.

"Most of the time."

"Most."

"Well okay, so we did the first time. But I told you. He's married. It's not like we have to worry about that."

"That doesn't—"

"That's the best part. Like I said, safe." And with that, she turns and does a little backward jog away from me, loose brown curls bobbing around her sweatband, a tight Cheshire Cat smile spreading across her face.

By the time we reach the light of Shadowwood Lane and make a sweaty path to the kitchen in my own cookie-cutter Georgian, where we pour out two large glasses of bottled water with a twist of lemon, Donna tells me all the details, a few of which I'm not comfortable knowing. Like the fact that Perry Ferguson has a fondness not only for suspenders but also for silk ties that, in the heat of passion, he winds around Donna's thin tennis player's wrists. I picture her preparing for this as her last act of undressing—sitting on the hotel bed, carefully unhooking the safety chains and heavy engraved clasps of her collection of gold bracelets, placing them in a shimmering stack on the nightstand alongside his wristwatch, then holding her hands up to him, penitent and willing.

"C'mon, Jessie. Haven't you ever thought about what it'd be like to be with another man after all these years?" she asks, grinning at me because she already knows the answer to her own question and is lost in some private memory of a recent rendezvous. "And don't lie to me. I know you have."

Just two months earlier, Donna and her husband David celebrated their tenth anniversary by taking a weeklong cruise to what the glossy brochure described as "exotic, picture-postcard ports of call in the Caribbean." She'd seemed happy then. I couldn't imagine what had happened to make things go so wrong.

"Hell, I'd forgotten what great sex feels like. But this man? This man is just so yummy." She actually licks her lips.

She has me on that one. I feel like a twelve-year-old at a slumber party, eager to ask her best friend's older sister what it's like to French-kiss a boy. I want her to tell me exactly what it feels like to be held in an unfamiliar way, to be touched by unfamiliar hands, but in the end, I lose my nerve. I'm beginning to be embarrassed by this whole conversation, as if Donna has removed her sweatshirt and paraded topless down the middle of Shadowwood Lane.

Donna, on the other hand, seems to take a certain pride in savoring the moment, as if she's just been named Infidelity's Woman of the Year and is glad that I, friend and confidante, am there to witness it. She sits in my kitchen and drinks her water in big, noisy gulps, then slams the glass on the table. She stares dreamily at my ceiling while sucking her lemon slice.

I study the view from my kitchen window. The dogwoods the Lawn Doctor planted last year are just beginning to bloom. Beyond them, with the first rays of cloud-filtered sunlight, the shiny brass heads of the automatic sprinkler system pop up like so many ground-hogs, spraying a rainbow-tinted mist across the row of thin trunks with every rotation.

"I've been dreaming that Turner will be killed in some kind of accident. That he'll, well, that he'll die," I say, all too conscious that my husband, even on a Saturday, stays true to his daily routine and must be standing in front of our bathroom mirror upstairs, razor in hand. "What do you think that means?"

Funny thing is, she acts like she doesn't even hear me. She's tying her shoe, the shrunken lemon slice still stuck between her teeth.

If I'm lucky, Donna's feeling the same way about the revelation of her affair and will have some sympathy for my predicament. Maybe she's wishing she'd kept her own story to herself. This can be just between us. We can forgive each other. Act like it never happened.

I study my nails, square-edged and ragged, taupe polish flaking at the cuticles. Upstairs, I hear a door slam. Donna is still tying the lace of the same shoe. She's tied it no fewer than four times.

Donna pops the lemon slice out of her mouth and peers at me in a way that suggests she thinks I'm a complete idiot. "Oh for God's sake, Jessie," she says. "That husband of yours will live to be a hun-dred. His kind always does."

"What's that supposed to mean?"

"You know, all that mother-and-apple-pie crap, wholesome as

white bread. The kind that's never had a day of fun in their whole lives and resents anyone who has."

"Think so, huh?"

Needless to say, Donna and my husband are not the best of friends. He says she's "flighty." She thinks he's, and these are her exact words, "got a metal rod up his ass." I can't disagree with either of them.

"Well," she says, pausing dramatically, "maybe your dreams mean you really want to kill the son of a bitch. You just don't have the guts to do it yourself." Then, "God, Jessie, I may be cheating on my husband, but at least I don't want to kill him. Not yet anyway."

 *THREE*

My husband Turner is a creature of finely tuned routines, his life dictated to him by clocks and calendars and the Things to Do reminders he punches into the electronic scheduler he carries with him a good sixteen hours of every day and places on the nightstand, within reach, just in case he wakes up and needs to remember something important. He reminds himself of everything. And not just stuff from work. Everything gets punched in. When to renew his driver's license, tee-off dates with his golf friends, all his various appointments to get his teeth cleaned and to check his blood pressure, his cholesterol, his prostate, and the growth patterns of any suspicious moles. He's got everything planned five years from now. A tinny, piercing alarm goes off every Friday evening, signaling that it's time for him to watch *Wall Street Week*.

Punctuality, consistency, neatness, consideration for others. These are the traits that define his life, and, I sometimes think, are the only ones that do. He's the kind of man civic clubs can count on to volunteer for fund-raising campaigns and can trust to watch the till at bake sales and carnivals. I've often pictured him as a schoolboy, all his crayons sharpened and stacked in a school box, his head bent over a coloring book, taking great care to stay inside the lines.

He is, at fifty-four, a commercial loan officer at First Glenville National Bank. He long ago earned the rank of vice president, though one could argue that the title was bestowed more in tribute to his seniority and his tenuous social connections of long past than in recognition of any outstanding performance.

The First Glenville National Bank is itself an anomaly, having survived the past decade, but just barely, without being gobbled up by some giant multistate megabank. Once recognized as the oldest and most prominent bank in Glenville, Georgia, it now ranks a solid last place in the market, muscled aside by competitors who've wired up ATMs on every corner and, in their drive throughs, give out handfuls of I LOVE MY BANK! stickers for customers' children and gourmet dog biscuits for their pets. At the branch of First Glenville National Bank where Turner works, the brick is starting to crumble, the roof leaks, and the surrounding lawn, once lavishly landscaped, is turning to sand. No wonder nobody wants to buy it.

When I look at my husband sitting across from me at the dining room table, calmly slicing his potatoes with the same solemn expression he might have while calculating the amortization of a loan, I am seized with the sudden desire to make grave but preposterous announcements.

By the way honey, I found out today I have cancer. Would you please pass the salt?

Or, upon my collapsing to the floor, *Dear, don't let me spoil your dinner, but I believe I'm having a heart attack.*

Something tells me that even news of some medical calamity would not break his composure, that he would view it instead as the kind of situation necessitating a cool head so the proper insurance companies can be notified, the proper forms can be filed.

We have become one of those couples that spend their days moving around within the institution of marriage like the planets orbiting the sun. There is an unseen and unfelt gravitational force that keeps us locked together in our own elliptical paths, but we remain far enough away from each other so we won't collide. The space across our long, well-polished dining room table is becoming wider and wider.

Despite what my dreams insist on telling me, my husband is a good man.

Turner Maddox is a good man.

Decent.

Hardworking.

A pillar of the community.

That's what everyone says. Good is what he is, going about his life quietly and with the kind of single-mindedness touted by business consultants and motivational speakers. He reads paperbacks that inevitably have exclamation points in their titles. *1001 Ways to Motivate Your Team!* or *Plan, Proceed & Win!* and so on, ad nauseam, and reads them seriously. This is where he picked up the idea for that electronic scheduler. Some book told him he needed one, top of the line for the on-the-go executive and all that, so he ran off to the nearest electronic gizmos store to get himself that very model, though buying it may be one of the only on-the-go activities he's en-joyed in years. I have fantasies of stuffing that scheduler down the garbage disposal, all the dates of his future grinding away in bytes down the drain.

&

Many women complain loudly, and often, about their husbands leaving crusted toothpaste around the toothpaste tube or wet towels draped over the side of the tub.

Not me, not ever.

Turner wipes down every bathroom surface. Even leaves the toilet seat down, every time. He can't walk through a room without turning to straighten a picture frame, without running an index fin-ger over the edge of a table to detect the slightest hint of dust. Just once I'd like to walk into our bathroom and see his boxers hanging from the towel rack or short black whiskers on the porcelain—telltale signs of a masculine presence that I imagine must be associ-ated with raging testosterone and unbridled lust.

Turner is in bed every night by 10:30, asleep within ten minutes.

He wakes every morning at precisely 6:55, anticipating the alarm that goes off at 7; is in the shower by 7:10; showered, shaved, dressed and ready for each day by 7:35.

"I sleep just like a baby," he proclaims, and this is true. The whistling mews exhaled from his mouth in sleep may annoy me to distraction, but they're not loud enough to rouse him. Every morn-ing he wakes "rested and refreshed," the lines of his mouth upturned ever so slightly in his Rotary Club perfect smile.

By 7:40, Turner is standing in front of the toaster, orange juice in hand. Alarmed into ever more drastic culinary restraint by news reports, his doctor's advice, and the very real fact that not a small number of friends his age have dropped dead from heart attacks, he has, over the past few years, given up caffeine, eggs, bacon, butter and most margarines, red meat, cheese, and some artificial sweeteners. He spreads a thin layer of low-sodium marmalade on his whole-wheat toast.

He's out the door no later than 8:05 for his ten-minute commute to the bank, leaving the house every Monday through Friday in a dark gray or navy suit, the crisp corners of his starched white pinpoint-stitched shirts framing his neckline and wrists in the latest Wall Street Gone South fashion, his gold cuff links anchored in place and gleaming with engraved initials. Turner Quinn Maddox, both of which, the cuff links and the name, he inherited from his father. He wears this uniform even on casual days, when all the other employees, the bank's forty-year-old CEO included, are dressed in T-shirts or sweatshirts emblazoned with the bank's cheery dollar-sign logo.

When we first met, I'd never been around a man who wore starched white shirts on a daily basis, and I was drawn to them like a schoolgirl dazzled by the sight of her boyfriend in a prom-night tuxedo.

When we held hands, I enjoyed the scratch of the stiff fabric against my wrist.

When we kissed, I found myself reaching up to touch him, to dip my fingers into the slight space between his shirt collar and his neck, to run my palms over the sharp angles framing his silk ties. In those days, the sight of those shirts hanging in Turner's closet, fresh from the dry cleaners and still wrapped in plastic, could move me to tears.

The way I remember it is that Turner and I stumbled into a lasting friendship, a quiet and unquestioned closeness. I saw his solemn determination as sophistication, his steadiness as strength of character. His soft touch was a welcome change from the inept pawings of men my own age, and under his care, I was, for the first time in my life, at ease with the world and sure of my place in it.

During those first years of our marriage, we spent most evenings sitting in identical overstuffed chairs in the den, listening to National Public Radio and reading, looking up occasionally to catch the eye of the other, and smiling, as if to say in unison, *This is good. This is right.* In those days the stillness that filled the rooms of our new home was welcomed by us both.

Just before 10 P.M. every Friday night, he would take my hand and lead me to the bedroom, where we would undress in the darkness, sliding effortlessly, and without words, between cool, unwrinkled sheets. If I hadn't known he was married before, it would have been easy to have mistaken him for a virgin. Every touch was a question. Every kiss explored with caution, as if he feared a mere puff of breath escaping from his lips would leave me with wounds he could not repair.

I loved him even more for his gentleness and his timid caresses. Every tender moment was as if he were saying, *I treasure you.*

In retrospect, I also know that what I wanted then was to belong to something, and my being with Turner set the stage for all that— for marriage and children, to a membership in Glenville Meadows, to anything I wanted. Back then, I wanted a life straight out of *Southern Living*, one with dinner parties and a gazebo out back and a landscaped lawn that greeted visitors with a lighted pathway. In those days I would stare at the pages of that magazine and picture myself standing at the front door, baby on my hip, waving to my husband as he left for work in our minivan. I clipped recipes for five-course menus that featured exotic ingredients available only at the upscale supermarket in town. I studied mantel decorations and table linens, draperies and china patterns, club chairs and nesting tables. After reading an article about how handwritten letters and thank-you notes were becoming a dying art, I spent $300 on several sets of monogrammed correspondence cards made of Italian watercolor paper, a few of which I'm still using more than a decade later.

⅗

We were, after a respectable two-year courtship, married in the Glenville County Courthouse by a magistrate court judge. It wasn't exactly a wedding from a magazine cover, but it was a wedding and that's what counted.

Turner was forty-two. I was twenty-six. It was my first marriage. His second. We got married at the courthouse because he'd been through a big wedding once before and somehow convinced me that such a spectacle was a jinx to marital happiness.

At the time I admired him for this, for wedding me in this way. It was romantic and a bit impulsive, and despite the dingy surroundings of the Glenville County Courthouse and our less-than-photogenic presiding minister, I was happy about it all, happy to be pronounced his wife no matter where we were. Elopement, after all, appealed to my sense of drama. It was as if we were characters in a novel, mavericks escaping the trappings of our hostile families to make a secret life together. I also knew that from what I'd seen of the few remaining members of Turner's family, any event bringing my family and his family together in the same room—even briefly, and even in a very big room—would not be the best idea.

All you have to do is look at our family photographs to see the differences in our backgrounds. There are photos of Turner's family everywhere in our house. High-ranking military officers dating back to the Civil War. Laughing groups of handsome young men and lithesome young women in formal dress, dancing in gazebos and in formal gardens. Long-dead aunts giving violin concerts on the stages of private finishing schools. Boys playing cricket and rugby and lacrosse, sports no one in my family has ever heard of. Infants in christening gowns more elaborate than most wedding dresses, their tiny round faces already seemingly aware of the myriad of obligations ahead of them.

The few photographs I have of my family, pre-1940 or so, show an altogether different culture. Miners huddled together at the entrance of a shaft where a deadly explosion killed them all the next year. Toothless women in their thirties dressed in flour-sack dresses and surrounded by their children, all barefoot, always one of them with a finger halfway up his nose. Slack-shouldered farmers posed beside their prize possession, the family mule. Soldiers in ragtag clothing who were rumored to have been deserters, having fled the battlefield to change their names and become Wild West outlaws.

They're all dead now, all of them, but these images, though yellowed with age, speak volumes. The photographs of my family are not on display. They're all in the attic, gathering dust.

So off to the courthouse we went, Turner in his gray business suit and me in a new Laura Ashley dress.

The judge, whose teeth made a constant and distinct clicking sound, conducted the entire wedding ceremony from behind a desk piled high with business license applications and permits for selling alcohol. The remains of an egg-salad sandwich, which our ceremony had interrupted his finishing, was perched on the corner of one of these stacks. He read the generic, government-sanctioned vows that we repeated back to him.

"Do you take this woman (click) to be your lawfully (click, clack) wedded (click, clack) wife?" And so on.

During all this, I was sure I caught him sneaking glimpses at that sandwich, the smell of which, mayonnaise-full and slightly sour, was not wholly restrained by its rewrapping. Maybe he feared one of us would snatch it from his desk and, with arms interlocked, feed it to each other in the sloppy, romantic fashion of couples eating the first piece of wedding cake.

Our two witnesses were recruited from the musty corners of the county deed room across the hall. Our one wedding photo was an out-of-focus Polaroid coaxed from the judge after he scrawled his illegible signature on our marriage license and sent our witnesses shuffling back, not a word uttered by either of them, to the safety of their racks of maps. In the photograph, Turner's arm is around my shoulder, his face staring into the camera with a serious smile. I'm looking to my right, my head blurred, caught in a turn.

I remember being happy that day. Remember, in fact, that I turned to look at the rain that was still falling beyond the yellowing glass of the one window in the judge's office. Remember that Turner and I, emerging on the courthouse steps, erupted into laughter, as if we'd survived some important though badly scripted occasion.

&

After Turner and I eloped on that afternoon in May, he brought me to All Saints Episcopal Church, the church of his childhood, where we climbed the wide stone steps and walked, hand in hand, through the heavy engraved oak doors. I remember trying to tiptoe across the darkly polished floor. With my first step into the sanctuary, my feet felt conspicuously heavy, like I was wearing twenty pounds of lead lifts in my shoes. Each footfall generated an echo that reverberated from the floor to the vaulted ceiling and back again.

At the conclusion of that day's services, the priest, a longtime friend of Turner's, asked us to stand before the altar, hand in hand, while he recited the blessing for a civil marriage. I had planned to tiptoe the whole way, but when I stood up, my left heel lodged itself in a groove of the old floor, nearly causing me to pitch forward and out of my seat. I held on tight to Turner's arm as I righted myself. I wore the same Laura Ashley dress I'd worn to our courthouse wedding.

"Turner Quinn Maddox and Jessie Eleanor Kilgore Maddox, you have come here today to seek the blessing of God and of His Church upon your marriage. I require, therefore, that you promise, with the help of God, to fulfill the obligations which Christian Marriage demands."

We said our requisite "I do's" all over again, in front of the entire congregation, and they responded with the requisite "Amen."

The priest then took it upon himself to add a few words of his own choosing.

"Despite the fact that the happy couple was too impulsive to have waited for a proper church ceremony," he said, pausing to allow a wave of laughter to wash over the congregation, "their marriage is blessed by this church and is holy in God's eyes." A few of those seated said "Amen" again. That part wasn't scripted for them, so they looked around at everyone else to see if it had been the proper thing to do.

The announcement itself caused quite a stir among the society matrons who watched us from their cushioned seats in the sanctuary. I felt my face go as red as those cushions as they craned their sleek blue-tinted coiffures around the coiffures of the friends seated in front of them, all to get a look at the purportedly happy and impulsive couple.

Outside the church, under the bright canopy of a yellow ginkgo, a small crowd of expensively perfumed well-wishers swirled around us briefly before turning away to disarm the alarms on their Volvos, Saabs, and BMW sedans.

To the members of All Saints, I am these four things, which I list here in order of their importance. Number One: Mrs. Turner Maddox, loyal and faithful wife. Number Two: Secretary for the Glenville Hills Garden Club, most of whose members are in their seventies and attend services with us at All Saints. Number Three: Dutiful member of the Glenville Society Cotillion. Number Four: Occasional dinner party hostess, and not a very good one at that. I think that about covers it.

Someday in the future I see myself sitting in the sanctuary at All Saints—but in the front row then—hands folded in my lap while the blue heads seated behind me will be whispering.

She looks devastated.

And I will be.

Don't know how she'll get along without him.

I'm not sure about that either.

They seemed so happy.

After all that, I will be here still. I will find myself consoled by regular bridge club lunches and occasional out-of-town excursions, not with the couples who are our friends now, but with the other widows who will claim me as one of their sad little band and as their "latest project." Invitations will be extended to me out of courtesy, but not for long, and not to events where the seating arrangements are boy-girl-boy-girl and all twelve place settings must be used.

People will begin to speak in hushed tones whenever I leave a room.

Think she'll remarry?

I haven't thought that far ahead.

She's holding up well, don't you think?

⁊

After we married, I did what I thought *Southern Living* wives should do. I enrolled in a frantic succession of adult education workshops that promised to leave me an accomplished watercolorist, sculptor, violinist, poet, and flower arranger. I'd grown bored with community theater, I told myself, and had other artistic ventures to pursue. A making of a home for Turner and me. A making of our new life together. A new family.

Whatever I was searching for in those classes I never found, failing miserably on all fronts. So when the invitation to join the Glenville Society Cotillion arrived, I accepted. Turner had been drawn to my artistic side from the beginning, had even come to a few of our community-theater productions, but I never felt he took the theater or my art classes seriously, so the Glenville Society Cotillion was something he wholly approved of my doing. The group was founded in 1929 by his paternal grandmother as, in her words, "an appropriate social and community service league for the married ladies of Glenville society." It was because of Turner's grandmother that I was voted in unanimously, since no one could argue with a legacy like that. Now I spend at least one night every few weeks attending various committee meetings held at members' homes. We embrace each other upon arriving and spend the evening around candlelit dining room tables or in backyard gardens, trying to come up with the "good works" that will earn our club the proper status it deserves while transforming our town into "a better place to live and raise our families." Those are the rules in our membership handbook.

We easily afford membership in Glenville Meadows, where Turner plays golf on most Saturdays and Sundays, wearing shirts and slacks in shades not known in nature. He usually shoots in the seventies, but keeps this fact a secret from those bank customers and prospective customers he entertains on the links. This is another trick he picked up from one of his paperbacks.

"Your game must be a little off today, Turner my boy," they tell him as his ball hooks expertly into the woods.

"Must be my lucky day," they say as another of his shots goes plop into a water hazard.

It's a strategy that works, though he hasn't had to use it much in recent months. His bank is losing customers, not picking up new ones.

&

I saved all the keepsakes of our romance. The photograph taken from behind the judge's desk. The ticket stub Turner received when he left the car in a multilevel parking deck across the street from the courthouse. A matchbook from the Peach Blossom Café, where we stopped for a secret celebration lunch. I even tried pressing a tiger lily he'd sent me between sheets of wax paper, but after a few months the flower fell apart when I tried to pick it up.

On our marriage license, a shadow print underneath our signatures depicts a young couple holding hands and walking down a cobblestone road that leads to a horizon where a cheerful greeting-card sun is rising. That couple looked nothing like Turner and me, and that fact was strangely unsettling. They seemed to me the unattainable romantic ideal to which we, and all other newly married couples, should aspire.

"Lots of folks frame these," said the judge, who waved the document in the air, as if he had good reason to believe its brief flight around the room would ensure our wedded happiness. "Cost a little (click, clack) more, but they make a real nice keepsake," he said, giving the parchment a final shake before handing it to us.

I put everything in a lavender shoe box, tied the box with a white satin ribbon and put it in the attic, inside the large oak chest where I keep other mementos. A spelling bee ribbon from fourth grade. A stuffed bear won for me at a school carnival by a boy whose name I can no longer remember. Movie stubs and concert tickets and theater programs from dates that went nowhere. Two of my grandmother Kilgore's quilts. Photographs of onetime friends and confidantes who were promised devotion forever but are strangers to me now.

On Saturday mornings when Turner is out shooting nine holes with Frank Daniels, I sometimes go up to the attic and unlock that chest, to look and touch these things I've saved, trying to remember why I put them there in the first place. My whole life is wrapped up in these boxes, all stuffed into a bigger box I've packed with cedar chips. Sometimes I worry I'll have nothing more worth adding.

&

It was Turner's record of marital bliss, or rather the lack of it, that caused my mother the most concern. Yet over the years she's come to love him, often seeming to enjoy his company more than mine. It was clear that Turner's entrance into our family unexpectedly raised the invisible standard by which all of us would be measured. I have, on occasion, accused her of being a little in love with him herself.

My friends, meanwhile, were all a bit mystified at this matching of Turner and me.

"What on earth do you see in him?"

"What could you possibly have in common?"

In their well-intended efforts to dissuade me, they all promised introductions to onetime fraternity brothers (attorneys and accountants, internists and dentists) they judged less boring and, in their opinion, more suitable for marriage. My friends couldn't fathom the age difference between us, and since it was a constant source of frustration for me to try to explain it to them, I finally stopped trying and let them think what they wanted.

Turner's friends viewed things from another angle altogether. Few of his male friends and colleagues were still married to their first wives. The ones who were eyed Turner and me with great suspicion and, it seemed to me, a little envy. Turner was obviously having a midlife crisis and I was, for a time, automatically cast into the unenviable role of "that girl Turner up and married." The first wives treated me coldly, although in all fairness, their reaction to me was one more of avoidance than confrontation. When we were together, they spoke mostly to Turner, rarely to me, and seemed to make a concentrated effort to steer any conversation to recollections unique to their generation or toward any pre-Jessie social event they shared with Turner's first wife, Anna Wilcox Maddox, who, judging from the stories they told, was the pretty, funny, and graceful sorority sister they all claimed as their closest friend. The fact that Anna Wilcox Maddox, after only two years of marriage, ran off with the Glenville Meadows golf pro—her whereabouts tracked only through the occasional postcard—seemed to escape their collective memory. Turner's first wife, it appeared to me, must have inherited not only the respect that came with very old money, but also an expectation of eccentricity brought on by her wealth. Nobody was surprised when she decided to squire away the golf pro, just as nobody was surprised when, at her debutante ball, she raised her white taffeta skirt, kicked off her dyed-to-match shoes, and pranced barefoot into the fountains in the center of the ballroom, belting out the lyrics from a popular show tune.

Those friends of his who were divorced and remarried, some several times, were more generous, even though I couldn't help but feel they were welcoming me as they would a new painting to be hung over Turner's mantel.

To them I was this year's model, a transition between Wife Number Two and Wife Number Three. Oddly enough, this often seemed a more insulting way of being ignored.

I can't say I blame any of them. Not now anyway, which carries with it an irony of which I'm all too aware.

Turner and I recently attended the wedding of a friend who, at fifty-one, beamed with all the happiness of a Boy Scout as Wife Number Two, a twenty-three-year-old fitness instructor, sashayed down the aisle, heel to toe in her pearl-encrusted pumps, to stand by his side. During the ceremony, she repeated her marriage vows in such a perky, singsong voice that I expected her to lead the entire wedding party out of our pews and onto the lawn for a mid-afternoon session of step aerobics.

Afterward, at the reception, I found myself alone with her for an unexpected and uncomfortable few minutes. As I looked into her young and hopeful face, I could think of absolutely nothing to say, no common ground between us. So we simply stood there, both of us looking into our wineglasses and around us at others who somehow managed to strike up friendly and benign conversations. When she took a sip of her wine, her lips left a collagen-full pout, in a blinding shade of neon pink, that extended halfway down the side of her glass.

Thankfully, it wasn't long before she was rescued by a trio of her bridesmaids, tanned and finely muscled young women whose smiles showed off wide mouthfuls of extravagantly white teeth. In a huddle of overlapping white and pink silk taffeta, they wrapped their outstretched arms around the bride protectively and led her toward the gifts table, as if compelled in their duty as bridesmaids to rescue her from any awkward social situation occurring so early in her marriage.

She was so young, so confident about the possibilities of her life and of marriage, ready to face the world with this new husband at her side. That, quite frankly, alarmed me. I could see how a man could fall for that. And fall hard.

FOUR

Give them wisdom and devotion in the ordering of their common life, that
each may be to the other a strength in need, a counselor in perplexity, a
comfort in sorrow, and a companion in joy. Amen.

THE CELEBRATION AND BLESSING OF A MARRIAGE

THE BOOK OF COMMON PRAYER

The first time I saw Wanda McNabb I caught her rummaging through the center drawer of my desk at the Glenville Wellness Center. She'd arrived for her appointment a few minutes early, while I was in the employee lounge getting a fresh cup of coffee, and when I turned the corner and walked around the carpet-covered wall of my cubicle, I found her there.

"Excuse me, but who are you and what are you doing at my desk?"

"Pencil," she said, without looking up. "I need a pencil." She reached a hand farther into the metal drawer, beyond where it jammed in mid-opening. Her fingers fished inside blindly, moving aside rulers and rubber bands and loose change.

"Let me see if I can find you a pencil around here somewhere," I offered. She looked up at me then, calm blue eyes centered in a face that revealed nothing beyond the wide grin that was still, inexplicably, displayed.

And then I knew. Her 10:30 A.M. appointment was right there on my calendar, but since I meet with so many clients each day I like to take at least a minute of preparation, preferably five minutes, between sessions. Her abrupt arrival, or mine, had the effect of catching me completely off guard.

I recognized Wanda from her picture in the newspaper, where it appeared under the sobering headline, GLENVILLE HOMEMAKER QUESTIONED IN HUSBAND'S DEATH. Baxter McNabb, "local car salesman, former All-American and decorated Vietnam War veteran," said the *Glenville News-Tribune*, bled to death on the floor of Wanda's sewing room while waiting for the ambulance to arrive. One of the shots she fired at him pierced the left ventricle of his heart. CPR couldn't fix that.

When I first saw Wanda on that cold day last November she wore her blond hair, streaked with white, in a girlish braid that hung down her back and past the stretch waistband of her skirt, which, when she moved, floated toward her canvas oxfords in a succession of fluttering waves. Her legs, when so briefly uncovered, were unshaven and darkly purple with veins. She was fifty-three.

Wanda had killed her husband only three weeks earlier.

She fired four shots from a .32-caliber pistol to get the job done. The pistol was one of those ladies' protection models with a pretty pearl handle, and she kept it in her purse if she was going out, which she did rarely, or at home in a child's bedroom turned sewing room.

Lucky for her it was in the sewing room that night, at the bottom of a basket full of yarn.

There were, predictably, the obvious questions. Why she bought the pistol in the first place, how she was resourceful enough to get to it when she needed it most. But given scant evidence to the contrary, and no incriminating answers to those questions, the matter was resolved quietly, and with little legal fanfare.

According to the official record, Wanda's husband Baxter was planning to use her head for batting practice. She shot him only after he picked up an aluminum baseball bat and started swinging at her head. With his drunken bad aim, he broke a mirror, a floor lamp, and two porcelain dolls perched atop a dresser.

Various pieces of evidence were collected from the sewing room, and Wanda was, in an effort to reestablish law and order, charged with manslaughter and held for a week at the county jail while the police and the district attorney considered the heinous nature of her crime. Photographs of her bruised body were logged into evidence, and the severity of the blows was considered a major factor in her defense. So by the time the week was over, and given no public outcry to the contrary, the charges were dropped.

"You understand, ma'am," they all told her. "Just doing our jobs."

Wanda, they decided, saved her own life by killing her attacker. The fact that Glenville's city government had only a year earlier denied funding for a shelter for battered women weighed heavily on the collective conscience of our little town.

The one condition of Wanda's release, the nature of small-town ain't-we-progressive law and order being what it is, was that the district attorney strongly encouraged her to attend the Spousal Abuse Support Group here at least once a week and check in with me, her psychiatric caseworker, twice a month. Wanda was all too happy to oblige. As she told me later, "It was the least I could do, Jessie. I wasn't in any mood to argue with any of them."

I placed my coffee cup on a coaster I retrieved from the far corner of my desk, reaching across the desk and in front of Wanda to do so, which caused her to retreat from her hovering position. She slumped into my swivel chair, causing it to nearly tip over backward.

I held out a ballpoint pen to her, but she shook her head.

"Nope. Got to be a pencil." Her smile wavered for only a second, but she continued to look at me as if I was the intruder.

"Here," I said, plucking a fat orange pencil from a cup on a bookshelf next to my desk and holding it out to her. "It's the only pencil I've got." It was a carpenter's pencil, triangular, blunt and uneven at the point, probably last sharpened with a pocket knife. I couldn't remember how it had found its way to my bookshelf. Judging from the thin layer of dust that covered it, it was probably left behind when the clinic's inpatient wing was remodeled two years earlier.

Wanda studied the pencil, turning its awkward shape over and over between the fingers of both hands, twirling it like a baton. She looked capable of tossing it high into the air, jumping up from my chair, and executing a flawless cartwheel.

"This will do," she said finally, slamming the center drawer of my desk shut with such force that I feared I'd never be able to pry it open again. She pulled from a canvas handbag a thin spiral-bound notebook that was rolled tight and secured at either end with two fat rubber bands. On the notebook's cover was a glossy photograph of a white kitten sitting in a basket, one tiny pink paw raised to the camera.

"I like to keep notes," she said as she unrolled it, found her place and tried to smooth the page flat.

"Writing down your thoughts is a good thing," I said. "It helps."

"Which one of us is it supposed to help?" Wanda asked as she placed her notebook in the center of my desk blotter. Clearly she had no intention of moving from my chair, which, now balanced with her weight, let out a screech as she slid it closer to my desk. She looked like a student eager to fill her blue book with exam answers. I saw that maybe a third of the notebook was filled, and she had written on both sides of the wide-ruled paper, all in loopy, old-fashioned penmanship. There were occasional exclamation points or other notes scrawled in the margins. I wondered if she started writing when she was in jail, if they let her keep the notebook stuffed between her thin foam-padded mattress and steel bed frame. I guessed they hadn't, thin spiral wire being the sort of thing put to dangerous use in jail. All of the writing in her notebook was in pencil, but there were, at least from what I could see, no erasures.

"Maybe it'll help both of us," I said, resigned to the fact that I was going to remain seated in the client chair beside my desk, which, I noticed with some dismay, was distinctly more comfortable than my own. The ballpoint was still in my hand, my thumb on its trigger.

Wanda leaned back in my chair and squinted at the paper. She dated it at the top and started scribbling. She had an awful lot to say so soon after our first meeting. I had the distinct impression I was failing some sort of test and that she was going to make sure someone in high places knew about it.

I let her write while I sipped my coffee, trying my best to look patient. I watched the clock and made a conscious effort to stop clicking the pen in my hand.

Wanda wrote for five minutes, filling nearly three pages. She didn't look up until she was finished. "Thanks for letting me do that," she said, stretching her freckled arms over her head with a cracking sound. "But you don't need to be so quiet. I can write and talk at the same time, you know. Isn't that what you people try to do? Get us to talk? Shrink our heads?"

In the next cubicle, someone was sobbing. I heard the sound of tissues being pulled from a box. A piped-in synthesized version of "Eleanor Rigby" drifted across our suite. This is the clinic's futile attempt to mask the fact that our counseling sessions take place not in private offices with real doors but in cubicles where most anything said above a whisper can be heard by everyone.

Wanda threaded the carpenter's pencil through the first knot of her braid, at her neckline, where it stuck there like a misshapen hairpin. Then she folded her hands over the page she finished and sat there staring at me and patting her thumbs together as if to say, *Look here, I don't have all day. Let's get this over with.*

"It's okay. I understand," I said.

"What, exactly, do you understand?" she snapped. She extracted the pencil from the knot of her hair and held it poised over the paper, ready to jot down my response.

"I understand the need to keep a diary, to write down your thoughts and your feelings," I told her.

"It's not like I write down 'Dear Diary' before I start writing. That's not how I do it."

"It's still the same thing, Wanda. It's the same process."

"Do you do it? Do you write down all your feelings?"

"I have before, but no, I don't keep a journal now."

"Why not, if you understand it so much? If it's supposed to help both of us?" She scribbled something else on the page. I thought of all the unfinished journals that lay at the bottom of that locked oak chest in my attic. Stacks and stacks of them, all leather-bound and gilt-edged and purchased at stationery stores that cater to society ladies who chronicle their dinner party triumphs and the planting dates of the seedlings taking root in their patio gardens, the details of which—sundials and tea light luminaries and designer sculptures of turtles, toads, and rabbits—are copied meticulously from the pages of *Southern Living* and are, we all hope, worthy of such comparisons. The thick unlined pages of these journals intimidated me, seemed too good for the Bics I used, and whenever I've had the nerve to unleash my unconscious thoughts on them, I've been horrified at the results.

"The important thing is that you're keeping one," I said to Wanda, trying again to turn the conversation back to her and away from my own failure as a diarist. I was beginning to feel I'd lost the upper hand in this interview. In retrospect, I know I lost it even before the interview ever started.

Wanda didn't respond. Her right hand was moving across the page, the left anchoring the notebook to the table.

"I think it's important to write things down, to remember and understand meaningful events in your life," I said. In this, our first session together, I had wanted to establish a friendly rapport first without dwelling on the obvious reason she was here, and was, in fact, pleased with myself for introducing the issue in this way. I was under the distinct impression I was being subtle. Killing her husband had to have been a meaningful event in her life, though whether it was the single most meaningful event I wasn't sure.

As far as Wanda was concerned, I was way off base.

"You don't understand anything," she said, rolling up her notebook around the pencil I'd given her, then stuffing everything in her handbag. "I'm writing so I can forget."

So that's how Wanda became my client. She's the only one of my sixty-plus who isn't on Glenville Wellness Center–prescribed medication, though she has tried to convince me more than once that her inability to lose ten pounds is a dire psychiatric condition and she needs a stash of diet pills—"the good stuff, not over-the-counter"—to improve her flagging self-esteem.

Some patients draw you into their lives, whether you want, or are ready, to make the journey. Visiting my cubicle was a living witness to a horrifying tale, a real marital melodrama, and despite myself, I was hooked. I guess you could say Wanda and I, in the limited interaction this job allows, became friends.

I've thought about Wanda a lot during these past months. About the stories she's told me, the confessions she's made. I used to believe she never thought about killing her husband until he started swinging that aluminum bat. Maybe not even until the second she looked up from her sewing and reached for her gun in its yarn-covered basket. Even though I know more now about what really happened, I still cling to the belief that Wanda just snapped on that particular night, that she was, in that one brutal moment, defending her life.

These days, of course, Wanda looks as happy as the next person. Some days she looks even happier, as if the world has revealed itself to her in some brilliant new way. This, too, is why I need her. In my own life, I've forgotten what happiness feels like.

FIVE

S unday morning finds us in church, in our regular places in the center section of the vaulted and rarefied air of the All Saints Episcopal Church sanctuary. Eighth row middle, wedged between Mr. and Mrs. Walter Griffin on our left and Mr. and Mrs. Frank Daniels, and their bulimic teenage daughter, Kathleen, on our right. Turner, as is fitting in Glenville for a bank vice president and community volunteer, handles all the church's finances. Since he takes this duty seriously, as he does all other duties in his life, we find ourselves here on most Sunday mornings, standing and kneeling in unison with our friends, many of our neighbors, and a respectable number of Turner's colleagues, all of us repeating, at the priest's comforting instruction, the prayers that are to ensure our happiness in this world and our eventual acceptance into heaven.

There are two morning services at All Saints, the 8 and the 10:30. Turner and Frank Daniels usually reserve the 8 A.M. time slot for nine holes at Glenville Meadows, so Mrs. Daniels and I are left this one leisurely morning to ourselves.

On this particular Sunday morning, the day after my walk with Donna, I sat for nearly thirty minutes doing nothing but staring out my front window hoping for rain. The sprinkler system keeps feeding my lawn and my thirsty dogwoods, but I fear my geraniums, without a few helpful tips from the Lawn Doctor, won't live through the spring.

Turner and I are kneeling shoulder to shoulder when, during the first prayers of the mid-morning service, it occurs to me that my life will always be like this, that I will find myself here, eighth row center, kneeling this same way every Sunday morning until I die. I do not find this the least bit comforting. It startles me so much that my eyes pop open and for a split second I fear I'll be spitting up my breakfast all over the hymnals in the rack below.

Could it happen that fast? Close your eyes and lose forty years.

I look at Turner, afraid I've made some movement that will give me away, but his eyes remain closed, his face the very model of the prayerful penitent. Beyond him, at the end of the row, is Kathleen, pale hands covering her mouth, milky blue eyes staring straight ahead. Maybe she's feeling the same way I am, but for different reasons.

I close my eyes and try to fall back into the rhythm of the recited prayers, try to concentrate on the words I should say in return.

Since this is the Lenten season, I've decided I should make a real effort to give up something more sinful than chocolate, which is what I gave up last year because I couldn't think of anything else I wanted more and the priest said it counted. This year I'm putting myself to a real test—to give up my unsettling thoughts about my husband and my marriage. I've begun to enjoy them entirely too much, even more than chocolate, but so far, it's clear my plan isn't working. I should have stuck with chocolate again this year.

I scan the church bulletin and find it's full of the usual stuff. The order for the service, the prayers to be read. On the back page there's an assortment of birth and anniversary announcements, calls for prayers for those members of the congregation who are hospitalized or are recovering from illness. There's also an announcement for a Come One, Come All Church Cleanup Day, scheduled for the following Saturday. "Bring your buckets and brooms, your pails and your gloves, your rakes and your lawn blowers. Lunch will be provided!" Turner and Frank Daniels, I know without asking, will pack up all the cleaning supplies in our respective households and be there promptly at 9 A.M. as requested.

Donna Lindsey isn't sitting in church having thoughts like this, you can bet on that. She is, I know for a fact, seated this very morning with her husband and children in the progressive-thinking Methodist church across the street, probably in the back row where the whole family can slip out unnoticed if the services run long and they risk missing the kickoff, tip-off, or tee-off in whatever major sports event is being broadcast.

If I know Donna, she's spending this morning's services thinking about what she's going to wear to work on Monday. She's probably sitting there in her pew planning out her entire week's wardrobe. This silk skirt with that rayon blouse. Shoes, earrings, and bracelets all to match. Her favorite silk scarf saved for Tuesday night, when she plans to meet Perry Ferguson.

In Donna's church they read the scriptures from one of those modern Bible translations, the kind where the Twenty-third Psalm's "my cup runneth over" becomes, in the new version, "you fill my cup to the brim." A thoroughly modern translation perfectly suited to a thoroughly modern woman like Donna. I know this because I attended that church before I married Turner, back when I didn't think twice about voting a straight Democratic ticket.

SIX

When we make the turn onto Shadowwood Lane after Sunday services and lunch at Glenville Meadows, Turner behind the wheel, my mood brightens at the prospect of spending the afternoon alone in my own house. I know that as soon as Turner pulls the Explorer into the garage he'll hop out and get behind the wheel of his thirty-two-cents-a-mile company Chrysler, doubling back to meet Frank Daniels at the Glenville Meadows driving range. His swing was off this morning, he tells me, so he needs the extra practice. I plan to repot my wilting geraniums.

To get to our house, you drive north on Sulumor Avenue, past the sprawling new multiplex that's a supermarket, deli, coffee bar, and video store all jammed together under one roof and open twenty-four hours a day, even on all the big holidays. Past strip mall after strip mall filled mostly with nail salons, tanning booths, and $6.99 all-you-can-eat Chinese restaurants. Past the Strip itself, a three-mile stretch of blacktop crammed on either side with fast-food franchises and pizza delivery shops. Past row after row of abandoned cotton warehouses that in the 1980s were rescued from demolition and divided up into offices for accountants and mail-order firms and real-estate moguls who thrived inside their exposed brick walls until a good number of them went broke by the early 1990s. Past Sumer Stables, which offers $2,000-plus equestrian camps in the summer for ages five to eighteen and boards a good number of the riding ponies of Glenville's future debutantes.

Most of the women I know in Glenville, with the notable exception of Wanda McNabb, are either former debutantes or trying their best to fool everybody into thinking they are. I'm the latter, and so is Donna Lindsey. I got into Glenville Meadows and the Glenville Society Cotillion by way of marriage, and Donna has been waiting for years to do the same. David's application for membership is pending, and it looks like he'll get in this time. You don't have to have old money to get in anymore. You can be a self-made man. If you can pay the club dues, nobody, except maybe my husband, pays much attention. But being a debutante, now that's something else entirely. That takes real money—daddy's money—and everybody knows it.

You'll see the Glenville Hills branch of First Glenville National Bank (that's where Turner works) at the corner of Sulumor Avenue and Heritage Drive. Take a right onto Heritage Drive. Go two miles and you'll start passing real-estate development after real-estate development, all with fancy names that sound alike and glossy brochures that look alike, all designed to match Glenville's modestly affluent with the homes of their dreams.

Five BR, 4½ BA, master suite with his/her walk-in closets and Jacuzzi. Marble and Corian countertops, ten-foot step ceilings with true artistic workmanship!

If that's what you dream of, you'll find it here.

Heritage Ridge, Ridgeview, Ridge Point, Ridgefield, Fieldstone. All marked with stately hand-carved, hand-painted signs encased in stone, not quarried locally but imported, and doing their best to announce to passersby that anyone without an exact destination in mind will be pulled to the curb by security guards and shot on sight. You'll pass all these before you get to Heritage Knoll, and you'll make three left turns before you get to Shadowwood Lane.

"How in the world do you find your way home?" my mother asked, wide-eyed, the first time she visited. "From the street they all look the same to me."

We see the ambulance when the Explorer noses downhill toward our cul-de-sac. Houston Collier, ruddy-cheeked and out of breath, is standing in the middle of the street, watching the rear of the vehicle, hands deep in the pockets of his wool trousers. It's warm this morning, but he's wearing several layers of sweaters. Every time I see Houston he's got on the same pair of brown wool trousers, and every time they look looser. His body is shrinking away, day after day.

"Hmmmm. What do you think's happening." The way Turner says this I know it isn't really a question, so I don't give him an answer. We slow to a stop, and Turner's window slides down.

Houston shuffles toward us. A pair of fuzzy blue house slippers protrude from underneath his rolled cuffs. Behind the lenses of his thick, black-framed glasses, his bloodshot eyes peer at us through the open window, then turn away, restless but hopeful, as if he is trying to figure out where the EMTs have deposited his wife. Soon enough, we all watch as the collapsible legs of the gurney that carries Mildred disappears between the open doors of the ambulance, her own pair of pink fuzzy slippers sticking out at the end. Maybe she and Houston, upon his retirement, were given these slippers by a well-meaning relative who thought that wearing something bordering on the ridiculous would cheer them up in their old age.

"Everything okay?" Turner asks.

"My wife. She's had some trouble. Need to take her in for some tests."

"Ahhhh well, you can't be too careful." Turner says this like he's relieved, as if he had expected to hear that Mildred was attacked by a gang of thieves who, as we chat here in the street, are ransacking our house.

"She'll be fine," Houston says, and gives a nervous nod in my direction. "She has these spells, you know." Mildred has ulcerative colitis.

"Well, you be sure to let us know if we can do anything to help," says my husband. "If there's anything—" His electronic alarm starts whirring away in his pocket. It's time for his afternoon tee-off.

One of the EMTs hops out of the back of the ambulance and makes his way toward Houston in a sprint that dissolves, as he crosses the street, into an awkward skipping gait. "Ummmm, sir," he says, clearing his throat. "If you want to ride in the back with her, that'll be all right."

I catch myself thinking, with some alarm, of how young he is, this man who, at least for the moment, is responsible for the health of my neighbor. He stands there beside our car, thick arms swinging back and forth, as if he plans to transport Mildred to the hospital strapped to his broad back.

"I guess I'd better go on, then," says Houston, who, as he moves away from us with the hand of the young EMT steadying him at the elbow, seems even older than his seventy-two years, all sagging shoulders and shuffling blue slippers. As he walks, a breeze catches the right leg of his trousers and it balloons out briefly to its original size, the size Houston's legs must have been when they were behind the desk at his big Atlanta law firm, where he was known for his tenacity in fighting with the IRS and not, as he is in our quiet cul-de-sac, for his skill in making it to his mailbox without tripping over the silver-tipped cane his wife insists he use.

"He doesn't like to use it because he thinks it makes him look old," Mildred told me once when I found her seated on one of those little rolling gardener's chairs, leaning over sideways on it at a precarious angle and yanking weeds from a bed of yellow tulips. "If he doesn't use it he's going to trip over those smelly old pants of his, fall into one of my flower beds, and break his foolish neck. Sometimes I think men are the more vain of the sexes, don't you dear?"

"Keep us posted then," Turner calls after Houston.

The EMT helps Houston climb into the ambulance beside his wife, then closes the rear doors and flips some kind of lever, locking them both safely inside. Turner and I pull into our driveway as the ambulance drives away, slow and without its siren.

That night I dream Turner and I are ice-skating across one of the small ponds at Glenville Meadows, near what Turner has described as "the especially treacherous sixth hole" of that pristine golf course. In the dream, I think about how this might be the event Turner's horoscope for today has predicted, one in which the stars said "strange customs would prevail," because the idea of that golf course's water hazard freezing over deep enough for ice-skating is absurd. In this part of the South, a few flurries of snow are enough to close down all the schools and send everyone scrambling to the supermarket to fight over the last cartons of milk and remaining loaves of bread. Here, an inch of snow is considered a blizzard. A few inches more can shut down our entire town for nearly a week.

I'm wearing a pair of red wool mittens, and Turner is holding my left hand in his. We're pretty good too, considering neither of us has ever ice-skated. Everything, from the trees sparkling with ice to the sky that's alive with the still-falling snow, surrounds us in blinding shades of white, as if we are poised together in one of those little water-filled globes that you shake upside down and then watch as the giant fake snowflakes fall to cover the scene below.

There isn't another person in sight. A long black scarf covers my head, and when, much to my surprise, I do a perfect figure eight on the ice, the ends of the scarf whip across my face. When I untangle the scarf and turn to look at Turner, he is skating off in the other direction, where I know the ice is thinner and won't hold his weight.

I try to scream but can't. I watch as my husband, silently and without a struggle, slips through a crack in the ice and disappears from sight.

45

Just a bad shot, honey. Nothing to be concerned about, he yells to me as he goes under. *I'll be back in a jiffy.*

I wait there, my ankles unsteady on the thin blades. In the dream, I'm sure he'll resurface, that he will, in fact, emerge, shivering but not in need of swift rescue. He'll make his way back to me carrying a handful of golf balls he recovered from the bottom of the pond—coming back from the dead water to bring his wife a present.

 *SEVEN*

n Wednesday, four days after Donna Lindsey tells me she's regularly screwing her young haberdasher at a hotel strategically located twenty miles away, she calls me at my office to cancel our walk for the upcoming Saturday.

"I'm sneaking away for the weekend," she purrs. "Okay, *we're* sneaking away."

The fact that she saw Perry Ferguson the night before is, I'm sure, the reason for her undeniably cheerful mood. I can almost see her winking at me through the phone lines, confirming that at some point since our initial conversation, I've been drafted, unwittingly, into the role of co-conspirator.

"A whole weekend? This sounds serious."

"Guilty as charged. We can't get enough of each other." As if to prove her point, she lets out a loud, unmistakably sensuous sigh.

I try to keep my voice upbeat and giggly to match hers. She makes it sound so easy. At the center of my desk are files for seriously ill clients I've been unable to locate. I figure I lose about ten or fifteen of them a year for a variety of reasons, which is, from what I understand from my colleagues, about average. They stop taking their medication. Some move, not bothering to give a forwarding address. Some stop treatment because family members refuse to keep paying the bills. Others simply wander away from Glenville and disappear into the streets of the nearest large city. There are some, of course, who wind up dead, not all of them by their own hand.

While Donna babbles on, I look at my watch. There's a staff meeting blocking out most of my afternoon. Lunch is out of the question. I can't imagine having enough time to meet a man for drinks, much less sneak away with him for a whole weekend.

"I'm not sure we can say we're shopping for the entire weekend," I say, only faintly aware that I'm interrupting something Donna is saying. "The mall isn't open around the clock, you know."

"He didn't ask you about last night, did he?"

"What?" I'm flipping through the case file for Roberta Hall, a former heroin addict who's stopped showing up at the clinic for her daily methadone dose and has, so far, missed two appointments with me. Roberta's relapsed four times in the past two years, so I'm not very optimistic about how or where I might find her.

"David, of course," Donna snaps. "Hey, would you pay attention? I'm pouring my heart out here."

"I've got a lot of work this morning, Donna," I say, a little too impatiently. "But no, he didn't ask. I didn't even see him." I continue to scan Roberta Hall's file, noting that her three children were, years earlier, placed in three separate foster homes, one in Glenville and the other two in neighboring communities. Maybe she's visiting them. That's one possibility, though not a likely one. I can't remember if the court allowed her to visit her children or even if she knows, or cares, where they are.

"Told you so."

It is Donna's concerted opinion that her husband will never question her whereabouts, that he'll take the boys out for hamburgers or pizza every time she announces an absence, even one for unexplained reasons. Maybe she's right. From what I can tell, Donna and her husband are spending an increasing amount of time away from each other. When David isn't out looking under the hoods of Glenville's finest luxury automobiles (he owns Lindsey Motors, which specializes in foreign imports), he's out at the local airport, looking under the hood of his one true love—Delia, his 1947 Cessna. He's been working on that plane for the past five months. Tinkering with the engine, touching up the original paint job. He takes the boys with him most of the time, giving them jobs that sound important enough for them to tell their friends about later.

"That baby's a King KX99. Chrome discs, a new carb. Good tail wheel on her. Won't be long now," he tells me over the boxwood hedge, and all of it sounds pretty important to me too. He gives me a variation of this report every time we meet on our respective trips to our mailboxes, both of us sorting through handfuls of sweepstakes announcements and credit card solicitations.

As far as I can tell, Donna and Delia have never met.

I probably should mention here that in addition to thinking Donna is flighty, Turner also doesn't see eye to eye with David on most things. Just after the Lindseys moved here some nine years ago, when David Jr. was only a few months old, Turner's bank nixed David's application for a loan to open Lindsey Motors.

Turner insists the bank did the "prudent" thing.

"I got the door slammed in my face" is how David remembers it.

Needless to say, relations have been strained ever since. "Those foreign cars are always falling apart," Turner proclaimed during a summer barbecue Donna and I planned in an effort to patch things up between our husbands. "Maybe so," David responded, raising his beer in a toast. "But anything that falls off a BMW is of the highest quality." The irony of not funding a loan for an auto repair shop that specializes in cars that are always falling apart was lost on my husband.

"Hey, you haven't offed Turner yet, have you?" This jolts me back to the conversation at hand.

"Very funny, Donna."

"C'mon, would you lighten up? I'm just messing with you. Besides, since you're not listening to a word I'm saying, I might as well have some fun."

"Do you need me to watch the boys?" I anchor Roberta Hall's file under a glass paperweight on my desk and, in the spirit of friendship, try to concentrate on our conversation in some helpful and meaningful way. I also decided some days ago to bring up the subject of Donna's children the next time we had one of these conversations. I don't know what I was thinking. Maybe I thought the mere mention of her children would, in an instant, cause her to think about the consequences of her behavior.

David Jr. is nine. Gavin is seven. Every year the Lindsey family Christmas card features David Jr. and Gavin in some adorable holiday setting. The two of them rolling out cookie dough at the kitchen counter, their faces and Christmas sweaters smeared with flour. The two of them attempting to build a snowman on the front lawn when only a half-inch of snow had fallen. One year, when the boys were much younger, Donna dressed them both in reindeer costumes and photographed them pulling a sled. I've been wondering how much longer the boys will be willing to be used as props in their mother's effort to spread holiday cheer.

"Thanks, but no," she says to my baby-sitting offer. "They're going to my mother-in-law's. And David is looking forward to a bachelor's weekend. He'll sit around in his underwear and eat potato chips. Watch football. Maybe go out and add another layer of grease to that dumb plane of his."

The story she plans to tell is that she has to attend some kind of retail sales training course at her store's corporate headquarters in Atlanta. Whether such a course exists or not I don't know, but it does have a ring of believability to it.

It occurs to me then that all this giggling might mean Donna is drunk. "Where are you calling from?" I ask, suddenly imagining her sprawled across a ghastly chintz bedspread in a room at the Bay Island Hotel, her blond lover kissing the sweat from between her breasts.

Donna's choice of hotel is, in itself, suggestive of all things exotic and forbidden. The Bay Island Hotel is located near neither a bay nor an island, but just off Interstate Exit 124, its neon sign boldly announcing the availability of heart-shaped Jacuzzis, mirrored ceilings, and in-room adult movies. It's the type of place where the guests try to register inconspicuously, enter and leave their rooms separately and in separate cars, and where, across the street in the parking lot of a Cracker Barrel, the nondescript sedans of paid-by-the-hour private detectives are likely to be parked at any time of the day or night, camera lenses zooming in on any activity that might later be useful for their clients in divorce court. Exactly the type of place where no one would expect the powder blue minivan of Donna Lindsey—wife and mother of two, homemaker, and part-time jewelry salesperson—to be parked on a Tuesday evening and especially not over the weekend. I imagine that, in keeping with the hotel's name, each room is decorated with at least one framed view of tropical paradise, the ocean rippling out vast and mysterious under a multicolored sunset.

Donna doesn't answer right away. She's laughing so hard she can hardly get her breath.

"For God's sake, Jessie, get a grip. You think he's doing it to me this very minute?" More laughter. "It's ten o'clock in the morning. I'm not a complete slut."

I start to apologize, but before I can, she adds in an exaggerated whisper, "Ooooh yes, b-a-a-by, right there—" This, no doubt, is a phrase uttered often at the Bay Island Hotel.

At least this time I get the joke.

"You know something, Donna? I really think you're losing your mind." But we're both laughing by now. "Maybe you should come in for an appointment. Get your lithium refilled."

"Yeah well," she says. "It's good to go crazy now and then, Jessie. You should try it sometime."

⋇

Donna's call unnerves me. I'm overcome with an irrational fear that Donna, with her cavalier attitude about the entire matter, will make some massive blunder that will lead to the discovery of her infidelity and that David, in turn, will blame not her but me because I'm his friend too and haven't told him about it. In one of those leaps of imagination that connect one irrational fear to another, I fear she'll be sitting down to dinner with her husband and children one day and will, in an effort to focus attention away from her own guilt, announce that their next-door neighbor has been having decidedly "not normal" thoughts about her husband and that maybe it would be a good idea if the boys played only in their own yard from now on, away from my destructive influence.

What I end up doing is closing Roberta Hall's file, locking it in the left drawer of my desk along with the file on my other lost patients, and heading for First Glenville National Bank. Maybe seeing my husband—seeing him alive, that is—will help restore some sense of normality to my day and will do something to assuage my own strong guilt. We might even have lunch together.

Turner's secretary, Louise Farmer, waves me down from the other side of the bank lobby. I give a little wave in return.

Mrs. Farmer started working at the bank when she graduated from high school and now, long past the usual retirement age, has taken dictation, typed memos, and kept bank secrets for no fewer than five vice presidents. Her gold-rimmed bifocals are so thick that they magnify her hazel eyes to alarming proportions, and it is for this reason, I'm sure, that they usually rest not on her nose but against her substantial bosom, the ends of a sparkling gold chain attached to each earpiece. Underneath her sprawling secretarial desk is a small electric heater that, with the bank's thermostat set at an unwavering seventy-two degrees, keeps Mrs. Farmer's ankles toasty year-round. One day I fear there'll be a headline in the *Glenville News-Tribune:* SECRETARY'S HEATER SHORT-CIRCUITS; BANK BURNS TO GROUND.

For the most part, the atmosphere at the bank is friendly and informal, with everyone and their spouses on a first-name basis, but Louise Farmer, no doubt in deference to her longevity, is known only by the more formal Mrs. Farmer.

Mrs. Farmer leans toward me conspiratorially, as if she plans to tell me Turner has been trying to enlist her in an embezzlement scheme. "You won't believe what happened this week," she says. Since Mrs. Farmer is one of those women who nearly always speak in whisper tones, I find myself leaning a little too close to her in order to avoid asking her to repeat herself. I can barely hear her over the throbbing of her portable heater, whose motor seems to have kicked its coils into overdrive, as if it somehow senses she has moved a few feet away.

What happened, I soon learn, was that Mrs. Farmer had a new desk delivered to her on Monday morning. After the men from the moving company carted off her old desk, they brought in her new desk, a shiny new multiple-piece unit with a dark mahogany finish and brass drawer pulls. What the movers forgot to do, or as she tells it, *refused* to do because they weren't told they had to do it and had other desks to move into other offices across town, was to attach the typing arm of the desk to the desk itself. They dared to leave both pieces there, unattached, in her office, which is just outside Turner's office, figuring their job was done. That's the word she uses. They *dared* to do it.

"They brought it just before noon, when I take my lunch hour, so I had to leave it there," she says. "But when I got back, what do you think I found?"

"I can't imagine."

"What I found was Mr. Maddox under my new desk putting it together himself, with his own two hands. I nearly tripped over him." She goes on to describe how Turner was flat on his back, suit coat off, tie loosened around the neck of his starched white shirt, bolts and washers within his reach on the carpet.

"Do you know what he said to me while he was under there?"

Without waiting for me to guess, she tells me. "He says to me, 'Mrs. Farmer, I'd give anything if I could spend my days doing work like this.'"

I turn to look at Turner, who, behind the floor-to-ceiling glass wall that surrounds his corner office, is sitting at his desk and, thankfully, not under it. He holds up a finger to indicate he'll soon be off the phone.

"Turner's always liked puttering around the house," I say.

Mrs. Farmer plucks the bifocals from her face and holds them in front of her chest for a moment before letting them fall on their chain. Drawing her arms across her chest as if she's encountered a sudden chill, she totters away, the scent of lavender lingering in her wake.

As I look at Turner in his office, I picture him in his new occupation of choice. He's wearing a workman's shirt and tight-fitting jeans, not a gray suit. His hands are callused instead of smooth, and a tool belt, not an alligator one, is strapped around his waist. He's holding a trowel in one hand instead of a telephone, a carpenter's level in the other instead of a Mont Blanc pen.

Then I see a large black wrecking ball crash through the window behind his desk and swing a silent, deadly path toward his head.

EIGHT

R ight then and there I decide I need a geographic solution,
an escape from everything that is, or will be, my life in
Glenville. I want to run away and never look back. The only
thing I need to do now is figure out how.

By the time I get back to my office, I decide to run to the
only place I know better than Glenville—home to see my parents.
They're only a two-hour drive away, still living in the same five-
room stucco and concrete-block frame house where I grew up,
in the unchangeable landscape of Randolph Gap, Alabama. My
sister's in Randolph Gap too, with her husband and son, living
in one of those manufactured homes projects where everybody,

especially my sister, tries to pretend they're not living in a trailer park. It's not much of an escape, but it's the only place I can think of to go. Randolph Gap may be only a two-hour drive away, but it might as well be a million miles from what I've come to call home.

I also know there's no danger of Turner asking to join me because he always makes excuses for not visiting my parents, preferring instead that they visit us, which has happened exactly twice during our marriage and never for more than an afternoon at a time. My mother doesn't mind his absences. She treats him like the obedient, well-mannered child she's always wanted.

"Of course the poor boy doesn't have time to visit," she tells me. "He's got a bank to run. He's got responsibilities," indicating to the rest of us that responsibility is something obviously lacking in our own lives. "Turner's a good man," she'll say. "I don't know why you can't be more like him. I don't know why you can't be content with your life, why you can't find some direction for yourself. A woman your age. It's high time you did."

Meanwhile, the good man himself is planning his good deeds.

"I'd like to go with you, sweetheart, but I've already promised I'd help with the Easter cleanup. You know they'll need every hand they can get."

Turner never says "sweetheart" unless he's trying to get out of something. I'm convinced he threw in the "every hand" part to make me feel an additional twinge of guilt. If he'd been paying attention, he'd have noticed I wasn't inviting him to come with me but telling him I was planning the trip.

₲

The first thing I hear when my mother picks up the phone is not her voice but a series of high-pitched wails that screech octave after octave toward a cacophony of piercing screams. Years ago, when I was doing a research project to complete my certification at the Glenville Wellness Center, I observed a roomful of unmedicated schizophrenics, all wildly lost in their own private delusions and all expressing quite vocally the nightmares that were swirling around their waking lives. The sounds those patients made were one step closer to sanity than this.

This is a sound I haven't heard in years, and it can mean only one thing. My sister Ellen is home, and her birds are with her.

"Hello!" my mother yells into the phone. There's a shrill echo of "Hello . . . HELLO!" Then, "Shush, all of you, and stop all this racket. I can't hear a thing."

Predictably, the avian chorus responds with more mimics of "Hello, hello . . . HELLO!" I can see my mother standing in the front hall, the phone pressed hard against her ear as an unruly assortment of African grays, Amazons, budgies, and macaws hop and flap their wings in their cages and on their perches, hanging on to her every word as if she's hiding backstage and feeding them all their important lines.

"Hello, Mother. You sound like you're in a jungle."

"Who is this? Speak up if you want me to hear you!"

"Jessie. It's Jessie, Mama." I hear what sounds like glass breaking.

"What a nice surprise."

"I said you sound like you're in a jungle," I repeat, louder this time. In the background, I can hear a series of whistles.

"Shush up, all of you! I'm trying to talk to my daughter." As if this will help.

"I might come see you this weekend, if you don't have any plans."

"Hello, HELLO," comes the echo again. "Answer the phone phone PHONE!"

"We never have any plans, dear, you know that. But you can go to church with me," she says, her mood improving immediately with the idea that she can get me back into a "proper" church, which means the Randolph Gap Holy Rock Church and no other. "Sister Inez would just love to see you again."

"You, you, YOU!" the voices scream.

Great. If I'm smart, I'll plan to sneak out of the house before daybreak on Sunday.

Sister Inez is Inez Sneed, who was my piano teacher for six long years, bringing tedium to my young life in thirty-minute, biweekly intervals. In her self-imposed task of training another generation of charismatic church piano players, Sister Inez dispensed with the more traditional methods of piano instruction, preferring instead to lead me through tortured and faltering by-ear-only renditions of "Just As I Am" and "Amazing Grace." Inez Sneed, when I knew her, was a perpetually sour-faced woman who sported a stiffly sprayed beehive and whose body proportions resembled an aluminum can. My mother has labored for years under the mistaken impression that getting me and Sister Inez together in the same room after all this time will inspire me to take up the piano again and, in the process, rededicate my life to church performance. My most vivid memory of Sister Inez is of her hovering over my right shoulder, a thick wooden ruler ready to coax my stumbling fingers into pounding out the correct chords. My lessons usually went something like this: "Amazing grace, how sweet the sound," then WHACK! for not striking the C chord the way Jesus intended.

My mother's fondness for Turner aside, she's also convinced that Sister Inez's son Harvey has been pining away for me for over two decades, even though I can't remember him ever seeming interested in me, or in any other girl for that matter. But according to my mother, it is because I left Randolph Gap that Harvey never married and, at forty-one, spends every weekend driving his mother to the grocery store, the beauty parlor, and, of course, to church.

When Sister Inez's arthritis forced her to retire from giving piano lessons, Harvey was appointed her successor. He set up shop in a dilapidated room at the top of a steep staircase above Dillard's Shoe Store, and now spends most afternoons watching the children of Randolph Gap run their sticky fingers up and down the worn keys of his mother's ancient upright, his white loafers tapping out the rhythm. My mother considers it my duty to make an appearance in Randolph Gap every few years to remind Harvey that life is worth living.

"Guess who's here," she announces with sudden enthusiasm. "I bet you CAN guess if you try."

When I don't answer immediately, she can't help herself from telling me anyway. "Ellen's here. Got here last week. And Justin! She's got Justin with her."

"From the sound of it, Justin's not the only one who's there," I say. A lone bird is still captivated by the telephone and making an annoying ringing sound. It sounds remarkably phonelike. I wouldn't mind if my mother put me on hold to answer it.

"Oh that," she says with a laugh. "That's just Dexter. Does this every time the phone rings. He just loves the telephone."

"Sounds like they all do."

"Well, you know birds. They do the cutest things."

The idea of visiting my parents while my sister Ellen, her gloomy seven-year-old, and her array of feathered companions are camping there at the same time is not an appealing one, but I should have thought of that earlier.

Justin probably won't say three words to me the entire weekend, but will sit brooding in a corner, looking at me as if I'm a toad deserving of dissection.

The birds will peck my eyes out while I sleep.

My mother will drag me to Sunday morning services at the Randolph Gap Holy Rock Church, nagging me the whole morning about how Episcopalians (which, when she pronounces it, sounds like she's describing us as "pistol aliens") are nothing more than lapsed Catholics, and Catholics, "as any decent Christian person knows, have everything wrong from the beginning." A few years ago she even sent me a newspaper clipping in which a columnist jokingly referred to Episcopalians as the "frozen chosen." She sent it along with a note that read, in her pinched block lettering: "Frozen is better than burning forever, but that's not how you were raised."

Am I this desperate to get out of the house for the weekend? To get away from my husband? Maybe this is what it feels like to be crazy. It's nice, reassuring almost, if you can surround yourself with people who are crazier than you are.

"How about if I leave after work on Friday? I'll be there before dark." I can see us sitting at the dinner table, the yellow eyes of a dozen birds surveying the contents of our plates and eagerly following the movements of our silverware.

"You're calling long distance?" she asks. The fact that I haven't lived in Randolph Gap in more than twenty years, and, as a result, routinely call my mother long distance, seems to be a constant surprise to her.

"You can get discounts, you know. Special rates for calls after seven."

This is my cue. Over the years I've learned that if I don't have ready reasons to flee, I can be trapped on the phone with my mother for more than an hour, listening to the events of her day in excruciating detail.

"The Winn-Dixie had ground chuck on sale today, two forty-nine a pound. I don't think that's such a great price, but I bought five pounds anyway." My mother's freezer is full of such bargains from the meat counter, most of it so deeply buried that it bears little resemblance to whatever label she's taped to its aluminum foil wrapping.

Are these the kinds of conversations that are supposed to bring mothers and daughters closer together? I worry that they are, that these are the only conversations my mother and I will ever have, that we'll never discuss anything more important than grocery store lists and sale catalogs that arrive in the mail. Believe me, I've tried. I've tried to make chitchat about what brand of coffee I buy, about whether I should plant petunias or begonias, about which recipe and which soup mix I prefer for chicken-and-broccoli casserole, about how much I paid for the towels I got on sale at the big outlet mall, but I just don't get it.

When my mother isn't prowling the aisles of the Winn-Dixie on sale days, she convinces my father to drive her to a wholesale shopping outlet ten miles away. "It's farther than your father likes to drive, but they have the best bargains. One of those cans of green beans lasts us a week!" She plans these excursions days in advance, down to every last detail, and always reports to me every item on her list. My father ambles down the wide aisles after her, and she instructs him to load her Volkswagen-size cart with things like twenty pounds of American cheese, eight whole chickens, cases of Saltines, and cans of tomato soup, pinto beans, and sauerkraut, each of which weighs as much as a bowling ball.

How much I pay for things is a perennial favorite among my mother's conversational topics.

"How much do you give to get your hair cut?"

"How much are your car payments?"

"Where did you get that cute little cotton blouse with the pearl buttons?" And, more important to her, "Did you get it on sale?"

"Do you know that buying generic detergent instead of Tide can save you a bundle?"

"I really have to go now, Mama. See you Friday." I try to sound cheery about it, but hang up anyway. I feel tired already.

My mother's voice takes me back to memories of why I left Randolph Gap in the first place. I was seventeen and headstrong, armed with an academic scholarship that would propel me toward a very different life. For years I fought desperately to create the *me* I always dreamed of being—the *me* that never would have been had I stayed home.

When people asked what my father did for a living, I told them he was an engineer, an architect, or the owner of a string of successful convenience stores. Occasionally, and probably as a result of my watching too many episodes of *Dallas*, I grandly referred to him as being in the oil business, a profession I believed was bound to carry with it some mystique of wealth, power, and sophistication. What he really does is manage a combination gas station, car wash, and minimart called the Stop 'n' Shoppe, the extra "pe" added in a bizarre British affectation I've never understood. It's not even a very successful minimart as minimarts go, having the misfortune to have been built in a location later bypassed by the interstate highway.

The Stop 'n' Shoppe is the kind of place where you'll find a thick coat of dust floating over the tops of unsold baby food jars, past-due expiration dates on the potato chips, long and crumb-filled cracks in the uneven linoleum. Despite the fact that it doesn't do the kind of business that would keep its cash registers full, it is robbed with an alarming frequency, usually by teenagers who haven't yet mastered the fine art of picking a good place for a heist.

When it happens, my father opens the register and, without objection, gives them what they want. The most one of them ever got was $125.75, the bulk of it in quarters from the hand-operated wand car wash out back. The last kid who robbed the place was so young he could barely manage to wave his pistol menacingly and, at the same time, use the other hand to lift the paper sack he'd stuffed with rolls of quarters. The bottom of the sack ripped open by the time he made it to the parking lot and he was on his hands and knees trying to pick up the quarters when police officers apprehended him. Yes, crime comes not only to the fluorescent-bathed aisles of the more conveniently located, surveillanced megamarts in Randolph Gap, but also to the quiet and musty counters of the Stop 'n' Shoppe.

When my father isn't at work, he spends most of his after-dinner hours watching television or shooting pool at the Green Duck, the roadhouse-style bar located across the parking lot from the Stop 'n' Shoppe.

When I was a child, my father made a game of sneaking me in to see the bar's mascot, a menacing four-foot-tall stuffed duck that greeted patrons at the door. That duck was a particularly repugnant shade of green, reeked from all the beer that had been spilled on him over the years, and was, I remember, taller than I was at the time. He wore a yellow derby. I was repulsed and attracted at the same time, and not knowing what to do with those contradictory emotions, I believed what I felt for that duck was something like love. I would have stood there staring at that green duck all day if they'd let me.

"Now, Carl, you know I can't let that child stay in here," the bartender would say, and my father, grinning all the while, would take me by the hand and lead me out the door.

Once I had my driver's license, my mother sometimes sent me to the Green Duck for an altogether different purpose: to fetch my father from his bar stool. "Come back in a few years, honey," the bartender crooned, "and I might just take you dancing."

A few years ago, on one of my rare visits home, a fit of misplaced nostalgia sent me back there again to see the object of my childhood affection one more time. The duck was there all right, though it had been banished to a back storage room, his smelly green shell of a body lying on top of a loose stack of boxes, his head tossed in a corner.

"I can't believe you even remember that old thing," said the bartender, who poured me a beer on the house. "Hell, nobody's asked about him in years." Nobody remembered how he was decapitated either, but a few of the patrons guessed it must have happened in a barroom brawl a few years earlier.

In his youth, my father dreamed of leaving Alabama forever by joining the Army and heading overseas to fight the Germans. But by the time his basic training was over the war itself was over, and he made it only as far as California, where he spent his tour cleaning bedpans in a military hospital and dreaming only of coming back home to Enterprise, Alabama. It would take him a few more years to get away from home for good, even though the farthest he got was Randolph Gap, where he met my mother. Late at night, when he's watching one of those World War II documentaries on cable, his eyes tear up with a nostalgia for things only imagined—the disarming of land mines, air raids over Berlin, marches across the French countryside, an encounter with a lovely French mademoiselle on a bicycle—and he is, for a moment, happy.

When friends asked about my mother, she was a dress designer or a painter of some modest renown, when she is, in fact, a housewife whose passion is making macramé handbags and painting gourds with lopsided daisies and sunflowers. She takes the handbags and gourds, which are marketed as country crafts, to the Randolph Gap Swap Meet every other Saturday.

My mother sends love gifts to television evangelists, teaches Vacation Bible Schoolers how to make lumpy clay ashtrays for their parents, and, with missionary zeal, frequents grocery stores and strip malls across north Alabama, where she puts pamphlets with titles like "Will You Be Ready for the Rapture?" under the windshields of parked cars and into the hands of hapless shoppers who aren't quick enough to see her approach. I don't know where she gets her stash of these crudely printed tracts, but for some reason the cover always features a pen-and-ink drawing of a woman with a sleek pageboy, her hands raised to her face in terror, her mouth poised for a bloodcurdling scream. In other words, a woman who is most decidedly not ready for the rapture, a woman who will have to pay the price for her wickedness. The fact that this woman resembles me has not escaped my mother's attention.

During my sophomore year in college, she sent me one of her macramé handbags, a black shapeless thing with a large calico-print flower sewn to the front. Since the package was from my mother, I knew better than to open it in my room, where my roommate Amy could spot it. Amy was a former high-school drum major transformed into self-described dilettante, who chain-smoked Camels, wore black, and slept with her French professor, and for that I adored her. I took the package to a corner of the student center and pulled back the heavily taped lid as if it contained a bomb. When the lid was bent back just far enough for me to see what was inside, I promptly stuffed the entire package into the nearest trash can.

I later told my mother I never received the package, that it must have been lost in the mail, and to this day she reminds me that the post office in that "high and mighty" school I attended is rife with either incompetence or thievery, or both. She also remembers that it cost her $4.49 to send the package first-class and that she could easily have gotten $10 cash, or a tabletop charcoal grill, for the handbag at the Swap Meet.

Sending me that macramé bag was my mother's thinly disguised attempt at making me homesick, a condition she believed would lead me to reevaluate why I left home in the first place, inspiring me to catch the first bus back to Randolph Gap and, in doing so, "get my life back to normal." Running off to college and giving up a promising career as a church pianist was not, in my mother's opinion, something any "normal" girl would do. That macramé bag, I knew without even opening it, was filled with her rapture pamphlets.

When friends asked about siblings, I told them that my sister Ellen was studying abroad and that she spoke three languages. In reality she was, by age fifteen, being shipped off regularly to juvenile court on shoplifting charges and being kept away from sharp objects. After each of these episodes she was hauled into church by our mother, who made her memorize Bible verses by the dozen and go to the altar after every service to repent. All this time I was spending sunny afternoons sprawled across a quilt in the quadrangle of my "high and mighty" college campus, rehearsing for a minor role in a Chekhov play and trying to decide what dress to wear for the drama club's spring dance.

I lied about everything.

I invented myself as I went along.

Back then, I didn't feel guilty about it at all.

&

Donna Lindsey's weekend plans sure sound better than mine. At least I can live vicariously through her, imagining that I have a life more adventurous than my own.

After work on Wednesday, a day that despite my best efforts does not live up to its promise of what my daily horoscope called "a romantic rendezvous with a fellow Libra," I decide to walk next door to Donna's house. Maybe she'll let me in on some sexual technique that women of our generation are unaware of but men of Perry Ferguson's generation practice routinely and are now using to keep women of our generation in a frenzied state of reckless abandon. I'm convinced he's been using something like that on Donna.

David and the boys are on the front lawn engaged in a three-way softball throw. When he sees me break through the opening in the boxwood hedge, he stops what he's doing and misses the ball David Jr. throws to him, which, in turn, prompts a stereophonic chorus of "Awwww, Dad." The boys dutifully say their hellos, but it's obvious they fear a girl is about to break up their game.

"You about ready to take Delia up?"

"Got her strobes running."

I nod thoughtfully, like I know a thousand and one things about strobes. David must realize I don't know a thing about airplanes other than what he tells me. He's like the classic absentminded professor, spouting off about quantum physics to the waitress who's served him a grilled cheese sandwich.

While David and I talk, the boys stand beside their father, shifting from one foot to the other and punching their fists into their ball gloves.

David prattles on, saying something about "ceconite wings" and "wheel pants." After a few minutes, he picks up on the fact that the boys are quickly losing patience with both of us. "Well then, make yourself at home," he says. "Donna's making dinner. She'll be glad to see you."

By then both boys are sprawled on the grass, arms and legs flung out as if they've been gunned down there on the sunny lawn and have nothing better to do but bleed to death nobly. Gavin holds his ball glove over his face like his big brother, imitating David's every move, but whenever he tries to moan he breaks into a fit of giggling. As I turn to walk away from them and up the front steps, David Sr. lunges toward both boys, pinning them to the grass in a spontaneous show of fatherly affection. It looks like the kind of picture the Heritage Knoll development would use in one of their marketing brochures, and for a moment, I imagine myself in this family portrait—a husband and two boys, football on the lawn. Leaving them there fills me with a loneliness I can't even begin to describe.

I find Donna standing in front of her stove. She's gripping the handle of a skillet, seemingly oblivious to the fact that the hamburgers she's frying are seared black and sending thick plumes of smoke over her head toward the smoke alarm, which I expect will go off any minute.

I walk to the stove and turn off the burner.

"Don't you just . . . just . . . hate your life sometimes?"

Tears stream down both of her cheeks, which are bright pink from standing so close to the stove, and she is sniffling and staring at me with an eerie, desperate look. I've seen that look before. Lots of times. But never from Donna. I can't think of a thing to say.

I'm the one who's supposed to hate her life, Donna. Not you. C'mon. You're the only hope I've got that life exists out there somewhere. But I don't tell her this, thinking it might just make things worse.

A few weeks after Donna and I first met, she started calling me up late at night, once a month or so, and, without a hello or any other introduction, asking me questions like "What do you think about husbands?" Donna's conversations often begin with some quirky, cryptic question like that—never a mention, God bless her, about my grocery list. That's how our friendship started, and it's one of the reasons I love her.

"Your husband or mine?" I'd say.

"The *idea* of a husband," she'd tell me, turning philosophical.

I didn't have an answer for that.

"Well, I was just wondering," she'd say. "I like mine okay enough this week, but last week was another matter." Then she'd be off and running, telling me about it all, about whatever happened that week or the week before, revealing the most intimate details of her marriage to me a week at a time. She often jokes that our talks are cheaper than making an appointment at the Glenville Wellness Center, and, as she puts it, "a hell of a lot more fun."

"Well, I do," she says to me this time. "I hate my life a lot of the time."

I put my arms around her and let her cry. I hear the front door open, the heavy drumming footsteps of her husband and children, still in play, unaware of what's happening. The television is switched on, and there is laughing, more tossing of the football. They're hungry now, and ready for their burgers.

❧

That night I dream I'm high above Glenville, flying through the clouds with David Lindsey as he takes Delia up for her virgin flight. He looks comfortable behind the instrument panels, switching this button and that, checking all the dials. Holding her steady while I enjoy the view.

This is something, isn't it? he shouts over the steady flip-flip-frop-flip-frop of the propeller.

Yes. Yes it is.

David is thirty-four, four years younger than I am. His dark brown hair is long enough so that it curls at the back of his thickly muscled neck, and on most afternoons a shadow of new whiskers frames his square jaw. He's attractive, but in an average-guy, big-brother sort of way that other wives, even other husbands, don't find threatening. In my dream he smells of motor oil and deodorant soap and, in the limited intimacy we have because his wife is my best friend, he kisses me on the cheek when I arrive at the hangar. Despite myself, I can't help but wonder what a real kiss from him would feel like.

At that height Glenville looks like an architect's model. All Styrofoam buildings glued together in neat rows, city block after manicured city block, surrounded by tiny plastic trees that are forever green. Streets dotted with matchbox-size cars on their way to the jobs of their upwardly mobile owners. A leisure class of people the size of toy soldiers, mowing their painted lawns and walking their toy dogs.

Just think, the developer's pitch would be. *YOU could make all this happen. YOU could make this your legacy!*

The whole scene falls away from us as we climb higher and higher, home seeming more remote and more unfamiliar than ever before.

Donna's having an affair, you know.

There. It just slips out.

She's admitted it. "I'm sleeping with that young guy in menswear." That's exactly what she said.

Like in many dreams, we're carrying on this entire conversation but our mouths aren't moving. David can read my thoughts and I can read his. It's a dangerous thing, this thought-reading. I'm making a conscious effort not to think about the two of us hiding out in one of those little Styrofoam houses below, my body wrapping itself around his.

Yeah, I know all about that. It just figures. That's what he's thinking. About his wife's affair, that is. He hasn't picked up on the other part yet.

So what are you going to do about it?

Don't know, don't care.

What? But—

Don't much matter what I do, does it? She's the one's got to decide.

This is not what I expected to hear.

But you've got to do something!

Says who?

Me. Everybody! You're her husband, for Christ's sake.

Is that right?

What's wrong with you? Of course you are.

I try to remember if David was hit on the head earlier in the dream and if that's what's causing this lapse in his memory. Boink, and tweety birds are flying in circles, making you forget all your troubles.

Aren't you married? he asks, and puts a hand on my thigh. His hand is warm and welcoming, his fingers gripping the bare flesh under my skirt with just enough pressure for me to realize it isn't a casual gesture on his part. There is something intended.

I think about this. My own little Styrofoam house is down there somewhere, but I can't figure out where. All I can think about is his touch.

Hell if I know, I tell him. *I can't remember the way home.*

 *NINE*

They say in their heart, "I shall not be shaken;
no harm shall happen to me ever."

PSALM 10:6

THE PSALTER

THE BOOK OF COMMON PRAYER

For my second appointment with Wanda McNabb, I made sure to circle it in red on my desktop calendar and to stay in my cubicle until she arrived. It was a petty thing to do, staying planted in my chair just so she wouldn't get there before me, but I felt it was important to keep our sessions on a professional level. Sitting in my own chair, behind my own desk, was a start. I decided I might even surprise her by taking some notes of my own.

"Brought my own this time." It was Wanda, who waved a handful of red pencils. With one fluid movement, she whirled around, fell into the chair beside my desk, and let her canvas handbag drop from her arm to the floor with a thud. A jumble of objects bulged from the opening of the bag. The same rolled-up notebook she carried on her first visit, a ruffled plaid hair bow, what looked like a miniature photo album, and a skein of yellow yarn pierced through with two long silver knitting needles, the latter making me wonder if her .32-caliber pistol lurked underneath.

Wanda still gripped the pencils in one hand. In the other she carried a small plastic box decorated with a turkey in a jaunty Pilgrim's hat. She deposited the box on the corner of my desk. "Here," she said, tapping her pink fingernails on the cartoon turkey. "Everybody's got a sweet tooth this time of year." She wrapped her fingers around the box and, with great effort, popped the top. Inside were six oatmeal cookies.

"You really shouldn't have, Wanda," I said. It always makes me nervous when patients give me things, probably because in the past patients who have come bearing food have been certifiably more unstable than Wanda. Over the years, I've thanked them for their offerings of cookies, fudge, and peanut brittle, but it all went in the trash as soon as their appointments were over.

"Fresh from the oven this morning," she beamed. "Go ahead. Try one. Cookies are good for what ails you. That's what I always say."

"Thanks. I'll save them for lunch."

"Take a few home to your husband if you want. Way to a man's heart, you know." She smoothed her batik print skirt and folded her hands in her lap. Wanda McNabb, I thought, knows a lot about getting straight to a man's heart.

"You're ready to write today, I see."

"Oh, these?" she said, waving her pencils. "I guess I am. But not right now. Let's get better acquainted first." She was doing it again. She'd been in my office no more than five minutes and I already felt like she was the one in control.

"Okay," I said, shifting uncomfortably in my chair. "Why don't you tell me how you've been feeling lately. You've been sitting in on the group sessions, haven't you?" I reached for the security of my coffee mug and held it cupped in both hands, trying to assume a scholarly, unemotional tone.

Wanda reached back to adjust the clip that held her hair in a ponytail. From somewhere in our suite, a phone was ringing, unanswered.

"Do you think I should cut my hair?"

"I don't know, Wanda," I said. "What I really want to hear about are your sessions. Do you enjoy talking with the other women? I've already been getting rave reviews about the cookies you bring." Maybe *enjoy* wasn't the right word to use in a situation like this, but I'd hoped the sessions were at least somewhat helpful, maybe even cathartic. I made a note to call Carol Andrews, who hosts the weekly meetings of the Spousal Abuse Support Group, to get a full report on Wanda's progress.

"But yours is short. Don't you like it short?" Wanda turned her head this way and that as she studied the cut of my hair.

"Well yes, I do. It's easy."

"Easy hair. You think that's what I need?" She placed her pencils on the edge of my desk, where they broke formation and clattered in either direction. Then she unhooked the clip in her hair and, separating it into three long strands, began twisting it into a thick braid. "Nothing but trouble, trouble, trouble."

As I watched her braid her hair, I remembered how it felt to sit on our front porch on a sweltering summer afternoon, wedged between my mother's knees while she steadied her rocking chair and braided my own once-long hair. In those days, my mother and I had at least that in common.

"Not many women have hair like yours, Wanda."

"At my age, you mean. Not many women my age wear their hair this long."

"I meant it as a compliment, Wanda. Not like that."

"Baxter never wanted me to cut it. When we first married, he'd spend two hours after supper every Saturday night washing and combing it. He'd sit behind me on the bed, his legs wrapped around me, his hands in my hair. He could be gentle like that when he wanted to be. For such a strong man."

It was the first time she'd mentioned her husband. It was hard to imagine the man who threatened to bash her head in with a baseball bat ever initiating so tender an act. The same man she sent reeling backward toward the open door of her sewing room with the force of four bullets.

Wanda finished the braid and, holding the ends together with one hand, fished in her purse to remove one of the rubber bands coiled around her rolled notebook. Her hands moved fast with the intimate repetition of the act, wrapping the rubber band around the braided end of her hair—snap, snap, snap.

"That was the Baxter I knew," she said. "You only know what you've read in the newspaper and whatever it says in that file you keep on me." When she reached a hand to smooth a loose curl that fell over one ear, she closed her eyes. I wondered if she was lost in the memory of her husband's touch.

"You knew him better than anyone."

"I guess I did," she said, "but that's not saying much."

She began to tell me. She talked about Baxter in the kind of detail my mother would have relished. She told me what he liked for breakfast—homemade biscuits and sausage patties, two eggs over medium, orange juice, and half a cup of black coffee. How early in their marriage he worked during the evenings and weekends to build bookshelves, spice racks, and even the cradle that, over the years, rocked their four children to sleep. How he would scream and cry in the night with nightmares of his years in Vietnam. She talked about all these things as if she were reading a children's bedtime story.

As she was leaving, she reminded me to take the cookies home to my husband if I wasn't going to eat them. She turned in the hall and, reaching around her back, caught the end of the heavy braid in her hand. "You know why I want to cut this?" she asked. "I mean, besides it being a lot of trouble?"

I shook my head.

She tugged hard at the braid, then let it go, causing it to swing across her back. For one brief moment, she looked like some exotic animal, whipping her mane back and forth as she paced inside her cage. Then she leaned against the door frame, slipped her hands into the wide pockets of her skirt. She looked like any other woman her age, like someone who would be completely at ease in a notions store, flipping through books of dress patterns.

"This hair," she said, "is full of too many memories." And with that, she turned to walk away, leaving me to imagine her sitting in a hairdresser's chair, lobotomized not with an ice pick under a neatly plucked eyebrow but with the reassuring snip of the hairdresser's scissors.

TEN

So on this rainy Friday afternoon, my bags packed and already in the back of my Explorer, I find myself on the road home to Randolph Gap.

This morning I was jolted out of bed by another dream. In the dream I was in bed, just lying there on my back in that sweet, not-quite-awake state, thinking of nothing in particular but the feel of the cool sheet draped over my body and tucked, biblike, under my chin. For some reason, both my feet were sticking out from underneath the sheet, but when I stretched out, wiggling my toes, it was as if the feet at the foot of the bed weren't mine at all but belonged instead to a woman with well-manicured toes. The nails glistened with small squares of red lacquer.

When I turned to look at Turner in bed beside me, I saw his mouth open in a snore, a dribble of spit at the corner of his cheek. His graying hair was plastered to the pillow.

The next thing I knew I pulled my pillow from underneath my head. For some reason my hair was wet, like I'd only minutes before thrown myself into bed after wandering around the front lawn in a thunderstorm, and then there I was, smothering Turner with the pillow.

He didn't resist at all. He just lay there peacefully, like he'd been expecting this to happen all along. I figured he'd kick and scream and tear at me with his fingernails like people in the movies do when they're being smothered with a pillow. Not Turner. He didn't put up a fight at all. I remember thinking I hated him for not fighting, for not even trying to leave me with at least a bruise as proof of my bad intentions. That's when I woke up.

In my dream, just before I placed the pillow over his sleeping face, I was absolutely convinced that if I didn't lower that pillow over his nostrils and press down as hard as I could with both hands, he would do it to me first.

&

The voice on my tape deck drones on about the essential incompatibility of men and women. One of my New Year's resolutions is to read at least one new book every month, preferably one of the classics I never got around to reading in college but feel I need to read in order to be a more well-rounded, more literate member of society. Listening to a book on tape while driving is my compromise to actually picking up a real book. I can sit back and enjoy the ride, not having to waste valuable driving time scanning the dial in search of radio stations.

I haven't had much luck keeping my other resolutions, so I bought this new book as my reward for keeping one of them. It's a self-help, pop psychology kind of book, not exactly a classic, but it is, after all, a book and that's what counts. My other resolutions were:

Number One: To, like Wanda McNabb, lose ten pounds.

Number Two: To clean my house each Wednesday evening because I suspect that the two women who visit my home on Thursdays, armed with cleaning supplies, bad attitudes, and our burglar alarm code, have figured out that the spotless areas of the house are Turner's and the sloppy ones mine, and they resent me for it.

Number Three: To be a more loving and attentive wife.

Needless to say, I'm failing at these three.

On the tape, Richard Blumegarten, Ph.D., fifty-seven weeks on nonfiction bestseller lists everywhere, tries to explain to me how the male mind works.

Here's his advice: "Men seek love, commitment, and security just like women. What women need to learn is that men just have different ways of expressing their innermost needs."

Minutes later, in his assessment of the female mind: "If a woman is in a bad mood, what she really wants is to talk to you openly and honestly. If she can talk about it, she can face her feelings in an open and honest way. She can release her anger."

The quotes on the tape's jacket proclaim it "a definitive study of the dynamics of modern male-female relationships," one that will "dramatically improve the way you relate to your partner." They promise that anyone reading, or in my case listening, to this book surely will be transformed, will, in a few easy-to-learn steps, "open that bright and shining door to better, more loving communication."

I see myself transported to some idyllic setting, a place of soothing colors and nonconfrontational furniture arrangements, calmly explaining to Turner that in my darkest heart of hearts I daily wish him dead. In my daydream, he nods in complete understanding. Not that he wants to be dead. He's just happy I'm sharing with him, that we are, at last, communicating in an open and honest way.

⁂

As I pull into the long gravel driveway of my childhood home, the rain slowing to a drizzle, the sky dark enough so that I have to switch on my headlights, I lower the window on the driver's side and stick my head out.

With the rain hitting my cheek and the cool wind blowing my hair, I am sixteen years old again, being driven home from my first real date. The roar of a thousand singing cicadas greets me. I close my eyes and breathe in the melancholy gin-soaked smell of damp pine needles and the wood smoke drifting from the chimney in my parents' house just beyond the curve. I can almost remember how it felt when, on a warm late afternoon in March, my date twirled a strand of my auburn hair between his fingers. Can almost see his look of awkward surprise when, only three weeks later, I didn't stop him from unbuttoning my blouse in the backseat of his father's Oldsmobile.

He was a sweet, pimply-faced boy named Andy Leonard, who, some years later, was killed in a hunting accident, leaving his wife and three children to mourn the fact that he'd been so drunk he forgot to wear his reflective orange vest.

After many more nights of breast holding and other fondling in his father's Oldsmobile, the act itself took place on a squeaky leatherette sofa in his older brother Freddy's trailer. That sofa, as I recall, was a vivid aqua blue and was no bigger than a love seat really. When we were stretched out together on it, Andy's legs dangled off the other end. It was the middle of July, and it must have been at least 110 degrees in that trailer, even though it wasn't even noon yet. The oscillating fan by the room's small aluminum-framed window made a lot of noise but was only blowing warm air as it spun past us with each half-rotation.

I had slipped out of the house under the pretense of going swimming in the Black Warrior River. The way I saw it, it wouldn't do for me to go off to college a virgin. And besides, I was bored with Randolph Gap, bored with Andy Leonard's fumbling attempts at seduction. I was anxious to get this whole deflowering thing over with so I could move on to bigger and better things.

My general malaise, combined with a healthy dose of misplaced teenage hormones, was, I'm sure, prompted by the fact that I'd just finished reading *Sweet & Savage Kisses*, one of the classics of the bodice-ripper genre my friends and I were reading then. On my way to the trailer that morning I bemoaned the fact that I didn't have a lacy white nightdress, since that was the type of garment usually ripped off the heroines in these novels after they'd been wandering around the moors in the wind and rain, thinking that a true and passionate love, a love they cheerfully would die for, would never come to them. The black bikini I wore under my T-shirt and shorts would have to do.

I wasn't quite sure if I'd done it right, or if Andy had done it right. I distinctly remember feeling my legs were terribly awkward, always in the way. *Sweet & Savage Kisses* never addressed that particular topic, and not knowing what to do with my legs left me feeling surprisingly embarrassed and ill-equipped to handle the whole experience.

From that book and others like it I'd picked up on some of the basic things that take place during sex, but I did not, at that age, understand how the language of those books made everything sound vastly more romantic than what was apt to happen in real life, especially to a sixteen-year-old girl in a trailer in the middle of July in Randolph Gap, Alabama. In my dreams, in my virginal twin bed late at night, I sighed as my lover left a long trail of hot kisses from my neck to my navel and then continued downward to what I'd heard described as "the center of my womanhood," whatever that meant. From girlhood speculation and scant information gleaned from friends who had brothers, I was also somewhat prepared for the presentation of "turgid manhood" these books mentioned. But what I was supposed to be doing with my legs in these new and unfamiliar positions remained a mystery to me.

Andy wasn't much help. Judging from the many times he uncomfortably shifted above me, he was having similar trouble figuring out what his correct position should be, especially since the sofa wasn't long enough to accommodate his six-foot-three-inch frame and he kept sliding backward, away and out of me. It made me wish I'd read all of *Sweet & Savage Kisses* instead of just poring over the passages my friends had underlined in red ink and had, in the margins of particularly steamy scenes, drawn loopy red hearts and smacked their lips against, leaving bright pink kiss prints. I was sure the legs issue must have been addressed at some point and I, in my haste, had missed it. So, apparently, had all of my friends.

When it was over, Andy squeaked to a sitting position on the sofa, which he now clearly blamed for the clumsiness of the proceedings. He quickly pulled up his jeans, poured himself a glass of lemonade, and left, sweaty and shirtless, to sit on the trailer's concrete steps.

I dressed and slipped out the back door, leaving him to sit there in the July sun and contemplate the fact that because of a knee injury he would be spending his senior year sorting and selling nails, tent stakes, and lightbulbs at his uncle's hardware store instead of running plays on the football field and being gazed at lovingly by half the cheerleading squad and talent scouts from the South's leading universities. When I got home, I locked myself in the bathroom and washed the blood out of my bikini bottom. We saw each other off-and-on during that long, hot summer, our dates usually taking place in that trailer. He told me he'd write me at college but never did.

For over fifteen years I forgot all about Andy Leonard.

Then one morning I saw it. Turner and I were sitting at the kitchen table on a bright Sunday morning, each of us already dressed for church and each reading a section of the newspaper. Turner was reading the *Glenville News-Tribune,* and I was reading a few clippings my mother had sent from *The Randolph Gap Ledger,* our hometown newspaper. So far there were two weddings, four recipes, and a story about using manure to fertilize your garden. Then I saw it, a four-inch-long story buried in a corner of page four of the previous week's issue:

RANDOLPH GAP HUNTER KILLED

A local father of three was killed here Saturday in what police have determined was an "unfortunate hunting accident."

Steven Andrew Leonard, 35, of 564 Cottonwood Way, was shot and killed by one of three companions who accompanied him on a deer hunting trip into the Randolph Gap Wildlife Preserve. Police are trying to determine which of the three guns fired the deadly shot, but after a thorough questioning of the men, all friends of the deceased, it appears the shooting was not intentional.

"We're still investigating this terrible tragedy, but it appears this was an unfortunate hunting accident where the parties involved were not observing proper safety regulations," said Randolph Gap Police Sgt. James Malone. "Mr. Leonard was not wearing a regulation hunting vest, which very well could have prevented the shooting." Malone also reported that a "substantial quantity" of alcoholic beverages was found in the vicinity of the hunters' overnight camp.

Because it is a state-regulated wildlife sanctuary, hunting in the Randolph Gap Wildlife Preserve is strictly prohibited during any season. Malone added that Mr. Leonard's hunting companions likely will face charges of misdemeanor trespassing and illegal hunting.

Mr. Leonard is survived by his wife and three children. Funeral services are pending.

On that morning in September, when I read that Andy Leonard had been killed in the woods, his chest ripped open in a pine thicket at the edge of the Randolph Gap Wildlife Preserve, I sat at my kitchen table and cried. I cried for Andy Leonard, for first loves, and for the loss of an innocence I could hardly even remember.

When Turner saw I was crying and asked what was wrong, I told him it was nothing. Just PMS. Nothing for him to be concerned about.

He patted my hand sympathetically.

I'd moved on to bigger and better things all right. And I was miserable.

ELEVEN

My mother meets me at the door, nearly colliding with me as she rushes out to greet me. After a sidestep of a hug between us, I maneuver my way, suitcase in hand, into the front hall. Missy, my mother's arthritic poodle, teeters toward me, her unclipped claws scratching the hardwood floor like grappling hooks. It is Missy's habit during my visits to follow me around the house and stare at me adoringly.

Outside the house, my mother's passion for holiday decorating has hit fever pitch. Plastic Easter eggs are strung from the budding branches of nearly every tree in the yard. In the shrubbery and the still-dormant flower beds, more eggs, some of them bursting at the seams with sickly looking plastic chicks or ducks, are arranged in small baskets. My mother uses neon green Easter grass to fill in where no real grass is growing. On either side of the driveway are six blow-up Easter bunnies clad in vintage-1970s tuxedos. A seventh bunny is stationed near the front door of the house itself.

"Come on in this house. Everyone's just dying to see you," cries my mother. She hauls me through the door with such a grand gesture I half expect an entire parade of long-lost relatives to be standing there in a receiving line. But there's no one in the hall but my mother and, as far as I can tell, no one is making their way to meet either of us. No one except Missy that is, who, upon arriving at the door, leans her wooly rump against one of my shoes.

Otherwise the house is deadly quiet, the stillness interrupted only by the occasional whistle of a lovesick bird in the other room and the crackle of pine logs in the fireplace. My mother has such a love of fires that she's been known to build a roaring blaze even during the summer, when she has to switch on both air conditioners to enjoy it.

She leads me through the living room, past the kitchen, and to the bedroom my sister and I shared as children. We pass a half-dozen large cages and waist-high perches, our arrival announced with a nervous ruffling of feathers and a succession of frantic little dances. I have an unsettling premonition that this is what it will be like to visit my mother after my father dies—being welcomed a little too enthusiastically into the quiet, well-dusted house of a woman who spends her day talking to birds and is out of practice with human visitors. Missy is making a valiant effort to keep up with us. The house smells of birds and, faintly, of dog piss.

In a corner of the living room, in front of the TV, Justin is sprawled on his stomach, legs planted squarely behind him. His hands grip the controls of a video game and his face is contorted in fury as he wages an onscreen battle. On the screen, one of the fighters uses a sword to lop off the cartoon head of his opponent and we watch as it lands with a bloody splatter in a wicker basket. Justin does not look up as we pass.

I could find my way blind through this house. Except for the temporary transformation of my mother's living room into an aviary for my sister's birds, nothing here has changed in more than thirty years. The same swath of black velvet, stretched between thin strips of beveled wood, hangs by a gold cord over the same, though many times reupholstered, sofa. The image on the velvet is one of a winged, golden-haired angel walking behind a child who is crossing a rickety wooden bridge at night.

On rainy afternoons when my sister and I had nothing better to do, we would sit and stare at that velvet painting for hours, wondering if there was a guardian angel watching over us. If there was an angel who would smile as she led us over rocky ledges and across unsteady bridges. An angel who would whisper in our ears the warning signs of any approaching danger.

My sister Ellen was fearless as a child, sure that her guardian angel (she named hers Matilda) was watching out for her every minute and would spare her any dire consequence resulting from her daredevil behavior. Looking at that angel on the wall affected me differently. Guardian angel or no guardian angel, I decided early on that the world was a dangerous place, that caution was required at every turn.

My mother stops and motions for me to place my suitcase outside the closed bedroom door. The look on her face tells me to be quiet about it. She speaks only when we reach the kitchen. Missy slides to the floor and, through weepy hair-clotted eyes, looks at me apologetically.

"Your sister's sleeping. She's not feeling well," my mother whispers.

My sister routinely does not feel well, which my mother always attributes to an attack of her nerves. Sleep is her cure of choice.

What my mother won't admit is that my sister's habit of falling into bed at all hours is a well-rehearsed signal. Something is about to happen, or already has happened. She's lost her job. She's out on bail. Divorce is imminent. Any number of things can bring on one of my sister's nervous attacks. The very fact that she's left her husband Cecil to fend for himself in Lot 14 of the sprawling and ever-changing landscape of Mountain Acres Estates, and is keeping Justin out of school with only two weeks left before he is to finish first grade, is an even clearer indication that trouble is brewing somewhere on the horizon.

⅋

"Let me fix you something to eat." My mother is standing in front of the stove waving a large cast-iron frying pan in the air.

"I'm really not hungry, Mother."

She moves to the refrigerator and, frying pan still in hand, reaches in to palm two eggs from the refrigerator door. My mother does not view an offer of food as a true invitation. We've often warned visitors that a refusal of her cooking might end up with crockery sailing across the kitchen. On her refrigerator four magnets shaped like watermelon slices tack down the corners of an eight-and-a-half by eleven–inch sheet of paper that, judging from the black streaks across it, has been copied many times, like a chain letter, from some anonymous source. The sheet proclaims: Emergency Phone Numbers. There are some two dozen listings underneath.

> *When your faith needs stirring, call Hebrews 11.*
> *When you grow bitter and critical, call 1 Cor. 13.*
> *If you are depressed, call Psalm 27.*
> *When your prayers grow narrow or selfish, call Psalm 67.*
> *When men fail you, call Psalm 27.*
> *If your pocketbook is empty, call Psalm 37.*

I plan on looking up Psalm 27 myself, since the cure for two of the maladies listed—men and depression—obviously are connected in some important way that has eluded me. At the bottom of the page the sheet advises:

> *Emergency numbers may be dialed direct and are toll free! No operator assistance is needed! All lines are open to Heaven twenty-four hours a day! If you feed your faith, your doubt will starve to death!*

My mother is forever collecting these kinds of inspirational messages. I'm surprised she hasn't already sent me this one by mail.

"I'll scramble up a few eggs. You always liked eggs."

"Okay, sure. Eggs are good." There's no use arguing with her.

"Is that a new bracelet?"

I study my wrists. "No. Same I always wear."

"I just love that bracelet. Turner has such good taste in jewelry."

This one I picked out myself, a fact I've pointed out to my

mother repeatedly, and always with the same reaction from her: "You paid that much?"

"I bet that friend of yours—what's her name?—gets some really good deals on all her jewelry, even if it is only costume," she announces. "They always give great employee discounts in places like that. My friend Juliette gets great bargains on all her towels and sheets because she works at that big store down in Birmingham. Even gets them monogrammed for free."

"Donna. Her name's Donna."

"Ask her about getting you a discount sometimes."

"All right, Mama," I say, picturing Donna at her kitchen stove, crying and hating her life.

"You look tired. Why don't you stop working with those crazy people and stay home to be a good wife to Turner." She cracks the eggs into a small blue bowl. "It's not like you need to work."

This is something new.

To say that the sexual revolution and the general acceptance of women in the workplace are ideas that never quite caught on in Randolph Gap would, I guess, be true to some extent, but to leave it at that offers an incomplete understanding of the mentality that exists here. The point, at least to my mother and almost everyone else I know in Randolph Gap, is that people work only if they have to.

If your husband, or your wife, earns a good living, you don't have to work. If you're still drawing a check for an accident that knocked you off a scaffold two years ago, you don't have to work. If you slip on a wet floor in the produce section of the big new supermarket just off the interstate and, in your recovery, threaten lawsuits and win a tidy settlement from the supermarket chain, you don't have to work. Not having to work has nothing to do with being male or female. It's like winning the lottery. Your prayers are either answered or they're not.

"You could visit one of those fertility doctors, you know," she says. "Be like those women on TV having quintuplets. People will give you all sorts of things if you had five babies at a time. One family even got a new house. I saw it on the news. All the babies lived, too. Little things, about a pound apiece, but they lived."

"Who's been talking to you? It wasn't Turner, was it?"

Her back is turned to me while she uses a fork to whip the eggs, her shoulders shaking with the whirling action of the eggs in the bowl.

"Absolutely not. I'm just worried about you, that's all. I can tell by looking at you that something's not right. It doesn't take somebody telling me something for me to know something's not right with my own daughter. The very idea is ridiculous. That's what it is. Besides, why would he say anything to me?"

Whenever my mother tries to lie, she becomes overly defensive, her voice rising at the end of each sentence, and she tends to babble. By the time she rambles into "say anything to me?" her voice hits such an operatic note that I fear the antique ceiling fan overhead will fly off its hinges. I can see it landing in the center of the table, slicing off my head in the process.

It's also a sound that, inevitably, stirs up the birds in the adjacent room. A series of similarly high-pitched wails of "to me, to me, TO TO TO ME" echo my mother's voice.

"Those birds just crack me up," she says. "You really should get one. It's just like having a child around the house."

&

Something, of course, did happen to prompt all this debate about the risks of my chosen profession. On Tuesday afternoon, a client and I had what could, I guess, be called an altercation. It was just one of those things. Certainly nothing to get upset about.

His name is Melvin Spivey and when he showed up for his two o'clock appointment, I could tell something was wrong. I didn't need some sort of multiphasic test to tell me that. He didn't look good out of his eyes.

"So tell me, Melvin, how are you sleeping?"

Melvin's vacant, ashen-ringed eyes stared at the carpet floor in my cubicle. His forehead was a mass of despairing wrinkles and his hands gripped his knees until his knuckles turned white.

"You haven't been sleeping, have you, Melvin?"

Melvin did not look at me but kept his eyes fixed on the blue carpet. He didn't answer either, but he didn't have to tell me he hadn't been sleeping. I knew he hadn't. I pictured him sitting on the edge of a stained and lumpy mattress in his pay-by-the-week room at the Whispering Pines Motor Court, listening to the loud tick of the alarm clock and the rhythmic thumping of a bed in the room next door. I couldn't much blame him. I probably wouldn't be able to sleep either.

Melvin's hands slowly kneaded the fabric of his jeans. I made a note in his chart that he was nonresponsive. Another that he wasn't sleeping.

My questions were getting nowhere. Melvin just sat there. I checked his chart. He was taking a fairly high dosage of an antipsychotic, and his dosage had been increased since his last visit. He was on several other medications too. An anticonvulsant to counteract the muscle spasms that are a side effect of the antipsychotic, a mood stabilizer, plus something else to help him sleep. Sleeplessness is another common side effect of antipsychotic drugs. Some patients, when they are able to sleep, have nightmares that are more bizarre and disturbing then the conditions for which they are being treated.

I realized that Melvin wasn't moving much. The muscle spasms in his neck, which he'd had last month and the month before, were gone. Even the anticonvulsant hadn't put a complete stop to them. I knew then he wasn't taking his medication. That explained a lot. I made another note in his chart.

"Is there something you want to talk to me about, Melvin? Something you want to tell me?"

Melvin made fists with both hands. I could hear him grinding his teeth. I moved my chair toward him an inch or so, bending my head lower in an effort to get a good look at his eyes, to try to connect with him in some meaningful way. I reached out my hand to him, wanting, I guess, to pat his arm reassuringly, to let him know someone cared.

That was when he bit me, grabbing my left arm with both of his stubby, white-knuckled hands and sinking his teeth through the fabric of my new yellow silk blouse, just above my wrist.

❧

"I can't believe you want to work somewhere where people go around biting each other," my mother says as she spoons lumps of congealed, half-cooked egg onto my plate. She opens a loaf of sandwich bread and arranges two misshapen slices next to the eggs.

"Where's Daddy, anyway?" I ask, trying to avoid this conversation, and the meal. "Is he working the late shift again?"

"You could at least work in a proper office somewhere, or in a department store like your friend. Donna, that's her name, isn't it? People don't go around biting each other in department stores."

"This is the first time it's happened, Mama. And it's not like people are running around biting each other. He bit me. I didn't bite him back." People are, on the other hand, running around Donna's department store screwing each other, but I keep that bit of information to myself. Biting is bad enough. I don't want to get my mother started on the subject of screwing.

"Well, if that lunatic bit me, I'd have knocked some sense into him on the spot."

"He wasn't taking his medication, Mama. He didn't know what he was doing. It's not his fault." Poor Melvin is this very weekend being held in the clinic's inpatient wing until a forced round of medication, at an even higher dosage, makes its way into his bloodstream. He probably doesn't even remember biting me.

"It's okay. Really. He hardly even broke the skin." That wasn't exactly true.

"Pull up your sleeve. I want to see."

"It's nothing. Really, Mama."

Missy, slumped at my feet, gazes up at me with cataract-covered pupils. She does her best to get my attention with a series of exasperated sighs.

My mother hovers over my shoulder, waiting for me to roll up my sleeve and produce the evidence. "I cannot understand how you're taking this so lightly, as if nothing ever happened. You'd think all that education of yours would have taught you something."

I unbutton my cuff and push back my sleeve to reveal a large square bandage. Underneath are four tooth-shaped punctures, two of which are larger and deeper because Melvin has a significant overbite and his two front teeth hit their target more accurately than the others.

My mother unceremoniously rips off the bandage and pulls my arm close to her face so she can study the wound.

"The very idea," she says, turning away in disgust. "People biting each other like animals. What's this world coming to is what I want to know. They ought to lock this man up and throw away the key. And don't you go letting your father see that. He'll have a fit."

I repaste the bandage to my bruised arm, unroll my sleeve to my wrist, and button it. I sit there in silence, eating my eggs.

TWELVE

The fact that my mother is encouraging me to visit a fertility doctor is even more unsettling. As if I need to hear that now. As if that could solve all my problems.

Turner and I wanted children. Still do, I guess. But I'm still not ready to deal with any more doctors.

I've had four miscarriages during my marriage, the most recent happening this past October, the same month Wanda McNabb killed her husband. The thought of being pregnant again fills me with sadness, loneliness, and guilt over the babies I lost. My mother tells me I should be over it by now, that I should feel blessed to have the chance to carry another baby, but I can't get past it. I don't know if I ever will.

By mid-October, I was fourteen weeks pregnant. Only fourteen weeks, not far enough along to feel the baby kick but far enough for people to notice that I was developing a rounder belly. Far enough along that, according to all the prenatal books, my baby was fully formed, even at only three to four inches long, complete with its own unique set of fingerprints. The morning sickness I'd had in the first few months was starting to go away, and my breasts felt heavier.

Since my other three miscarriages occurred before I was three months along—"spontaneous abortion," the doctors called it—we thought we'd done it this time. We couldn't bear to keep the news to ourselves any longer, so we told everyone. While our neighbors were setting out their pumpkins and other Halloween decorations, we had a big party and pinned up blue and pink balloons everywhere in the house, on the front porch, and on the mailbox. Donna Lindsey and my mother, even Mrs. Farmer at the bank, began planning baby showers.

Then, in that fourteenth week, I went to my obstetrician on a sunny Thursday afternoon for a regular checkup.

"We should be able to hear the baby's heartbeat today!" he said as he dashed into the room while donning a pair of surgical gloves. "This is an exciting time for you. For all of you," he said, patting my belly affectionately.

Turner went with me to the doctor's office but sat in a chair in a corner of the examining room, holding my clothes and looking afraid to move. I loved him then for his anxiousness, for his timid manner in the presence of our baby's heartbeat.

The doctor listened. Adjusted things. Listened some more. It seemed the cold surface of the doctor's instrument moved across every gooey inch of my gel-covered belly.

"We need to order an ultrasound," he said. "We've been needing to do one anyway."

"I thought we'd hear the heartbeat today," I said. "That's what you told us."

"Well, these things are tricky sometimes. Nothing to be concerned about. That baby's just curled up in there as tight as a bear in a den."

Two days later I went in for the ultrasound. Turner held my hand as the technician, who announced that her name was Debbie, rubbed more conducting jelly over my abdomen, and said, "Okay, folks, you ready for the show?" We both watched as the grainy picture appeared on the computer monitor. I'd planned to frame a photo of our baby in utero and give it to my mother.

"I can't tell what's what," Turner said. "Is that the baby? It looks like a satellite picture of a weather storm on the eastern seaboard."

"Hush up, Turner," I said. "This is serious."

"Well, it does," he said, and squeezed my hand.

Debbie the technician was silent.

"Tell us what's going on," he said, suddenly looking alarmed. "Is that the baby or not?" He pointed to a dark oval shape on the computer screen.

"Look, I'm just the tech here," said Debbie. "But I'm going to schedule you an appointment with your doctor first thing tomorrow."

"We just saw the doctor two days ago," Turner said.

"Well, you need to see him again."

That night was a sleepless one.

We knew something was wrong. Debbie would have told us if she'd seen the baby. Would have bragged to us that she could hear its beating heart. I found Turner in the den at four o'clock that next morning, calmly puncturing all the blue and pink balloons and stuffing them into a trash bag.

A few hours later Turner and I arrived at the reception desk of my doctor's office. We must have been the first appointment of the day, because there were no other women waiting.

"We'll show you right in," said the young nurse, who wore a smock decorated with diaper pins and storks. On my previous visits here, she had been giggly and chatty, telling me about her own two-year-old, who was driving her "pea-eyed crazy," and asking me what I planned to name my own baby. On that morning she was sober-faced and quiet.

Just by looking at her face, I knew.

I had to strip and put on the standard paper gown. I sat on the examining table swinging my legs and trying to keep the gown from falling off my shoulders. Turner sat in the same chair, again holding my clothes.

The doctor said I'd be scheduled for a D&C the next day, where they would scrape out my uterus, baby and all. A simple procedure, he said. General anesthesia, he said.

"Your baby is not alive."

Not alive.

Not alive.

Not alive.

That's all I could hear. *Not alive. Your baby.*

Your baby with its own fingerprints. Your baby with her ten fingers and ten toes and no beating heart. The room was spinning.

The week after the surgery, Turner went to work every day, the same as usual. Donna Lindsey brought me tea, and we rented movies I don't remember watching. I stayed in bed a lot. I was in a Demerol haze for the better part of the week. I never knew I could cry so much.

"If you pray, God will bless you with children," my mother had said, but that's not what I wanted to hear. I was tired of praying. I wanted my baby back, my baby with its fingerprints, its fingers and toes and a strong beating heart. We never even knew whether it was a boy or girl, though something in me believes it must have been a girl. I would have named her Margaret. Margaret Elise Maddox. My Margaret. We never even got to bury her. Never had the chance to mourn her properly.

These days all I can think about is that by now I would be eight and a half months pregnant. Margaret Elise Maddox would have been born in April. I could have come home to my parents' house with a new grandchild.

&

That first night in my parents' house I find myself, in dreams, walking up the wide front stairs of Caldwell's Funeral Home. The funeral director—lean, balding, and dressed in a tailored black suit—meets me at the door. His name is Fletcher Calhoun, and for twenty-five years he has overseen every important detail of the final tributes of Glenville's most prominent citizens.

We operate a turnkey operation here, he proclaims proudly. *Leave all the details to us.*

The main office of the funeral home itself is alive with ringing phones, the whirring of a fax machine, all the general clatter of arrangements being made to accommodate the newly dead. On the corner of one desk stands a towering arrangement of silk carnations in the shape of a cross. A blue ribbon, strung beauty-queen fashion, proclaims REST IN JESUS.

When we reach the casket showroom—Fletcher Calhoun calls it the Serenity Room—he holds the door open for me. Soft white lights, the kind found in the hospitality bars of hotels and airports, flip on automatically. There are maybe fifteen caskets arranged there on their pedestals, lids open to reveal the fluffy satin bedding. The more expensive models are bathed in the glow of overhead spot-lights. From a speaker hidden somewhere in the room, I can hear a harpsichord rendition of "Greensleeves."

Fletcher Calhoun describes each model. The walnut, the cherry, the bronze, the silver. Each has a name. Abiding Devotion. Tranquil-lity. Heavenly Comfort. All the kind of names given to thoroughbred racehorses whose temperaments are anything but calm.

When we come to the last model on display, I notice that the lid, unlike all the others, is closed. *This will be your favorite, Mrs. Maddox,* he says as he runs a bleached hand over the smooth mahogany. *I know you'll want the very best for your loved one who will spend eternity nestled on the pillows inside.*

He actually says this. *Nestled.* He tells me he plans to be buried in this very same model.

It's completely waterproof and rustproof. Guaranteed for one thousand years.

Is that important?

It is highly important, he informs me. *It is,* he insists, *a most loving tribute.* To purchase any other, lesser casket will lead Fletcher Calhoun to believe that I am interested not in a loving tribute, but instead in a thoughtless and insensitive rite for a distant relative I never liked but somehow find myself responsible for burying.

The handles, he tells me, *are plated with 18-karat gold.*

I make an appreciative sigh.

A most loving tribute indeed.

I ask him to open the lid. I want to see inside.

Imported lace. Handcrafted. He removes a dainty monogrammed handkerchief from his breast pocket and wipes away any trace of his fingerprints on the shiny surface. I wonder if it is his job to polish it daily.

I'd like to see inside, please.

Notice the delicate carvings. The intertwined hearts. And those cherubs!

Yes, but—

A vault of solid steel.

I reach to open it, my purse landing with a thud against the gold railing. The lid is surprisingly heavy and, at first, I think it might be stuck. Finally, it swings upward. What I see inside is my own body resting against all that imported satin and lace.

Fletcher Calhoun folds his hands in front of his body, all the composure of his lifetime of service at Caldwell's Funeral Home preparing him for this most delicate of situations.

THIRTEEN

Officiant: *O God, make speed to save us.*

People: *O Lord, make haste to help us.*

THE INVITATORY AND THE PSALTER

THE BOOK OF COMMON PRAYER

Wanda McNabb was married thirty-six years. Like many of her girlhood friends in Glenville, but against the wishes of her parents, she dropped out of high school to marry a boy who, despite his reckless efforts to do otherwise, made it home from Vietnam with all his anatomy intact.

Her four children were born within five years. Baxter Jr. a week after her eighteenth birthday; the twins Mollie and Annie when she was barely twenty; the youngest girl, Bobbie, when she was twenty-two. The children, along with Wanda's seven grandchildren, now live in cities more than a casual drive away from Glenville, far enough away from the headlines that made her a subject of town speculation and brought her to me.

Her children dutifully returned to Glenville for their father's funeral, arriving with a flurry of suitcases and baby carriers and cellular phones, but were turned away from their childhood home to search for the nearest available lodging. A large sign with its foreboding, Day-Glo message—CRIME SCENE: DO NOT ENTER UNDER RISK OF PROSECUTION—was tacked to the front door, and the door itself was crisscrossed with yellow police tape.

Four days later, when Baxter Sr. was safely buried and Wanda had been taken into police custody, they were gone again, pulling out of the long, unpaved driveway of the Whispering Pines Motor Court and heading toward the interstate in a dusty caravan of one station wagon, two Saturns, and a rental car.

"I don't blame them for leaving," Wanda told me during the first week of December. "I'd have left, too, if the police hadn't picked me up. I wanted to leave more than anything else in the world."

I considered this. I couldn't imagine myself sitting in a jail cell, holding my mother's hand and telling her everything was going to be all right when I couldn't be sure of that and all I could think about was visiting her behind bars for the next twenty-five years to life.

"They never talked about it, you know," she said. "For those few days they were here, it was almost like it never happened, like their father had dropped dead of a heart attack, or was in one of those ten-car pileups they're always showing on the news."

Her children, she told me, simply called up family and friends and, with sparing emotion, announced that their father was dead. They did not give details. When the clerk at the Whispering Pines

Motor Court, on hearing that the entire family was staying in town for a funeral, politely expressed his sympathies, Baxter Jr. told him, in all seriousness, "It was a long illness."

The funeral, she said, was well attended. "The church choir sang Baxter's favorite hymns and everybody came up to me afterward and said nice things and held my hand and asked if there was anything they could do."

All in all, everything was just as Baxter would have wanted it. People brought pies and fried chicken and casseroles to the motor court and, Glenville being the kind of place most people pass through on their way to sunnier destinations, the food was enjoyed not only by the McNabb mourners but also a New Jersey family of seven on their way to Tampa, Florida; a magazine distributor from Memphis, Tennessee; a newlywed couple from Chicago driving to the Georgia coast; and, of course, the Whispering Pines Motor Court clerk and his family.

It was as if no one knew what really happened, or even cared, at least for those few days. For reasons that had something to do with the police report being temporarily misfiled, the *Glenville News-Tribune* was a few days late in proclaiming the news. By the time they did, on the morning Wanda was questioned by the police—when, as she put it, "the coast was clear"—her family disappeared. She was left alone to face the stares of the neighbors who had so recently offered her their sincere condolences and homemade dishes. As she said, "At least they had the decency to wait until after the funeral before the rumors started flying."

The newspaper story made things clear enough, but the gossip following that revelation was the biggest news to hit Glenville in a long time. Many of the resulting rumors were ghoulish and horrific.

Wanda, they said, took her just revenge because she caught Baxter having an affair. With whom they couldn't say, but that didn't seem to matter. The story went that Wanda, in an act of passion, lost her temper, shooting him with some sort of automatic weapon and blowing his head clean off. That explained the closed casket because, as everybody knows, you can't sew a man's head back onto his shoulders and make it look natural.

Wanda, they said, killed him in some wild Satanic ritual and held a wineglass over his pumping chest wound as he lay on the floor of her sewing room gasping for air. She then gulped down a full glass of his blood and said a few prayers to Satan before she made sure he was dead and called 911.

It seemed there was a new rumor every day.

You just have to take our word for it, they said.

We have ways of finding these things out, they said.

The newspaper can't be expected to report such grisly details, they said.

Even though the town gradually began to accept the mundane reality of what had occurred, and Wanda returned home, there were still people who weren't quite sure what to believe. These were the people who grabbed the hands of their children and led them off in the other direction whenever they saw Wanda approaching in the supermarket or in the public library. Wanda even stopped going to church, figuring that those members of her congregation who branded her a Satanist would be forever suspicious if she did not, at an altar call one day in the future, admit that they were right and confess that her heart once belonged to the Prince of Darkness himself.

That was the hardest part of it all, she said. She and Baxter were married in that church and she hoped to have her own funeral there one day. She'd already picked out what hymns she wanted the choir to sing.

"All that week, people kept telling me what a good man Baxter was, how much he loved me and the children," she said. "It was true, but it still hurt to hear them say it, to be reminded of it."

I asked Wanda if she thought her husband was a good man, and if so, if that absolved him from picking up that baseball bat, if somehow that explained why she endured thirty-six years of violence.

"Yes," she said finally. "I do think he was, or at least he tried to be most days. What he did to me doesn't make the rest of it untrue."

 *FOURTEEN*

E yes still closed and not quite awake, I feel like I'm being watched. It's Saturday morning, and I'm in the narrow twin bed of my childhood, my toes jammed up against the white footboard decorated with stenciled daisies.

The first thing I see is a flash of blue feathers.

All of my senses kick in slowly, like I'm waking up from anesthesia.

There are feathers, then whole wings in my view. The wings are flapping and I feel the resulting cool breeze on my face, hear, finally, the cluck-cluck of the creature with the feathers. I fight back the urge to fling my arms protectively in front of my face.

I'd known it all along. Those birds are planning to peck my eyes out.

What I find is Justin sitting on the edge of my bed, a large blue-and-gold macaw perched on his shoulder. Justin's jaws are working lazily around the ears of a foot-long chocolate Easter bunny. The bird stares off in the opposite direction, like he wants me to believe it isn't his idea to wake me up in this manner, that he's had nothing whatsoever to do with this terrible rudeness. I rub my eyes with the knuckles of both hands until I see the flashes of light that convince me I can't be dreaming. I blink at my nephew, trying to will my pupils into focus. I can hear Missy scratching against the bedroom door.

"Well, hello," I mumble. "You're up early."

Justin glares at me like I've interrupted his train of thought. Only seven years old and, despite the bunny ears still protruding from his mouth, his whole demeanor projects the jaded, pale appearance of an aging rock star. I wonder if he has any friends his own age. If he has any friends at all besides these birds.

"Did a crazy man really bite you?" He says this with his cheeks full of chocolate, then sits there with his mouth still hanging open, as if the process of chewing has exhausted him completely, causing his jaw to become permanently unhinged. A foamy chunk of bunny ear sticks to two of his lower front teeth, both of which are mere specks of yellow in his gaping mouth. When I don't answer, he plugs his mouth again with the bunny ears. He's probably been sitting here for some time, waiting for me to wake up so he can ask me this question.

"Shouldn't you be watching cartoons or something?" I ask, relieved that my bruised and bandaged arm is still under the covers.

Beyond the closed door, I can hear a clattering of pans in the kitchen and the sound of something frying.

"I'm not a baby." He pulls the bunny ears from his mouth with a sucking sound and sits there with his thin pale arms crossed over his faded black T-shirt, which must be four sizes too big, the tail of it reaching past his knees. Justin's blond hair is cut extremely short, neatly shaved on the sides and over his ears, but one braided strand about four inches long hangs from the nape of his neck and is secured at the end with a pink barrette so tiny it looks like something I might have worn as an infant. A small gold earring gleams from his right earlobe, and on his left wrist there is a tattoo of a skull with a dagger stuck through one of its eye sockets. From the tip of the dagger drip several drops of blood that look alarmingly realistic.

"That's not a real tattoo, is it?" I ask, wary that my sister's parenting is seriously off balance.

"Mom says she'll let me get a real one when I turn sixteen, long as I pay for it myself."

"But what about this one?"

"Naaaah. It's one of those wimpy wash-off kinds." So I can get a better look, he holds his skinny wrist about three inches from my face. He turns his wrist back and forth so I can get the full effect.

"It's very colorful."

"I picked it out myself," he says, breathless with the excitement of what he perceives as a compliment. "And . . . and . . . when this one wears off, I'm gonna do a motorcycle." He looks at his wrist again, pleased with his choice of designs. The bunny ears slide back into his mouth.

My sister never was one to enforce standards of dress or manners on anyone, but this is going a little too far. I fish around on the nightstand for a tissue and hand it to Justin, directing him to wipe the chocolate off his fingers and mouth. He does it reluctantly, then wraps the soiled tissue around the body of the bunny and starts chewing at it again.

"So did you get bit or what?"

"It's not very nice to listen when adults are talking," I say, referring, of course, to the fact that he obviously overheard the previous night's discussion about Melvin Spivey. For a first real conversation between an aunt and her young nephew, this is not going well.

There is an uncomfortable, extended silence between us. It appears Justin plans to sit on my bed until he gets some sort of story out of me about the crazy man and the biting incident. Stubborn, and not unlike my mother in this regard. I'm being held hostage by a morose seven-year-old and his sidekick, who continues, in silence, to survey the scene from his perch on Justin's shoulder. One of them needs an eye patch to complete the absurd picture.

I have a sudden urge to start screaming.

I sit up halfway in bed and prop two pillows against the headboard.

"What's your friend's name?" I ask, hoping we can start over.

Justin does not want to change the subject. "Are you going to tell me about the crazy man or not?"

"Let's talk for a minute first and I'll tell you what happened, okay?"

He considers this. "Maxwell. His name's Maxwell."

On hearing his name, Maxwell stretches out his tail feathers in a long fanning arc that extends most of the way down Justin's back, bends his head close to Justin's chin, and clucks amorously. "Good parrot. Good bird," comes the raspy, inquisitive voice. Maxwell sounds like a bad imitation of George Burns, or maybe Groucho Marx, but then again, all these birds sound that way to me.

"Yeah, you're a good bird," Justin answers tenderly, reaching up to scratch Maxwell's chest feathers. The bird's head is black-and-white striped and topped with a bright green crest, which is a bold contrast to the back feathers that are royal blue interspersed with yellow. A long rubbery tongue darts in and out of his substantial beak. That beak could scoop out one of my eyeballs. Why my sister doesn't think a dog would be a more appropriate pet for a boy I'll never know. But it doesn't matter what I think. These two obviously like each other. Maxwell, basking in all this attention, raises his head, shakes out his feathers, and starts to sing, or at least it sounds like that's what he's trying to do.

"How old is Maxwell?"

"Mom says he's about sixty. The guy who owned him kicked the bucket. That's how we got him. He was really old. Lots older than Max."

"Maxwell's that old?" At that, the bird turns his amber eyes toward me. He actually looks offended.

"Mom says he'll live at least forty more years, maybe more. Are you going to tell me about the crazy man now?"

"Okay, but first of all, let's not use the word *crazy*."

"Why not? He's crazy, ain't he?"

Maxwell rocks back and forth on Justin's shoulder like an oversized version of one of those plastic novelty birds that people used to put in the backs of cars. When Maxwell dips forward he slides the tip of his curved beak inside Justin's shirt pocket, exclaiming a childlike "Ha, ha!" each time he withdraws it. It looks like they've played this game before.

"We don't like to use that word, Justin," I stammer. "Because these people are sick, just like when you have the chicken pox or the flu—"

"I've never had chicken pox."

"Well okay, that's not important. The point is these people are sick."

"Are you going to get sick now because he bit you? Are you going to go crazy?" My nephew looks at me with anticipation, no doubt expecting I'll soon show clear signs of madness, like in the movies when there's a close-up of some guy being bitten by a mosquito and in the next scene he's sweating with fever and showing unmistakable symptoms of malaria. "We learned all about germs in school," he adds proudly.

"No, I can't get sick. It's a different kind of sickness. Not the germ kind, but a sickness in his mind."

I'm not sure how much I should tell a seven-year-old about Melvin Spivey's illness. There's a running censor in my head.

"So he bit you because he was sick?"

"Something like that, yes."

"Did it hurt?"

"It did a little, but not for long." That's a lie. My arm is still sore.

"Didn't you want to beat him up? Do something to hurt him back?"

"No, Justin, I didn't. He was sick. He didn't know what he was doing."

Justin thinks about this for a minute. "That's silly. I always know what I'm doing," says the young skeptic. "So can I see it? I'm not gonna faint or nothin'."

Against my better judgment, I pull my arm from underneath the covers. My nephew stares at the bandage with a look of utter disappointment. Maybe he was expecting that Melvin had the teeth of a leopard. That my wrist would be lacerated beyond reconstruction. That he'd see exposed bone.

"C'mon, let me really see." Maxwell looks too, craning his head my way.

I have one more chance to redeem myself, to prove he's not been sitting here badgering me for nothing. I peel back the bandage to reveal the two neat rows of puncture wounds, a parenthesis carved into my skin. The surrounding bruise is beginning to turn a nauseating shade of green.

His response?

"Pretty cool, I guess."

With no further pronouncement on the matter, he heads for the door. Maxwell rocks back and forth on his shoulder, doing his seasick little dance.

&

I told Justin we didn't refer to people like Melvin Spivey as crazy. For the most part, that's true. But working at the Glenville Wellness Center is a lot like *M*A*S*H*, where they're always running for cover in mortar attacks and there's a truckload of wounded coming in and they're operating on some poor guy by candlelight and you just know there's another poor guy waiting to be operated on and bleeding to death in the process. In the middle of all that they can still find something to laugh about and people are playing practical jokes on each other and you know that if they didn't they'd all go stark raving crazy for real.

I remember precisely when this happened to me. I'd been a case manager three years and was seeing a patient I inherited from another counselor who, after six years on the job, joined the well-populated ranks of the clinic's burned-out and disillusioned and opted for a career as a checkout clerk at Wal-Mart.

My patient's name was Varina Nichols, but everyone at the clinic except me called her Snow White. Everywhere she went she whistled that silly song from the Disney movie, as if she were leading a parade of adoring, hardworking dwarfs to their next job site.

I was appalled that they did this behind her back. Whenever Varina entered the clinic at her appointed time, whistling slightly off-key, I was sure she could hear the twittering of my colleagues and would hold me directly responsible. Varina was in her late forties and had been institutionalized repeatedly after a number of close brushes with what the experts call "suicidal ideation."

One day, out of concern for the snickering that likely would follow the whistling Varina down the hall to the clinic's pharmacy, I followed her. While we stood in front of the pharmacist's window, she tapped her foot and whistled her happy tune.

After a few minutes of this, she lost interest in waiting and I watched as she began to glide across the floor toward a magazine rack, her arms floating upward as if she expected a flock of bluebirds to join her impromptu ballet. My coworkers were right. I was, indeed, treating Snow White. I half expected a group of tiny forest creatures to pop out from their hiding places in the air-conditioning vents and gather at her feet.

The pharmacist leaned through his little window and handed Varina's prescription to me. "Looks like you've got a live one on your hands," he said with a chuckle.

I frowned at him and stared down at the printout that was stapled to the white paper bag containing Varina's medication.

"Take this medication only as directed," it advised.

"This medication may cause some people to become drowsy, dizzy, or light-headed."

"This medication may impair your ability to drive or operate heavy machinery."

"This medication may induce a false sense of well being."

I turned to look at Varina, who by then was taking a bow, her performance ended, her face flushed and radiant.

Now there's a side effect I wouldn't mind having, I thought to myself.

And that was that.

That's when everything changed for me. I started to envy Varina's happiness, even if it was induced by medication, even if it was temporary. A false sense of well being, at least for Varina, was a hell of a lot better than the alternative.

For a long time after that, I saw my whole life as a search for this elusive and mysterious state of mind.

This chocolate may induce a false sense of well being, I'd say to myself as I tossed a few Snickers bars into my grocery cart.

This cheeseburger may induce a false sense of well being, I'd think as I grabbed a quick drive-through lunch and took the first juicy bite.

This home may induce a false sense of well being, I'd repeat as I lit candles and arranged vases of freshly cut flowers in preparation for our dinner guests, all clients of Turner's.

This caress, this marriage, may induce a false sense of well being, I would tell myself as Turner reached across the bedcovers to find me waiting there in the dark.

 *FIFTEEN*

"Have I ever shown you my babies?" It was the week before Christmas, some four months ago, and Wanda McNabb searched in her canvas bag for the photo album she always carried with her. "I know it's in here somewhere. I couldn't call myself a proper grandmother if I didn't have pictures to show off, now could I?"

After a few minutes, during which it seemed the entire contents of Wanda's purse was dumped on my desk, she retrieved it at last. The album's cover was quilted and trimmed in lace that was fraying at the edges. The words *My Family* were spelled out in yellow embroidery thread. It looked like something my mother would bring home from the Randolph Gap Swap Meet.

Wanda slowly thumbed at the pages. There were photos on top of photos in each page's bulging slipcover. She pulled them out one at a time, telling me who was in each photo and how old they were when it was taken. Just when you thought I'd seen the last photo, there was another one hidden underneath.

"You're lucky to have such a beautiful family, to be loved by so many people," I told her. "That means a lot." Looking at those photos of Wanda's children, I was trying not to cry. I'd lost my baby only weeks earlier, and the wound—of my own lost family—was still fresh.

"I guess so," she said. She sounded like she didn't believe it.

"The holidays must be tough for you this year," I said. "But think of how much fun you'll have with those beautiful grandchildren." I was doing my best to put a positive spin on things.

"Uh huh," she said, her voice cracking with a sob. She would, she said, be staying in Glenville for the holidays. She would not be going to Denver to have a snowy Christmas with Bobbie, not to Knoxville to be with Mollie, not to Savannah to be with Annie, not even the short distance to Bessemer, Alabama, to be with Baxter Jr. They wouldn't be coming to Glenville to visit her either.

I asked how she felt about that, even though it was obvious.

"They have their own lives now, and I understand that," she said. I handed her a tissue. "I mean, it's okay really. Their all have the flu, and their children all have the flu, and besides, they were just here in October anyway. They have their reasons." The reason for their October visit was anything but happy, but I didn't have to tell Wanda that.

It sounded like she was trying to convince herself more than me. I asked what she planned to do since she'd be alone. I hope I said it a little less bluntly than that, but I'm sure it didn't make her feel any less lonely.

"Oh, I'll keep busy," she said. "Probably go put a Christmas wreath on Baxter's grave, make sure the headstone is there this time. Last time I went by it wasn't." She launched into a brief tirade on the incompetence of the monument company designing the tombstone, how what they were charging her was highway robbery. Then she turned her attention to the cemetery itself, which, she said, had entirely too many rules about floral arrangements interfering with the grounds crew's mowing routine. She planted a white-blooming azalea near where the headstone would be placed and someone, she said, had the nerve to rip it out of the ground by the roots. She even received a rude note in the mail outlining the proper procedures "for placing tasteful remembrances of your loved one."

She wasn't planning on putting up a Christmas tree either. "Baxter always went out in the woods behind our house and cut one down. We never had nothing fancy or anything, usually an old cedar or sometimes a pine if it was full enough. Christmas won't be the same without one of his trees."

The more she talked, the more she cried, the more depressed I felt. I pictured Wanda sitting in her kitchen on Christmas Day, eating a turkey-and-dressing dinner out of a microwavable box or maybe joining some of our other clients for a free holiday meal served at the Glenville Civic Center. I wondered if her children would send her Christmas presents through the mail, if they were sending any presents at all.

Turner and I would spend a quiet Christmas alone, the two of us sitting around our tastefully decorated artificial spruce, nothing to say to each other except for the most perfunctory of holiday greetings, our presents opened with polite smiles.

Christmas at our house means the obligatory calls to the last remaining members of Turner's family. Then calls to my family. Then the two of us watching some incessantly cheerful holiday special on TV, until Turner falls asleep in his chair, then waking up, startled, and stumbling off to bed.

I longed to invite Wanda to my house for Christmas dinner, but that, unfortunately, was out of the question. I could just imagine how that evening would turn out.

It's so nice to meet you, Wanda, Turner would say while carving the Christmas turkey. *Jessie never introduces me to any of her friends from work.*

Well, it's awfully nice of you to invite me, Mr. Maddox. You have such a beautiful home.

Turner would smile indulgently, the way he always does when someone says this. As if he's thinking, *Yes, we know that already.*

I'd listen to them prattle on about how unseasonably warm the weather had been for the holiday season. About the pattern of the drapes in our dining room. About how Turner's late father and grandfather were bankers at the very bank where Turner works now, and that his grandfather, in fact, *had some small role* in founding the bank itself. About how delicious the turkey was, and *how juicy.* All the topics about which Turner can prattle on endlessly, and with anyone. I don't know how he can stand it.

I would be waiting for the big moment, for the exact instant when Turner figured out who Wanda McNabb really was.

So tell me Wanda, what do you do at the clinic?

Why Mr. Maddox, I don't work there. I thought you knew that.

No?

No.

Well what do you do then? Turner probably would be thinking at this point that Wanda was a visiting psychiatrist, someone I'd rescued from holiday on-call duty by inviting her into my home.

I bake a lot of cookies, Wanda would say. *I play bingo on Thursdays. I try to keep busy.*

Ahhhh, my husband would say, holding his fork in midair. *So you're the one who bakes those delicious cookies Jessie keeps bringing home?*

That's me.

And what about your husband? Couldn't he come with you today? Wanda, as Turner would have noticed, continues to wear her wedding ring.

Here we go.

He's dead.

Oh. I'm so sorry.

Oh, it's okay, really. They dropped all the charges.

A light begins to dawn.

Well, hmmmm, uhhhh—

But I did kill him.

And at that point, Turner would choke to death on his forkful of turkey. Wanda and I would finish our holiday meal, split a pecan pie for dessert, sing Christmas carols, and stay up all night, doing each other's hair.

Before Wanda left her session that day, we exchanged Christmas gifts. I'd never done that with a patient before, and could, in fact, have lost my job because of it, but with the way the session turned out, I was glad I brought something for her. She continued to bring me cookies on each of her visits, so I had a suspicion she was going to give me something, maybe a tin of sugar cookies cut in holiday shapes.

We handed our gifts to each other and sat there holding them, encouraging the other to open her gift first.

My gift was in a brightly wrapped box roughly the size of the photo album Wanda carried in her purse. I feared it might be an identical such photo album. I was afraid I wouldn't have enough favorite photos to fill it, small as it was.

I gave Wanda a dessert cookbook, thinking she might find a few more cookie recipes in it. I had a dozen or more of those cookbooks at home, all left over from a Glenville Society Cotillion fund-raising sale a few years ago. I didn't realize until much later what a sad gift it was, didn't realize then how much I would regret giving it to her. I gave a cookbook to a woman who lived alone, a woman who had no family to cook for, not even for Christmas. I only recently thought of this, and I hate myself for doing something so stupid. The fact that the cookbook was a *leftover* gift, not really a gift at all, was an additional burden on my conscience.

She didn't act disappointed. "This is just the sweetest thing," she said, leafing through the book and making appreciative "oooohs" and "aaaahhs" over glossy photographs of apple pie à la mode and three-layer cakes with buttercream frosting. "I just love a good recipe, as you know by now," she added, patting her stomach.

Before I finished unwrapping my gift, she started apologizing for it.

"It's not much. Just a little something."

Inside the box was an antique cameo pin. It was exquisite. I lifted it out of its box and placed it in the palm of my hand and there it perched, like some kind of delicate bird.

"Wanda, I really don't know what to say." And it was true. It was the most beautiful thing I'd ever seen.

I studied the smooth lines of the cameo, the delicate turn of her jaw, the hair pulled up in a Victorian twist. The woman's face was beautiful, but it also seemed sad. Here was a woman who, somewhere along the way, had met with great disappointment. I stared at it the way a young girl might stare at her first jewelry box, watching the tiny ballerina pop up to spin endlessly around on her toes when the lid is opened.

"It's beautiful," I said, clutching the pin in my hand, "but I can't accept it. It's too much, Wanda. Really it is." Reluctantly, I held the pin out to her.

Wanda raised her children during the years she and Baxter were married and had not worked outside the home except to sew the occasional prom dress for one of the neighbor girls, sometimes costumes for church plays. I knew that since Baxter's death she had no real income except for the veteran's pension she received as his widow. I was sure she couldn't afford a gift like this.

"That cameo belonged to Baxter's grandmother," she said. "She gave it to me on my wedding day, so, you know, I could wear something old. Now I want you to have it. Please, Jessie. Don't argue with an old lady."

I asked why she didn't want to save it, why she wasn't planning on giving it to one of her daughters or her granddaughters.

"She reminds me of you. Can't you see the resemblance?"

SIXTEEN

*A*fter Justin's early-morning wakeup call, I pull the covers over my head and try to think up reasons why I should feign coma and stay in bed all day. My sister, with her self-diagnosed nervous condition, can always get away with stuff like that, but somehow I didn't think it would work for me. Ellen could stay in bed all day and our mother would tiptoe past the bedroom door, put off the vacuuming, turn down the volume on the television, and at lunch would sneak inside to leave a sandwich for her on the bedside table. If I stay in bed past eight, she'll probably try to make up the bed with me in it. I roll over, yawn loudly, and stick my head out, grateful not to find myself surrounded by those members of my family who haven't yet seen what's under my bandage.

Ellen's bed looks as if wild dogs slept in it. The comforter is bunched up at the foot of the bed, the sheet twisted into a long cord that falls halfway onto the floor, and there are potato chip crumbs and what looks like the remains of several chocolate chip cookies settled into a bowl-like depression in the mattress.

I squint into the window-filtered sunlight and look around the bedroom of my childhood. There are framed photographs of Ellen and me on every available surface and hung in pairs, from waist level to the ceiling, on all four yellow walls. There are so many, in fact, that the room takes on the eerie appearance of a collector's gallery, like those pictures you see sometimes in the newspaper of rooms where someone has a thousand Barbies or five hundred antique cookie jars. My sister and I are a long way from being the children we were in this room we shared for fifteen years, but the faces that gaze back at me are children always and forever.

There are glossy, hand-tinted studio photographs, school portraits from every grade we attended at Randolph Gap Elementary School, and more than a dozen poster-size frames filled with snapshots trimmed to fit an assortment of poorly perforated rectangles, squares, and ovals.

Some are of me as a chubby and bald infant, then later as a toddler, holding a mixing bowl over my head like a hat, eating a spoonful of peanut butter. They're the type of photograph parents take of their firstborn when acts as ordinary as holding a mixing bowl over one's head and eating peanut butter are deemed extraordinary and worth capturing on film. Especially when the parents waited nearly nine years for their firstborn, and had, during this time, become accustomed to the idea that they wouldn't have children. Ellen was born two years later.

There's me, holding a newborn Ellen in my arms like a prized doll. Another with the two of us sitting on a Kodachrome-green lawn, the crinoline skirts of our Easter dresses fanned out around us as we clutch baskets full of plastic eggs.

There's the two of us opening presents underneath a glittering aluminum Christmas tree. The two of us seated together on a piano bench, Ellen banging both hands on the upper keys while I keep my fingers poised over middle C as Sister Inez's ruler taught me. The two of us on the beach during a rare family vacation to Florida, our plump pink bodies stuffed into identical bright pink-and-white polka-dot bathing suits, our toes sinking into the hot white sand. In that photograph, Ellen is charging into the surf, both hands out-stretched to catch the waves striking her eager legs. I'm standing back at a safer distance, my hands tugging at the ruffle of fabric around the waist of my bathing suit, watching and waiting for her to test the waters.

It's more than a little creepy. Of all the holidays and ordinary days that are frozen in time in this room, there isn't one photograph of either of us past the age of fourteen. Our mother collected and cherished us as children, but not as young women or, in my sister's case, as a mother herself. It seems both of us, at least in pictures, have long outlived our usefulness.

&

I've been home more than twelve hours and still haven't seen my sister. She was asleep when I got home, asleep still and snoring lightly when I eased my suitcase through the door, changed into my night-gown in the moonlight, and slipped into bed, but she was gone by the time Justin and Maxwell arrived this morning. Both Ellen and I are sound sleepers, so it's no surprise that I hadn't been awakened in the middle of the night by her escape, just as she hadn't been by my coming to bed.

If her previous bad behavior was any indication, she'd probably slipped out of the house sometime after midnight and was sleep-ing off a hangover in the bed of some laid-off construction worker she met after last call at Red's Tavern, Randolph Gap's preferred nightspot for the lonely and the misbegotten. She usually ends up with construction workers when she goes to Red's, but I know she's kept late-night company with out-of-town truckers, housepainters, short-order cooks and, once, a Presbyterian minister who was hav-ing a crisis of faith. The minister, after having been caught spending the night with my sister, was subsequently punished with a forced relocation to a much smaller church somewhere in Michigan. Justin was conceived after one such excursion to Red's Tavern, his father's identity known only to Ellen, providing she'd been able to narrow the field of possible candidates. I expect her to show up around noon, at which point she'll explain that she was up before sunrise and, knowing it was going to be a beautiful day, took a walk along the river and lost track of the time.

Ellen is an accomplished liar and can always come up with sim-ple and believable scenarios to explain her absences. Scenarios that have, over the years, somehow convinced our mother she has a sensi-tive, spiritual side that can be awakened only by quiet walks along the river, trips to the city library, or peaceful visits to the cemetery to place flowers on the graves of our grandparents—any occasion of which serves to settle her nerves. Ellen's guardian angel started dancing with the devil a long time ago, but our mother pretends not to notice.

"Quit being so hard on your sister," she'll say. "She needs her quiet time. You know how sensitive her nerves are."

Nerves indeed. To my knowledge, Ellen was never at any of these places when she said she was there, and especially not at the library, even though she would describe each place with a certain reverence, as if she was having a one-on-one chat with the Almighty. This when she really was waking up in a strange room with smeared mascara and a headache, trying to find her panties.

Our mother was especially fond of Ellen's trips to the cemetery, though I always thought Ellen used that story a little too often. On one particular summer day, our mother decided to visit her parents' graves a few days after Ellen said she had placed a large saddle wreath of roses on their shared tombstone. I don't know what possessed her to mention the wreath. She was usually too smart to include details like that. Details that could get her caught red-handed.

My father knew for years that Ellen was lying about her whereabouts but never said anything to either of them about it. Still, he did his best to convince my mother not to go.

"Well for heaven's sakes, Carl, why shouldn't I go? I want to see those roses. I bet they're just beautiful."

"Well, I'm not driving you if that's what you're thinking. It's too damn hot to be driving anywhere."

"I'd rather walk," she spat back, the clear message being she'd rather collapse from heatstroke than ride with him now, even if he were to offer. "And I'll thank you not to cuss in my house, Carl Kilgore. There's no need for it. No need at all." She was securing a straw hat to her tightly rolled curls one long bobby pin at a time, threading the pins through one side of the hat and then the other. In an artistic diversion from her regular macramé bag-making ventures, she'd decorated the hat with an assortment of flowers that were crocheted and sewn together with leftover yarn and quilt scraps. It looked like the kind of hat a child would wear on Halloween as part of a hobo costume.

My father let out a loud sigh and went back to his crossword puzzle. "Too damn hot to walk too," he mumbled under his breath.

She was gone a few hours. When she returned, she walked through the door with a determined calmness, placed her purse on top of the kitchen counter, and went about extracting a sponge, bucket, and a large bottle of bleach from underneath the sink. Her dark curls lay in wet and winding piles under her hat, one side of which had come unpinned and flopped around on top of her head.

She has to know Ellen lied to her this time, I thought. And if she knows Ellen lied this time it would stand to reason that she was lying all those other times too. I was nineteen, home from college for summer vacation, and that morning I was painting my toenails with Mango Tango, a rosy shade of orange that would match my new braided sandals. I didn't make a practice of ratting on my sister, mainly because I feared she would beat me up if she found out, but I didn't go around defending her honor either. During that summer she'd been picked up twice already for shoplifting, her pockets filled with lipsticks and perfume bottles from four downtown department stores. "I had to go to the altar and act all weepy four straight Sundays in a row to get out of that one," Ellen told me. "And even then, I had to memorize ten Bible verses. Can you believe it? Ten!"

I decided a second coat of polish could wait. I had to ask about those flowers. I placed my bottle of nail polish on the table, fanned my fingers and toes in front of me to dry, and waited for the explosion.

"People will steal anything these days," my mother said. "Common criminals is what they are, taking flowers from somebody's grave, somebody who never did anything to hurt them in all their lives."

I suggested that maybe Ellen simply placed the flowers on the wrong tombstone by mistake.

"Well, that's just ridiculous is what that is." She filled the bucket with tap water and added an assortment of pungent chemicals. "Your sister certainly knows her own grandparents' resting place. Such a sweet, sensitive child. Visits their graves as often as she can."

I don't think I have to tell you that she looked right at me with that last remark. Still, I didn't have the heart to tell her the truth, even if it meant I would redeem my own maligned character in the process. I visited our grandparents' graves back then too, just not as often as Ellen claimed she did.

My mother poured bleach all over the kitchen counter and started scrubbing in the way she always does when she's upset. She was sweating and crying, using one arm to scrub the counter and the other to dab at her eyes and forehead with a small ball of wadded and wet tissue. She was still wearing that stupid hat.

SEVENTEEN

The Celebrant and other ministers take their places at the body.
This anthem, or some other suitable anthem, or a hymn,
may be sung or said . . .

*Thou only art immortal, the creator and maker of mankind, and we are
mortal, formed of the earth, and unto earth shall we return. For so thou didst
ordain when thou createdst me, saying, 'Dust thou art, and unto dust shalt
thou return.' All we go down to the dust; yet even at the grave we make our
song: Alleluia, alleluia, alleluia.*

THE COMMENDATION

THE BURIAL OF THE DEAD: RITE ONE

THE BOOK OF COMMON PRAYER

few months after Wanda McNabb shot her husband,
everyone in her family started to believe that they were being visited from the grave. From the stories they passed on
to her, it seemed to Wanda that Baxter was going more places and

doing more things dead than he ever had when he was alive. The way she saw it, all this popping up in doorways late at night was the closest Baxter came to holding down a full-time job in years.

Baxter's sister believed Baxter had appeared to her as she waited to be wheeled into the operating room for a hysterectomy. It was an operation that was scheduled months earlier and couldn't be canceled, even if she was, as she put it, "still grieving for her lost brother."

Since she was so blessed, she was on constant lookout for signs Baxter was dropping in on other unsuspecting family members. She even suggested that because the visitations were becoming so frequent it was going to be up to her sooner or later to call the local television station. It was, she told Wanda, just like one of those "unsolved histories" on TV, about people coming back from the dead to seek their revenge by revealing who was responsible for their deaths.

"Before that day, if you'd asked me if I believed in ghosts, I'd have said 'No sirree. I'm a good Christian woman. I believe in Jesus, not in spooks and hobgoblins,'" Monteen McNabb Culberson told her family from her hospital bed the next day.

"But when I saw him with my own eyes, I just had to believe. And that got me thinking that if I believe in the Holy Ghost, which I do of course, and I believe in angels, which I do, then what's so unusual about my brother blessing me with this visit? My brother is an angel now, just like Gabriel. He's got as much right to visit me as any other angel." She repeated this story to successive audiences of family members and nurses as both groups changed shifts.

"Baxter," she asked, "is that really you?" And he just smiled and said, "Yep."

She went on to report to the family that Baxter looked "as

healthy as a horse" and that, true to life, he was wearing a new pair of overalls, a flannel shirt, and work boots. She also pointed out that he wore an embroidered name patch on the left front panel of his overalls, over his heart. This was, she said, exactly the kind of uniform he wore when he was first starting out in the construction business and before he learned to sell "high-quality, previously owned vehicles." She expected his name patch to at least have been bordered in diamonds and rubies, considering he was in heaven and all, but it was, much to her disappointment, held to the overalls with simple red thread.

Monteen asked her brother if they were feeding him well in heaven. It looked to her like they were.

"Awwww sis, you don't need to eat anything where I am," he told her. She didn't like hearing this at all. Her idea of heaven was that you could eat anything you wanted, as much of it as you wanted, without gaining an ounce. This disclosure, more than any other, concerned Monteen the most because it meant she'd have to go on a serious diet soon. She reasoned that if you couldn't gain any weight in heaven, you couldn't lose any either, and she didn't want to be stuck in her current size-18-on-a-good-day body for eternity.

"Oh, he looked so good," she crooned to her rapt audience. "Didn't have a scar on him either." Wanda figured Monteen added that last remark because she never liked her sister-in-law to begin with, and from what Wanda told me, she probably was right.

Monteen then asked Baxter why he wasn't wearing an angel's robe. "Awwww sis, they gave me one all right, but I just feel more comfortable in this."

All in all, she said, they had a wonderful chat. He stayed with her until the doctors came to roll her away to the operating room. He even moved to the side of her bed to hold her hand, which she described, tears in her eyes, as feeling like she was holding on to "the most wonderful cool summer breeze you've ever felt."

She said she felt grateful she had the presence of mind to ask him a few questions before she went under the anesthesia.

"Baxter, am I going to die in this hospital?" She said he told her no. "And he was right about that, as you can plainly see," she said, chuckling and pointing to herself, and then, in the next breath, reminding her family that it hurt her to laugh, what with her scars and all.

"Baxter, did you get to meet Jesus?" He told her he did, and that Jesus, much to his surprise, looked a lot like a buddy of his from Vietnam.

"What's it like to be dead?"

He laughed and said, "Awwww, it ain't nothin' special." Then, she said, he "just vanished without a trace and the next thing I knew I woke up and here I am." His visit taught her an important lesson. "I got a glimpse of the other side. I feel blessed that he chose me."

Not to be outdone by Monteen, other members of the family soon began reporting their own encounters with the ghost of Baxter McNabb. Monteen collected all the stories but remained convinced hers was the true, special visitation that, as she put it, "made him comfortable enough to keep coming back."

Three days after Baxter's visit to the hospital, Monteen's granddaughter Julie, who usually was the last to be picked at school-organized softball games, surprised everyone by hitting the ball clear over the fence in the school's back field. "Uncle Bax was helping me, I just know it," Julie told everyone. She seemed not to know that Baxter's skill with a baseball bat had special significance to Wanda, who, on hearing this story in the living room of Monteen's home, stepped out onto the front porch and vomited into the shrubbery.

Soon after that, someone observed that Monteen's dog had become fond of standing at the foot of the stairs and barking. "It's downright eerie," Monteen reported. "He just barks and barks, as if he knows Baxter is standing there on those stairs. That dog never liked my brother."

Later that week, Monteen's grandson Will received an A on a math quiz and this, too, was attributed to divine assistance. The fact that Baxter was no math scholar didn't deter them. "There's all kinds of smart people in heaven," Monteen offered. "I'm sure Baxter just asked one of them to help out."

Most of Monteen's family was more than willing to have Baxter around, as long as his visits worked to their advantage. Once, Monteen strolled into the den while her husband Bill was watching a Braves game. She intended to switch off the TV and persuade Bill to mow the lawn like he promised. But when she punched the OFF button on the remote control, the game stayed on.

"I just punched and punched that thing, but nothing happened. It didn't even blink."

When Monteen told this story, her voice dropped to a whisper, no doubt in reverence to the spirit world that manifested itself that day in her oak-paneled den.

Bill later confessed to Wanda that the batteries in the remote hadn't worked all day and that he'd forgotten to run to the store to buy more batteries, even though he'd told his wife he had done just that.

After Bill's fourth beer, he even started hamming it up for Monteen's benefit. He'd go to the kitchen and bring back two beers instead of one, popping the other and sitting it on the table between the two Barcaloungers.

"There you go, Baxter my boy. Jesus won't mind if you have just one."

Now and then Bill would lean toward the other chair and, as he recalled, "laugh and carry on and slap my knee like Baxter was saying the funniest thing I'd ever heard in my life." The whole time, Monteen remained seated in a chair on the other side of the room, her face ashen, her hands clutching the family Bible. Monteen knew in her heart that Baxter was the one controlling that remote, that he was sitting there next to Bill, drinking his beer and telling Bill jokes.

"They always watched baseball together," she said, as if that explained everything.

In early January, I asked Wanda what she thought about all this, if she really believed Baxter's ghost was visiting his sister's family. I knew the stories made her uneasy.

"I just wish they'd quit talking about it so much," she said. "As far as I'm concerned, they can believe what they want."

I asked her if she thought Monteen was making all this up, if her sister-in-law was doing it to hurt her.

"That woman is just plain crazy and always has been," she said. "Who knows why she's saying such things. From the way she tells it, you'd think Baxter never did anybody wrong in his whole life, that he's Jesus himself risen from the dead."

I suggested that maybe Monteen convinced herself of Baxter's visitations because she genuinely loved her brother, that this was her way of mourning his death.

"I'm the one who killed him. If he was going to come back and haunt someone, don't you think it'd be me?"

❧

In mid-January, two weeks after Wanda told me about the appearance of Baxter's ghost, she tried to explain why she'd grown weary of attending meetings of the Spousal Abuse Support Group. According to Carol Andrews, the group's coordinator, Wanda had already missed the last two meetings. Carol said when Wanda did go, she would stay in her chair, not saying much anyway. She was so quiet, in fact, that the other women in the group hadn't missed Wanda so much as they missed her weekly offering of cookies.

"If you can't talk her into coming back, see if she'll send us some cookies," Carol told me in her usual breezy way, then bounced off down the hall doing an imitation of the backhand slice she used to win our last tennis match 6–1, 6–2.

I was surprised to hear Wanda hadn't been going to her group sessions. I'd been meaning to check up on her attendance.

"I just don't have anything in common with those women," she said. "They cry all the time. It's depressing."

She was probably right about that. I told her the women needed to cry, that expressing their grief and their pain helped them get through this difficult time in their lives. Wanda never cried in my office. I wondered if she cried when she was alone, if the tears came when she climbed into bed, when it was so quiet the only sound she could hear was her own breathing.

I asked her if she'd shared any of her story with the rest of the group.

"They keep telling me they know how I feel, that I'm—how do they put it?—that I'm still in denial."

"They're just trying to help, Wanda."

"They don't even know me. They didn't know Baxter either." She crossed her legs, then uncrossed them again.

"Well, that's true, but they could get to know you if you'd give them a chance."

"What am I supposed to be denying anyway? I've never denied I'm the one who killed him."

To make matters worse, she said, the other women in the group seemed to hold her in high esteem because of what she'd done, which she found alarming in itself.

"They all look at me like I've won the lottery or something."

The women must have seen Wanda's picture in the newspaper, must have read the accounts of her husband's death. I had a brief vision of these fourteen women sitting around a large table, munching cookies and openly plotting the deaths of their own husbands, all fourteen of them jumping up from the table and running out to buy pearl-handled .32-caliber pistols identical to the one Wanda used.

"Why do you think that is?"

"How should I know?" She crossed her legs again.

"Do you think they see you as strong?"

"If they do, well then they really don't know anything." She uncrossed her legs again, using both hands to smooth out her skirt. She kept running her hands over the unwrinkled material.

I told her I thought she was still blaming herself, not Baxter, for what happened.

"Don't be ridiculous," she said.

I pointed out she didn't kill Baxter out of the clear blue, that the terrible and violent things Baxter had done to her had led to that day in her sewing room.

"Well, sure, things happened. I'm just tired of wallowing in it, that's all."

EIGHTEEN

When I stumble into the kitchen in search of coffee I find my parents loudly eating breakfast and having an even louder disagreement. From the kitchen I can see Justin sprawled in sleep on the living room sofa, thumb in his mouth, one leg hanging off the edge of the plastic-covered cushions. My sister's birds are in the room with him, and from their various perches they are grumbling and squawking to each other in their own peculiar language. Missy is curled up on a rug in the kitchen, snoring. My sister, as far as I can tell, is nowhere in the house.

I try to make myself inconspicuous, but I'm caught before I reach the coffeepot.

"Jessie, don't I take your mother everywhere she needs to go?" asks my father, who is gnawing his way down a strip of bacon.

"This certainly looks good," I say, taking a seat and trying to decide what to put on my plate. I have to act fast or my mother will start filling it for me.

"I can't rely on you for everything now, can I?" my mother asks in return.

"You always have, haven't you?"

"Well, I think it's high time I started doing a few things for myself, don't you think?"

My parents can carry on entire conversations by speaking to each other only in questions. I don't think it's wise to respond to either of them. If my sister's birds weren't around, I'd consider taking my plate to the living room and eating my breakfast on a TV tray.

"You think I've got one foot in the grave. Is that what you think? Lucy, short for Lucretia?"

It is one of my father's favorite things, especially in the middle of an argument, to refer to my mother as "Lucy, short for Lucretia." She was named Lucretia Elizabeth Stover, after her maternal grandmother, but she hated the name Lucretia all her life, refusing to answer to anything but Lucy. When she was twenty-one, she went to the county courthouse and paid to have her name legally changed. When my father married her, she became Lucy Elizabeth Kilgore, which suited her just fine. As long as there was never any mention of this Lucretia person she used to be.

"Oh for heaven's sakes," says my mother, who laughs in spite of herself and cuts her eyes in my direction. "See what I have to put up with?"

"Your mother," he says to me, "has developed a sudden independent streak."

What my mother has decided to do is buy a car. The fact that she does not have a driver's license does not seem to concern her.

A folded newspaper sits beside her breakfast plate, the contents of which have been ignored and are beginning to congeal around the edges. She pushes the classified section across the table at me. "Here, look at this." She's circled the ad of her choice with a green felt-tip pen.

1988 Lincoln Town Car, white with gray leather interior. 37,000 miles. One lady owner. Clean. $3,750. The phone number listed is a local one.

"Hmmmm." I'm trying my best to sound like I don't care one way or another. Like I'm not taking sides.

"Don't encourage her," says my father.

"The ad says one lady owner, Carl. A car like that deserves another lady owner."

"I don't know why driving around in my truck isn't good enough for you all of a sudden. Why you think we're made of money and you need to go riding around in some fancy Town Car." He pronounces the words *Town Car* with a distaste he usually reserves for words like *liberal* and *gun control.*

"She's ashamed of me is what she is. Doesn't want to be seen in the church parking lot in my truck. Thinks she ought to be riding on leather seats in air-conditioned comfort, just like the preacher's wife." My father indulges my mother's affection for the Randolph Gap Holy Rock Church and her occasional bouts of scripture quoting, even her insistence that he keep his beer in the basement refrigerator and not in her refrigerator where company might see it, but he's unwilling to let her churchgoing change his daily behavior too much. He seizes every opportunity to point out that it's his hard-earned money she tithes to the church every month. That it's his hard-earned money that helped pay for the preacher's new silver Cadillac. He alone must have paid for at least one of that Cadillac's whitewalls, he tells her.

"I've got a little saved up, Carl. I can pay for the car myself."

Despite his best efforts, I can see my father's resolve crumbling. When my mother makes up her mind to do something, it is of little use to argue.

"Well, I don't care what that ad says. I'm going to take a good look at it before you buy anything, one lady owner or not. And it better be clean."

My mother's face brightens with the knowledge that she's won this round at least, which, to her, signals victory on all counts is imminent.

"If it doesn't look good to me, that's that. Understand?"

She shakes her head obediently and picks up her fork, at last satisfied that she can eat. She folds her hands in front of her face and closes her eyes, which I know means she's offering up a fervent prayer—maybe one of the ones cited on her refrigerator door—that she'll get that Lincoln Town Car despite any conceivable objection from my father. My mother spends a good portion of her day offering up little prayers and big prayers like these, sometimes in silence and sometimes out loud.

Dear Lord, please let Sister Inez's biopsy show that tumor on her neck is benign.

O Lord Jesus, please let Jessie follow her calling and serve the church by playing the piano.

Dear Jesus, please let me find a parking place close to the entrance of the Winn-Dixie . . . and please let them have a good pot roast on sale.

These are just a few of the prayers I've heard her say over the years.

When she lifts her eyes, she looks at my father and me as if she's surprised to see us, as if we've just materialized at the table. She takes a deep, self-satisfied breath. "After we have a nice breakfast, I'll call to see when we can look at it." She says this in a tone meant to indicate she's in no hurry at all, that she'll place a leisurely inquiry later in the day.

"What I should do is call up Cecil and get him to come look at it with me, even if Ellen does pitch a fit," my father says, though my mother, her battle won, has by now stopped listening to him and is concentrating on her breakfast. "That boy may not know much, but he does know cars."

If I know my mother, she'll have that Lincoln Town Car parked in the driveway by sundown.

℞

"If you meet with opposition today, it is your charm, not argument, that can turn things around." That's what my horoscope advises me. Turner's says he should "take positive measures to curb unnecessary expenditures." I've been reading my horoscope ever since I was ten years old, in newspapers and in women's magazines and on the backs of the occasional restaurant place mat. I don't believe any of it, but I take comfort in knowing, if only briefly, what others predict the future will bring.

"Tell me what mine is," says Justin, who surprises me by coming into the kitchen and yelling this over my shoulder. I'd thought he was still asleep. He leans over the page I'm reading, a large blue-fronted Amazon perched on his forearm. My mother, as if we're being formally introduced, tells me the bird's name is Dylan. This one's intent on doing a little morning aerobics. He hops on one foot, then the other, over and over again. The Richard Simmons of the bird world.

Justin, ever informative, adds that my sister named the bird after "some dumb singer." When I reach over to pet Dylan on his green head, trying, I guess, to make my amends with these birds so they won't peck out my eyes while I sleep, Dylan snaps at me, catching my index finger in his sharp beak.

"He's just jumpy this morning," Justin offers. "He ain't around strangers much."

"You mean he isn't around strangers much," I say, sucking on my throbbing finger.

Justin stares at me as if he doesn't know what I'm talking about, as if he can't fathom why I've repeated what he just said.

"I don't know what it is about people and horoscopes," says my father, who looks well rested despite his late shift at the Stop 'n' Shoppe. "I can't figure it out. It's all a bunch of hooey if you ask me."

"Hoo-eeee," Justin echoes. "That's a funny word, Grandpa."

My mother goes to the sink to do the breakfast dishes, waving off any help from me, so I sit at the kitchen table and flip through the remains of the paper while finishing my coffee.

"You don't believe in horoscopes?" asks Justin, who pronounces it "horror-scopes."

"I don't see much use in them," my father says. "They just tell you what you want to hear."

"Read what it says about me," Justin whines, causing Dylan to stretch out his feathers and make a half leap toward the outstretched newspaper. He tears off a corner of it and shakes it around like a dog with a bone.

"What's your sign?"

"My what?"

"Well, it all depends," I explain. "Your horoscope tells you what it does depending on what the stars were doing when you were born."

"The stars were doing stuff when I was born?"

"Well, sort of." I was at a loss to explain this further. I'd obviously given Justin the idea that the stars were colliding around in the sky the day he was born, creating a celestial fireworks show in his honor.

"It's spooky stuff, Justin," my father says. He waves his fingers in front of his face, spooky style, as if to illustrate the mysterious power of the solar system. "The stars know what's going to happen to you before you do."

"Ain't nothin' scares me," Justin insists, then turns to me with his defiant young face, like he's prepared to punch me in the nose if I attempt to correct his grammar again.

I fight back the urge to do so, instead trying to remember when Justin was born. October 27, if I remembered correctly. A Scorpio.

"Okay, kiddo," I begin. "It says you're supposed to do everything your grandpa says, and that your grandpa is the wisest man in the whole world."

Justin blinks his eyes once, looks at me and then at his grandpa, and announces with a smirk, "Yeah r-r-r-right."

"You don't believe me? Read it for yourself."

My father laughs at this. "See? Stubborn as your sister Ellen was at that age," he says. "Stubborn as both of you, come to think of it."

"I'm not a dummy," Justin chimes in. "Tell me what it really says."

"Okay," I say, jerking the newspaper away from Dylan when he tries to rip off another corner. "This is it. You ready?"

Justin stares at me like I'm the biggest idiot he's ever encountered.

"You'll be the center of attention where social engagements are concerned. Show off your winning personality and fun things will happen."

"That it?"

"That's it. Sounds pretty good to me." Sadly, I can't imagine a time when Justin is truly the center of attention.

"Tell me what Mom's is."

I scan the listing until I find her sign. Aries. "Be assertive. If you proceed in a wishy-washy manner, you'll never get what your heart really wants." Ellen, who fervently believes in the power of horoscopes and in all manner of fortune-telling, would have loved that one. That horoscope, if she'd been around to hear it, would be proof positive that her decision to leave Cecil is the right move. She just has to be assertive about it and not give in when he comes crawling over here again, begging her to come home.

NINETEEN

I find my sister in the barn at the edge of the pasture. It's late Saturday afternoon, and my mother, father, and Justin have decided to take a look at that Lincoln Town Car with the one lady owner. My job is to stay at home and baby-sit my sister's birds.

"Hey Jess."

It's my sister's voice, coming from the loft in the barn. I left poor, foul-smelling Missy curled up on the small braided rug in the kitchen, where she's been snoring all morning.

I've retired to the barn to sneak a cigarette. The smoke is bitter but familiar, and feels hotter in my mouth than I remembered. I started smoking in college, partly at the urging of my dilettante roommate and partly because I was a drama major and thought holding a cigarette helped one strike dramatic poses. I quit at Turner's request a few months before we got married, but these past few months the old urge has returned, and I've sometimes found myself, after midnight, sitting on the brick steps in front of our house blowing smoke into the cooling night. I stash the butts in a flowerpot on the top step. No wonder my geraniums are wilting.

My sister tells me she arrived home just after daybreak but decided to sleep a few hours in the loft rather than risking an argument with our parents over the fact that she had, indeed, been out all night.

We sit on a crate near the barn door, two women in their thirties, one afraid of being caught staying out all night and the other sneaking cigarettes. If I were to leave Turner, I'd probably end up packing my things and coming here to Randolph Gap, something I swore I'd never do.

Every time I see Ellen she always has what she calls "a drugstore makeover." It's a different color every time. From Ash Blonde to Incredible Blonde to Sunset Blonde to Chestnut Blonde.

From the road, this barn looks like a picturesque country scene tourists stop the car and photograph, exclaiming all the while "Oh how darling!" or, "See there kids, that's the way life used to be." Inside, it looks like the kind of place where, in old movies about the South, a whiskey still gurgles away. To me, it has a quirky dilapidated quality, like some place where wanted criminals would be comfortable lounging around and plotting their next cross-country murder spree.

It's not even a working barn anymore, hasn't been for more than twenty years, and over the years it's been both junkyard and studio, filled with old furniture, rusting appliances, and the innocent victims of my mother's desire to express herself artistically. From where my sister and I sit, I can see coffeemakers with cracked glass carafes, what appear to be three rusted toaster ovens, one stereo unit complete with 8-track tape deck and a stack of 8-tracks with faded paper labels, several lamps with ripped shades and fraying cords, two rocking chairs with exploded wicker bottoms, and one refrigerator with its door removed from the hinges. An assortment of my mother's unsold gourds are hung from the rafters, strung together like so many goofy paper lanterns. Tied between them are dozens of gallon milk jugs, ready and waiting to serve some useful, but as yet undetermined, purpose. I don't think my mother has ever thrown away a plastic milk jug. She fills them with water and stacks them in the freezer like giant ice cubes; fills them with juice and iced tea; cuts the tops off others to use as makeshift flowerpots, or cuts circles in the sides and hangs them in the trees for birds to use as nesting boxes.

In the center of all this, my father has installed a pool table. It's propped up on concrete blocks, the felt surface ragged and stained with dark spots where rain leaks through the barn's tin roof. My father practices for his pool tournaments here, though the surrounding junk often prevents him from getting full extension of the stick.

"I didn't know you still smoked," Ellen says, reaching across me to take one from the pack.

"I don't. Not usually," I say on the exhale. "They're yours anyway."

Ellen is studying her nails. They are abnormally long and square at the ends. The one on her right pinkie sports some kind of glittering starburst design. Fakes, obviously. Three of them are broken off to the nail bed, the thick acrylic fibers torn from the real nails underneath. Ellen also sports a wide assortment of rings on every finger, some of which are stacked four high. I imagine she must have other rings somewhere on her body—in her navel, around her toes, on other places I don't care to think about.

"Had to kick some butt last night," Ellen says, frowning at the damage she suffered to her manicure.

This doesn't surprise me. When we were growing up, my sister was always getting into fights. She had a knack for it. Usually they were big sprawling brawls, confrontations that escalated fast from name-calling to hair-pulling to bloody noses. Once she chased nine-year-old Danny Johnson around the school softball field because he dared to kiss her, screaming that when she caught him she would break every bone in his body.

At least Danny gave her a reason to fight, or so she believed. Most of the time my sister's violent streak is unleashed by something less obvious. Someone looked at her the wrong way. Some "bitch" at the bar "was just asking for it." I used to think she'd outgrow it, but now I'm not so sure. I can see her in a nursing home, kicking the walker out from under a fellow resident and screaming obscenities at the orderlies. Like some of my patients, she sees enemies everywhere.

"There's a difference between regular fighting and really trying to hurt somebody," my sister explains, turning philosophical about her blood sports. "That bitch last night pulled a knife on me. Can you believe that? That's not fightin' fair at all. I had to throw a chair at her."

We sit there in silence, smoking.

We have, in much too short a time, run out of things to say to each other. Maybe she expects me to run off, armed and dangerous, in search of the party, or parties, who insulted her honor in the first place. I'm glad I'm wearing a long-sleeved T-shirt to conceal my bandaged arm. My sister would relish the story of Melvin's biting me but would be disappointed that I hadn't tried to maul him in return.

I want to know what's going on with Cecil. Why she's sneaking out of the house after midnight. Why she's drinking again. I want to know lots of things. Instead, I sit here in the cool shade of the barn door, watching a car sputter by on the road. I light another cigarette. It isn't unpleasant, sitting here with her, though I have the nagging feeling that I should be doing something, that I should be reaching out to her in some meaningful way.

"Let's go in the house," she says suddenly, standing up and brushing off the seat of her jeans. "I want to show you something."

&

"Did you know that you can get four hundred dollars apiece for these?"

We're in my parents' bedroom, and Ellen is holding up a small gold coin. It's a $5 gold piece, minted in 1905. There are maybe fifteen of the coins in the small box she lifted from the top shelf of our parents' closet. From the other room, I can hear my sister's birds still holding court—feathers brushing past the sides of their cages, claws scratching on their perches. When we passed through the kitchen, I looked at Missy still curled on her rug. At least she'd stopped snoring.

I take the coin and examine it. It looks like it's recently been polished. "So? Why are you showing me these?"

"Because this is my ticket out of here, that's why."

The fact that we are trespassing here, that we are looking at my father's private things, is all too prominent in my mind. Our grandfather gave these coins to our father when he turned eighteen, and he's kept them in this box all these years. As children, we knew they existed, but were allowed to look at them only with my father. Even then he watched us carefully, explaining that these coins were not toys, but "the genuine item." We were never to touch them when he wasn't around.

"Ellen, we shouldn't be here."

We're standing in my parents' room, in front of their open closet, with his neat line of blue-striped uniform shirts from the Stop 'n' Shoppe and her row of plain around-the-house dresses and a select few good-for-Sunday dresses. Standing too close to the worn shoes lined neatly in the bottom of the closet, to these clothes that smell of gasoline and of my mother's Tabu cologne. Even with my eyes closed, I could describe each item. I know that closet like I know my mother's kitchen. After forty years, little has changed in this small space since the day they married. I want to run from the room. I'm finding it hard to breathe.

"Daddy gave me these coins, Jess. He knows I need the money. He says any reputable coin dealer will pay good money for them."

Ellen explains that she plans to leave Cecil. For good this time. She's been planning it for at least six months, all the while trying to save up enough money to pull it off.

"I'm not going to sell them right away. They're here for when I need them. When the time is right." She takes the coin out of my hand and places it back in the box. "Just like money in the bank. Money that no-good husband of mine can't get his paws on."

⊰℅

My sister's reason for leaving Cecil is simple. At least it is to her.

"I can't stand to look at his ugly face one more day."

155

That's her summary of her marital difficulties. We're sitting on the back steps of the house now, smoking again. I figure we have at least another hour, and four cigarettes to go, before the Lincoln Town Car rolls up in the driveway.

Ellen, between puffs, is trying to peel off her remaining acrylic nails. With the lit cigarette wedged in her mouth, she squints as she holds each nail close to her face and tries to judge its weak spot. Every time she sticks the nail file under the acrylic and pushes she cries "Damn, that hurts." She does the same thing over and over, always with the same exclamation, until all the nails are off, their ragged edges scattered in a shiny pink pile at her feet.

During the course of her short marriage, Ellen has left Cecil at least five times.

Cecil had friends over to watch a football game.

He left his dirty sneakers, oily from his day at the garage, all over the house, and they stained the carpet.

She found suspicious-looking handkerchiefs in the hamper and suspected that he had a stash of pornography somewhere.

He took her dancing at the VFW on a Saturday night and openly flirted with other women. He even danced with two of them.

He liked his chili mild and she liked hers spicy.

These were her reasons for leaving. Somehow I knew Cecil would have different, and probably more logical, explanations.

When she leaves she usually comes home, to our parents' house, though once, during a summer two years ago, she and Justin packed a few clothes and Justin's Game Boy and CD player, threw everything in the back seat of her Honda, and drove straight to Florida. She never stays away for long, usually no more than a week at a time. Her trip to Florida lasted twelve days, but she reasoned that since

most of it was spent at Disney World, it constituted more of a vacation than an actual separation.

She didn't, to my knowledge, take her birds with her to Florida,
though she always brings them home to roost in my mother's living
room. I wonder how long she'll stay this time, but I know better than
to ask. I always get the same response: "I'm not going back, no way
José. This time I mean it."

My sister is like Donna Lindsey in the way she describes her
marital difficulties. Both of them make everything sound so easy.
Donna's solution is to have an affair. Ellen's is to leave.

It must be harder than they make it sound. Even in the movies
people fight long and bitter battles over their belongings or chase
down each other's lovers in fits of jealous rage.

Can a person just leave?

Is it possible to disentangle oneself so quickly?

Are the connections between people that tenuous, so easily broken?

People do it all the time, I know. I'm not, despite what Justin
might think, the biggest idiot in the world. I could leave too. Could
leave and tell everybody it was easy. Nothing to it. Best thing I ever
did. All that stuff.

I think of Donna and her plans to escape for the weekend, wondering if on this cloudy Saturday afternoon she's with her lover in a
darkened room at the Bay Island Hotel.

"Don't look at me like you don't know what I'm talking about,"
Ellen says, her index finger in her mouth as she chews away the remaining bits of acrylic covering her nails. "You don't look so happy
yourself, if you don't mind my saying so."

"I do mind." I get up from the step, throwing my still-burning
cigarette behind one of my mother's inflatable Easter bunnies, almost

hoping the lit tip will strike the bunny on its fluffy little tail and send it—Pop!—into a tailspin on the lawn.

I pace around purposefully. "I'm as happy as the next person, I guess." I make an attempt to smile.

"If you ask me, you should try to have another baby," she says. "A baby would take your mind off things."

"I'm not asking you."

I light another cigarette and look out at the field where my father is preparing to plant this year's garden. Over the years, the garden itself has grown from the three small rows he cultivated when we were children and expanded southward across the lawn where our swing set once stood. "See here, Jessie belle, this is how peanuts grow," he'd say, pulling up a scrawny plant and shaking it to loosen the clumps of dirt around the tangled roots where few, if any, peanuts were growing. "See here, this is how you plant beans," he'd say, tossing a handful of seeds into the ground. "One to push, one to pull, and one to grow on."

I imagine that Wanda McNabb is sitting alone in her kitchen on this Saturday afternoon, watching through the glass in the stove door as a new batch of cookies sizzles and flattens on the baking sheet. She's told me that during all the years she was married to Baxter, she never once considered having an affair, never packed her bags to leave him.

Here I am, the one who's supposed to have some insights into the mysteries of the human mind. Don't I deal with patients day after day, helping them resume lives that are supposed to be more troubled than mine? I'm the one who's supposed to have a genuine sense of well being. I'm the one who's supposed to have tomorrow under control.

I kick a small mound of pebbles at the edge of my father's soon-to-be garden, sending a shower of them toward the one tilled row of smooth ground.

"If you had a baby you wouldn't have to try so hard to look happy," Ellen says.

 *TWENTY*

My sister married Cecil Yeargan in a ceremony on the concert stage of the Randolph County Fairgrounds. The wedding itself was orchestrated by a country music radio station as a romantic warm-up for the band that was to perform on that warm September night. Ellen wore a calf-length cream dress trimmed with lace and carried one long-stemmed yellow rose. Cecil wore a cowboy's version of a tuxedo, with white-on-black stitching, a black leather bolo instead of a bow tie, and a black Stetson. Justin, who was dressed in a four-year-old's version of Cecil's cowboy chic, was the ring bearer. He stood beside my sister, stiffly holding a small white satin pillow and squirming like he had to pee. If the rings hadn't been strung together by a red ribbon and pinned to the pillow (my mother's idea), he'd have dropped them within seconds of reaching the stage.

There were no other attendants, so I was in the audience with my parents, where we at least had the distinction of being seated in the front row. Three empty seats were saved next to us, waiting for Ellen, Cecil, and Justin to walk off the stage a newly wedded family.

As my sister made a point of telling me before the ceremony, the best part about getting married this way was that, in exchange for getting married on stage as part of the radio station's "Hot Summer Romance" promotion, we all got to keep the front-row seats and stay for the concert that followed and it didn't cost Cecil a penny.

Before this weekend trip home, the wedding was the last time I'd seen my sister and nephew. I had met Cecil for the first time that day in my parents' driveway, but since we were running late and had ten minutes to drive twenty-three miles to the fairgrounds, we weren't formally introduced. Turner didn't come with me on that trip either, having, he said, to work over the weekend on some local industry recruitment tour he'd helped organize. So in fact there were four empty seats next to us, as my mother reminded me on the way to the fairgrounds tent.

All this happened years before I started enjoying my current fantasies of Turner's demise, and I was genuinely disappointed he couldn't attend. I remember telling myself it was nothing, that our separation for one weekend couldn't possibly be a signal of anything more significant than the simple fact that Turner isn't a country music fan and that he had to work that weekend.

"I wish you'd had a real wedding like this," said my mother as we took our seats.

The minister wore blue jeans, snakeskin cowboy boots, and a

sparkling jacket that, on the back, featured a sequin guitar bearing the radio station's call letters. He, too, wore a Stetson. A white one. I later found out he was a disc jockey with thousands of faithful female listeners, in addition to being a mail-order minister of some church of his own creation. Judging from the raucous applause, many of his fans were seated in the chairs behind ours.

Cued by his entrance, and emboldened by the beer they'd been testing in a Best of the Beers competition earlier that afternoon, a few of the women in the audience began to shout impassioned but unsolicited advice to my sister, who was by then holding hands with Cecil in a corner of the stage and looking nervous. She looked more nervous than I ever remembered seeing her.

A frizzy-haired blonde in a red suede jacket, who was standing at the edge of the fairgrounds tent with a beer in the grip of all ten of her rakishly long pink fingernails, started it all.

"Don't do it, honey!" she screamed, swaying precariously as the heels of her pink shoes dug into the gravel and sawdust floor.

Other women soon picked up the call, raising their collective high-spirited voices in discouragement of the hot summer romance on stage.

"You're making a big mistake. I know I did. Four times already!" cried a redhead wearing sunglasses, even though the tent was dimly lit and the moon was already visible in the darkening sky.

"Won't be nothing but heartache and washing his dirty drawers from now on!" yelled another.

Laughter and catcalls followed, all to the amusement of Ellen and Cecil, who looked considerably less nervous and laughed along with the crowd as they waited for the glittering reverend to lead them through their vows. At this point, other voices were chiming in.

"If you don't want him honey, I'll take him," a plump brunette from the fifth row called as she bent over in an attempt to give Cecil and the rest of us a glimpse of her impressive cleavage.

"Hey mister, you'll do just fine. My divorce is almost final!" rang another voice.

Then, from a short woman in the very back who was making her presence known by weaving to a standing position on her chair: "I'm still married darlin', but you can have me anytime."

Cecil, clearly enjoying this turn of events, stuck out his chest and gazed down at my sister proudly. When he whispered something to her, I figured he was saying something like, *See, I told you. You're one lucky gal.* She laughed at whatever he said.

One silver-haired lady who must have been pushing sixty stood up and bellowed at Cecil, "Come on sugar, you need a good woman like me, not some pretty young thing like her!"

My sister was a single mother, thirty-two at the time, which certainly wouldn't qualify her as young compared to most brides in Randolph Gap, but she took this and all the other comments from the audience in stride. If the woman who called her a "pretty young thing" had been nineteen, a lot of hair-pulling would have ensued, wedding or no wedding.

These people behaved like they were waiting for the pig races to begin, not for two people to get married. I feared this mayhem could continue for hours.

Thankfully, the master of ceremonies sensed this too.

"Come on, ladies," he said with a wide showman's grin. "You all had your chance at this good-lookin' fellow, but this sweet gal here has caught him and now I reckon she'll just have to put up with him, dirty drawers and all. So let's get this show on the road!"

The spotlights hit the stage at the exact moment the band began its unique rendition of "The Wedding March" set to a rockabilly beat.

My sister and Cecil, still holding hands, began to walk across the stage along a narrow strip of red carpet, Justin trailing behind them. The audience continued to cheer and whistle until somewhere in the middle of the song the band clumsily segued into "Love Me Tender," a tune so revered in Randolph Gap that it hushed even the rowdiest members of the audience.

All things considered, my sister's wedding was quite beautiful and moving in its own way. My mother, who sat beside me in her best church pew pose and tried to ignore the carnival-like atmosphere that preceded the service, was sobbing by the time the rings were exchanged. As she sat under the protective arm of my father, she made no attempt to dab at her eyes but sat there, eyes fixed on my sister, tears rolling down her cheeks.

Tears of happiness from the bride's mother I could understand, but why other women, especially older women who were long married, routinely boo-hooed at weddings, even at weddings of people they barely knew, was a mystery to me. They'd been through this before. They knew the drill, so to speak. I'd been to many weddings since my own and never cried, but that time I was surprised by an inexplicable rush of emotion. As I sat in my rusted folding chair in the front row, watching as my sister became Mrs. Cecil Yeargan, a wife for the first time, and as Cecil became a husband and father for the first time, I cried along with my mother and all the other women in the audience.

I was crying still when the disc jockey turned minister said "You may kiss the bride," and when Cecil wasted no time in wrapping both arms around my sister and pulling her five-foot-five-inch-with-heels frame up to his six-foot-three, causing her feet to dangle almost a foot off the floor. She kicked like an infant lifted into the air by a proud parent. One of her sandals slid off and tumbled across the stage.

We were given small bags of rice to fling at Ellen and Cecil as they descended toward us, but since someone underestimated the radio station's promotional supply, the shower of rice stopped abruptly after the sixth row. Feeling cheated, the crowd began throwing other things instead. Popcorn mostly, though there were a few gum wrappers, ice cubes and, I noticed, one condom. Thankfully, the audience had the good taste not to throw their empty beer bottles.

A small crowd gathered outside the entrance to the fairgrounds tent, where my sister, Cecil, and Justin exited between the rows of folding chairs. There was to be a short intermission between the wedding and the concert, and the crowd joined my family in congratulating the new couple. The first order of business, my mother decided, was to escort Justin to the bathroom.

Ellen reached a proprietary hand into Cecil's pocket and pulled out a crumpled pack of Marlboros. When she stuck one of the cigarettes between her parted lips, he cupped his hands around the end of it and lit it for her. The tip of the cigarette flared briefly in the strong breeze, then sputtered out again. My sister snatched the lighter from his outstretched hand and expertly lit the cigarette again.

"Give me that," she snapped. "And go get me something to drink. It's hotter than hell out here."

These did not sound like the words of a blushing bride. Something had soured her hot summer romance mood, though I wasn't sure what.

"Sure honey," said Cecil, still beaming, oblivious to any insult. "I'll be back in a jiffy." He stuffed his hands in the pockets of his tuxedo, adjusted his hat, and walked away in search of beer.

"Hold up, son," my father called after him. "Think I could use one of those myself."

The crowd of well-wishers milled around us, some stopping to offer congratulations but most simply standing around, now eager for the concert to begin. The jeering that had taken place before the ceremony was long forgotten.

My sister and I stood there in silence.

"You look beautiful," I said finally, not knowing what else to say. And it was true. Her long blond hair, sun-streaked and nearly incandescent under the lights of the fairgrounds tent, was lifted on both sides with French combs. Where the combs met at the back of her hair was a spray of baby's breath tied with a yellow ribbon. She looked more beautiful, more alive, than I'd ever seen her, even if she was bossing Cecil around like a shrew.

"Thanks," she said, exhaling a long stream of smoke. "Good to see you too, Jess."

I thought about all those nights we'd stayed awake as girls, whispering across the small space that separated our beds. Maybe that had left us, as adults, with nothing to talk about.

I could see Cecil and my father standing at the makeshift concession stand located at the edge of the midway, Cecil clumsily trying to hold on to four bottles of beer while digging in his back pocket for his wallet.

As they turned to walk toward us, Cecil laughing at something my father said, I saw for the first time how content they looked in each other's company. I imagined them leaving the fairgrounds arm in arm, planning fishing trips and hunting expeditions and pool tournaments. My father, who has always harbored a general distrust of bankers in general and of Turner in particular, had finally found a son in Cecil, who, as my father had already informed me, made an honest living as an auto mechanic. Turner and my father never looked that way together. Not once.

"Thought I was supposed to be the one crying," said my sister, and lit another cigarette.

I didn't know how to explain. Didn't know if I could explain. Here I was at my sister's wedding, not being able to think of anything to say to her, watching my father and her new husband, and thinking all of a sudden that my life was missing something. Missing something in the most profound sense. And I didn't know how to get it back.

"I was just thinking of how beautiful the moon is tonight," I stammered. I turned to look at the moon and was relieved when she turned to look too. It was, indeed, beautiful. A harvest moon, full and rising in the night sky, as bright and textured as a peeled orange.

"Hmmmm," my sister sighed.

My father and Cecil were getting closer, still laughing as they walked toward us, their feet kicking up tufts of straw and sawdust. The crowd that had pressed close around us on all sides started to break up as people began to take their seats inside the tent and the band tuned their guitars.

Ellen ground the butt of her cigarette into the gravel with one of her white sandals. Cecil handed a beer to each of us and someone suggested a toast.

My sister snatched hers away from him and, with her other hand, lit a third cigarette.

"Ewwww," she whined after taking a sip. "It's warm."

I was supposed to be happy. Everybody said so.

Going to my sister's wedding changed me somehow. Over the next few months and years, I began to see that Turner and I were friends still, rarely lovers, and the friendship itself was strained more often than not. On the night of my sister's wedding, I saw my life stretched out ahead of me—solitary, unchanging, and passionless—and I was afraid.

TWENTY-ONE

*God, the Father of all, whose Son commanded us to love our enemies: Lead
them and us from prejudice to truth; deliver them and us from hatred,
cruelty, and revenge; and in your good time enable us all to stand reconciled
before you through Jesus Christ our Lord. Amen.*

PRAYERS FOR THE WORLD

FOR OUR ENEMIES

THE BOOK OF COMMON PRAYER

When Wanda McNabb walked into my cubicle on the
first Monday in February, I hardly recognized her.
She'd actually done it. She'd cut her long blond hair
and what remained was a bright shade of strawberry. Maybe my sister's method of reinventing herself through new hairstyles wasn't so
pointless after all. It seemed to have worked its magic on Wanda.

"So?" she said, twirling around, her new hair bouncing around
on her shoulders.

"It's beautiful, Wanda," I said. She looked ten years younger and she smiled like a woman who had looked in the mirror that morning and finally, after many years, liked what she saw. I didn't think my own hairdresser would ever be capable of performing such a transformation with me.

"I can't believe I actually did it, but I did, didn't I? And it feels good. Really good." Wanda, to be certain, was talking about more than her hair.

"Oh, and you've got to see this." She reached into her handbag and extracted a thick braid nearly two feet long. It was tied at either end with rubber bands. I could see her notebook's curled edges protruding from her handbag, which, predictably, was at her feet. She held the hair in front of her and let it swing back and forth.

"Wow."

"Yeah, wow," she echoed. "I can't believe I carried all this around for so many years." She handed the hair to me. It had taken her seventeen years to grow it so long.

The braid, still streaked with its natural gray, was surprisingly heavy. I remembered what she'd told me, during one of our first sessions, about how this hair held too many memories. I touched it, running my fingers along the knots. I thought of Baxter, in those early years of their marriage, sitting behind her on their bed, combing her wet hair, turning it over and over in his hands until it was dry.

"I think I finally lost that ten pounds. Easiest diet I've ever tried."

I pictured her sitting in the hairdresser's chair, the long blond tresses falling, limp, into a stranger's hands.

"What are you going to do with it?"

"Stacey, she's the one who cut it, said I should sell it. Said there's good money in human hair."

"Really?"

"That's what she said, but I wanted to show it to you first."

I could see a customer in some distant city, stopping on a sunny day to peer into the window of a wig shop, admiring Wanda's hair, maybe walking out of the shop wearing it pinned to the nape of her neck where her real hair ended.

"Are you glad you did it?"

"Doesn't it look good?" A worried expression settled across her face.

"You look wonderful, Wanda. Really." She relaxed. "It's just that you said you wanted to cut it because it held too many memories, right?"

"I did?"

"Yes, you did."

"I guess that's true."

"So," I asked, "did it work?"

I wondered if it could be true, if memory could be excised from the body, if a surgeon's skill in removing a bullet buried deep in the flesh could erase the memory of the shooting. Wanda, as far as I knew, was still living in the house she'd lived in with Baxter during their long and embattled marriage and didn't have any plans to move. It seemed to me that house would hold more memories for her than her hair ever could.

"You know how people who've lost an arm or a leg feel like it's still there?" she said. "It happened to one of Baxter's buddies from Vietnam. What's that called?"

"When someone loses an arm or a leg?"

"Yeah, but it's like their mind is playing tricks on them. They think it's still there."

"I think it's called phantom limb something or the other."

"Yeah, that's it. Well, Baxter's friend Billy lost a leg, and for years afterward he kept thinking that his leg was still there, just like always. He said he could feel it itching and everything, but when he reached down to scratch it, there was nothing there." As she talked, she absently reached her left hand behind her back to where her braid would have hung had it still been attached.

"Do you feel that way about your hair?"

"Yeah, I guess I do. I can still feel it against my back, and when I got in the shower this morning I reached for it just as natural as that poor man reached for his missing leg."

I told her it would probably take some time, but I wasn't sure if this was true. I'd lost my Margaret, and I still hadn't gotten over it. The surgeon's skill in scraping out my uterus hadn't cut away the memory of her.

"Don't know if Billy ever got over it. I bet if he's still alive, he's still reaching down to scratch that leg."

 *TWENTY-TWO*

I sit alone outside for the better part of the next hour, brooding and smoking. As I light the final cigarette in the pack, I look up at the darkening sky. It's just after four, well before dark, but a chain of thick clouds stretch as far as I can see in either direction, turning everything to shades of gray. The wind, which an hour earlier was a pleasant kite-flying kind of breeze, is beginning to gust, blowing my hair into my mouth and sparks of cigarette ash into the folds of my T-shirt. The miniature windmills at the edge of my father's garden are rattling violently, fan blades whirling, and the plastic Easter eggs suspended from the shrubbery on the front lawn are cracking against each other. A few of the eggs are blown apart and tumbling—a purple half here, a pink half there—across the un-mown lawn. There are sure to be news bulletins on all the local TV stations, warning of some impending disaster of which we are, for the moment, blissfully unaware.

Inside the house, Ellen is listening to music from a country music station that promotes itself as "Your home for boot-stompin' country." If I'm not mistaken, it's the same station whose glittering disc jockey performed her fairgrounds wedding. In the short time between songs, when the noise dies down and before the disc jockey announces the next song, I can hear thunder somewhere in the distance.

I'm sitting here thinking about the advice of Dr. Richard Blume-garten, Ph.D., that what women really want when they're feeling miserable is to talk about it. Telling Turner that I've come to enjoy the prospect of his being dead and that, in fact, I'm constantly surprised to find him alive, would, I'm sure the illustrious Dr. Blume-garten would say, go a long way toward ridding me of this pervasive unhappiness. I've been tempted before to spill my guts, to call Turner in for *a serious talk*, to sit at either side of our dining room table and hash it all out.

Turner dear, I know you think I love you, but that just proves you're a big fat idiot.

Turner, I've come to realize that my life is just an empty, gaping pit of despair and I wish you were dead.

Would that be honest enough?

The problem is, I don't think I could do it. And try as he might, I don't think he would understand if I did.

Don't I give you everything? he'd counter. *Don't you have everything to make you happy?*

Or, more likely, *You weren't always like this, Jessie. Dealing with crazy people all day long is making you crazy too.*

So I don't see the point of saying anything.

If I confessed, I'd unburden my own conscience but leave him bewildered at best, maybe even a little miserable. Is this what you're supposed to do with misery? Dump it on other people so you can get rid of it and then go about your happy life as usual?

Would Donna Lindsey, if she were suddenly overcome with guilt, call her husband in "for a serious talk"? Confess her affair? I don't think so, and not just because it isn't likely Donna will ever be overcome with guilt. The instincts of self-preservation and entitlement that led her to the affair in the first place are too sharply tuned for her to ever indulge in such nonsense. As she said to me recently, "Men have been getting away with this for centuries for one reason. Because they're smart enough to keep their mouths shut."

The other possibility, of course, is that Turner would view my confession as less than serious, as Donna seems to have done when I told her I'd been picturing Turner having, as I euphemistically put it, "an accident." And that, ironically, would leave me with the unsatisfying feeling of having unburdened my conscience for no good purpose.

I decide my only option is to adopt a more carefree attitude toward life and love, to join Donna and my sister in their wild, full-throttle searches for happiness.

I'll run off for a libidinous weekend with a department store salesman who's young enough to still be embarrassed about buying the condoms.

I'll drink shots of tequila at Red's Tavern, leaving behind all thoughts of my own husband, and skip off drunkenly into the night with another woman's husband.

If Donna and my sister are any example, these are the things bored wives do in their spare time, even if they end up making a mess of their own lives in the process.

I should crank up the Explorer and sneak off to Red's this very afternoon, where I will, with a clear conscience, select the first construction worker within reach. Of the choices available to me, it's almost worth trying.

I'm trying to decide what kind of beer I'll have at Red's when the front door flies open and Ellen sticks her head outside. Her lips are moving, but I can't make out what she's saying. From inside the house a man's tenor voice wails about losing the love of his life. I can't hear all the lyrics, but it sounds like they could be loosely translated as, *I know I'm a loser, honey, but I'm all you've got.*

Ellen disappears inside the house again, and the music stops. She sticks her head out the door again.

"You better get in here."

I crumple the empty cigarette pack into the pocket of my jeans and make a concentrated effort to look happy.

"Hurry up," she says, making an agitated circling motion with her hand.

"What's gotten into you all of a sudden?" I hear another rumble of thunder from the west, beyond the darkening clouds.

"In the first place, that husband of yours called." I wonder how she'd been able to hear the ringing with the music so loud.

"He's on the phone now?"

"Nope. Long gone."

"Why didn't you come get me?" I'd tried to reach Turner twice already since I arrived home. I don't really look forward to talking with him, but the idea of his calling and not wanting to talk with me angers me.

"It's not my fault your husband doesn't want to talk to you," she says with a smirk, anticipating the reaction it will cause. "Strange too, considering how happy you both are."

I don't want to take the bait.

"Fine," I say. I'm standing in front of her, ready to go inside, but she's blocking the doorway.

"He said, and I quote, 'Tell her that Donna, that so-called friend of hers, left nine messages on the machine.' I wrote down the number."

Donna, as far as I know, is supposed to be spending a naked weekend with her twenty-something salesman. Something must have gone wrong.

Ellen, her news reported, is still blocking the door.

"What? There's more?"

Ellen looks confused for a moment. She wrinkles her brow, and then, as if she's just remembered it, adds: "Oh yeah. One more thing. You need to help me in the kitchen. That smelly old dog of mama's is stone-cold dead."

⁂

Ellen sits at the kitchen table filing what's left of her nails. I kneel on the braided green rug where Missy spent the morning snoring. The stench of urine is overpowering. I pull the neckline of my T-shirt over my mouth and place my other hand on the dog's flabby rib cage.

"What's the diagnosis, Doctor?"

"She's dead, I think. I don't feel a heartbeat."

"I told you that already. Did you learn all this stuff in school or are you just naturally bright?"

I can't believe it. My sister's enjoying this.

"Just get me a towel." Surprisingly, she throws her nail file on the table and gets up to do it. The birds in the other room start squawking the minute she passes through the room.

"A dry one," I yell after her.

As I wait there on the floor with poor smelly Missy, I remember something I've heard since I was a child. "Death always comes in threes," my mother would announce, and anyone who was around to hear her say this would nod in agreement. They knew all too well that this was true. They'd been counting off deaths three at a time all their lives, just like my mother. They remembered when people died this way too, by connecting any one death to another. It didn't matter who the people were. They could be friends, neighbors, even celebrities. As long as my mother or her friends were able to connect them to their lives somehow, almost any death could count as part of their dark triad.

My mother remembers exactly when her aunt Susie died because it was two days before President Kennedy was shot. The same afternoon Kennedy was shot Inez Sneed's husband Luther collapsed in front of Woolworth's and, as my mother retold it, "was dead before he hit the pavement." They all missed watching the Kennedy funeral on TV because they were burying Luther instead.

For me, Missy was Number 1.

If my mother and her friends are right, there's sure to be two more deaths within the week. If a dog counts, that is.

⚛

The phone rings six times before I get an answer.

"Yeah?" The voice is tired. Groggy even.

"Donna?"

"Uh huh. Jessie? Is that you? Thank God."

"What's going on, Donna?" I say. "Turner said you've been calling the house all afternoon. Where are you?"

I already knew where she was. When I called the number she left, the man who answered the phone seemed genuinely shocked that I wanted to talk with someone staying at the Bay Island Hotel. People staying there usually don't tell anyone where they are, and if they do, they don't want to be disturbed. The hotel manager probably thought I was a jealous wife who was on to her husband's shenanigans.

"At the moment, I'm in bed. Well, sort of half on the bed and half off, but in the bed vicinity. That counts, doesn't it?"

"Tell me what's going on. Are you alone? Are you okay?"

"Yes and no. I'm quite alone, thank you, but not exactly okay."

Donna soon reveals that she and Perry Ferguson met at the Bay Island Hotel as expected and that they spent the night together there engaging in all manner of rambunctious activities. This morning, after engaging in more such activities and working up healthy appetites, he kissed her good-bye and set out on foot for the Cracker Barrel across the highway, his intention being to bring back to the room two breakfast plates-to-go and two cups of coffee. Then he and Donna would sit in bed naked, eat eggs off each other's plates, and, in the process, get each other all worked up again for their next round.

At some point in the middle of all this they also had a serious discussion that revolved around their not returning to their respective homes after the weekend was over. They had, she tells me, planned to run away together and—she actually says this—"live happily ever after."

They planned, she says, to move someplace where nobody knows either of them, maybe Montana, taking nothing but their credit cards and the things they packed for the weekend. They're soul mates, she says, and can't live without each other. She'll give up custody of her boys if she has to, but it's worth it. The boys know she loves them, and once she and Perry are on their feet again, she can patch things up with them, and with David, and petition for custody. The fact that her affair had, in one short week, turned from "yummy" sex to undying love, a love she is willing to risk everything for, is something I'd missed entirely.

"Donna, have you completely lost your mind?"

"I don't think so. We're really serious this time."

"You two talked about this before?"

"Sure. Lots of times."

It occurs to me then that Donna said she's alone in the room. Something must have gone wrong.

"Tell me what happened, Donna."

"Perry's dead, that's what's happened. At least I assume he's dead. I don't see how he couldn't be dead, or hurt real bad."

An image of an enraged David Lindsey, breaking down the safety-latched hotel door with gun in hand, pops into my head. Maybe even a homicidal Mrs. Ferguson. The two of them forming an unlikely partnership as they searched for their cheating spouses.

"What? Oh God, Donna, what happened?"

I wish then that I could hang up the phone, forget I'd ever returned this call. I don't like where this story is going.

"Okay," she says, sobbing now. "So he went to the Cracker Barrel, right? But after an hour, he still hadn't come back to the room. I waited another thirty minutes or so, thinking maybe there was a long line at the restaurant, that it was just taking longer than we expected."

"And?"

"All sorts of things were running through my head. That he'd been struck by a car and killed as he was crossing the highway. There's a red light because it's just off the interstate, but it's a busy road, and it *could* happen. Or maybe he'd been mugged in the parking lot, that—"

"So what actually happened, Donna? Do you know?"

"So then I thought, 'Get a grip on yourself. You're being ridiculous,' so I finally got dressed. I walked all the way over to the Cracker Barrel, looked in the gift shop and the restaurant, even stood outside the men's bathroom, but I couldn't find him anywhere. Something must have happened. Oh God, this is just horrible. I don't—"

"Go on, Donna," I say, slowing my words. Trying to calm her in any way I can. "Tell me what happened next."

"So I ran back to the room as fast as I could, locked the door, and I've been here ever since. I'm scared to go out again." She says she couldn't possibly risk going to the police and reporting him missing, because that would connect her to him. The room was in her name alone—a single, with a king bed—and she paid with her American Express card, so there wasn't even any record of his staying there.

"And he's still not back yet. I've been sitting here like this for hours."

Donna hasn't even considered the possibility that Perry fled the scene. More likely, she just doesn't want to consider it.

"Is his car still in the parking lot, Donna? Did you check?"

Donna loses it then, wailing the most pitiful and horrifying sound I could ever have imagined.

"He could have been car-jacked!" she screams. "Anything could have happened! Oh God, oh God, oh GOD, this can't be happening.

He wouldn't just leave me here like this. He wouldn't! He loved me. I know that. I know it for a fact."

It sounds like she's banging the phone against the nightstand.

Nothing is working. I can't even remember half of what I've told her. I wonder how long it will take me to drive to the Bay Island Hotel, if I can make it there before dark. If I should go at all. I look across the kitchen floor at poor Missy, whom I've wrapped in a towel to await burial. In the living room, my sister is singing to her birds in whiny, lullaby fashion.

"Do you want me to come get you, Donna?"

"I just want to stay here a while and sleep. Then I'll get up and go home, I guess. Say I decided to come home early." She blows her nose, sniffles softly into the phone. "Act like nothing happened." She starts sobbing again.

I can't imagine Donna pulling herself together enough to arrive home as if nothing has happened. David is sure to notice his wife's unraveled composure.

This is the part about adultery I know I couldn't handle. Little lies and big lies, lies to cover up lies. If I were having an affair, I'd always be expecting the bomb to drop, expecting certain punishment for all my bad behavior.

"Are you sure you don't want me to come?"

She tells me no. She needs to be alone. She just wanted me to know what happened. Just needed to tell somebody, needed to say it out loud so she could convince herself that it really had happened.

Would Donna really have left her husband and children and moved to Montana to make a new life with Perry Ferguson? I guess she could have pulled it off, made that sound easy too. I think about our visit a few days ago, when I found her standing over her kitchen stove, burning her family's dinner. Problem was, Perry Ferguson hadn't played along, probably sufficiently spooked by all this talk of "living happily ever after" that he'd run back to his wife. Donna's plan wasn't his plan.

"Did you love him, Donna? I mean, do you really think that's what it was?"

"I don't know. Maybe I did. That's sure what it felt like."

TWENTY-THREE

Q. *What are the principal kinds of prayer?*
A. *The principal kinds of prayer are adoration, praise, thanksgiving,*
penitence, oblation, intercession, and petition.

THE CATECHISM

THE BOOK OF COMMON PRAYER

It never occurred to Wanda McNabb not to forgive Baxter for the things he did. She didn't know any other way. "You've got to take the good with the bad," she once told me. "That's the only way to deal with a husband."

In early February, I decided it might be a good idea if Wanda and I started having our Monday sessions over lunch, instead of in the more formal setting of my office cubicle, and it was during one of these lunches that she told me this. This was more than a little unorthodox, and I knew I'd already crossed the boundary between counselor and client, but by that time Wanda's story had seeped into my bones. I couldn't let professional ethics interfere with our friendship, or so I thought then. It would be good for Wanda, I reasoned. Good for me, too. Lunch was my treat.

I took her to O'Malley's, one of those restaurants that can best be described as a burger place with a liquor license, where the primary culinary attraction is that they stir up a dozen varieties of margarita. The waitresses visit your table in roving packs. If it's your birthday, they sing and cheer and serve, with great fanfare, the O'Malley's Marvelous Birthday Treat!, a three-scoop brownie with hot fudge, on the house. It is Glenville's newest and, at least for now, most popular restaurant, and I usually end up eating there once a week whether I want to or not.

At O'Malley's, Glenville's businessmen hang their jackets from the backs of their ladder-backed chairs and sit armed with cell phones in their pockets or within close reach on the bar. Once let loose from their office cubicles, they band together on the pretense of having a working lunch. With ties slung over their shoulders they eat their fried onion strips and specialty burgers and watch ESPN on any number of televisions suspended from the exposed beam ceiling.

Wanda looked nervous the minute we stepped into the crowded, swinging-door foyer. We were pressed close against a line of a dozen or more young women who, judging from the packages they carried and the presence of a very pregnant woman at the center of their chatty group, were there for a baby shower. Given the shortage of tables and the need for several befuddled busboys to push together four tables to make room for the gift-bearing group ahead of us, it took fifteen minutes before we were seated. I tried not to look at the group of women now seated on the other side of the restaurant, tried not to imagine myself as the honoree of such an event.

Wanda fidgeted with her silverware, holding each piece up to the light and inspecting it for spots. She moved her napkin from the table to her lap, then back again. She stirred her tea, added another packet of sugar. Stirred it again. She opened and closed the menu at least four times. Wanda is one of those women who, like my mother, find it hard to sit still in restaurants. Every time one of the waitresses elbowed her way through the saloon doors of the kitchen, Wanda swiveled on her side of the booth and turned her head in an effort to get a look at what was going on behind those doors. My mother once tried to explain it. "I control what goes on in my kitchen," she said, narrowing her eyes. "I'd feel better if I knew what was going on in this one."

I studied Wanda's movements. She used her napkin to polish her fork, then with a sweep of her hand, brushed a few crumbs from a corner of the table.

"What if the bad outweighs the good?" I said.

"What?" Her eyes surveyed the entire table surface, looking for more crumbs. She looked at me as if she was disappointed not to find me giving my side of the table the same inspection.

"You take the bad with the good? Isn't that what you told me?"

"Oh. Yeah, I guess I did." She picked up her tea and took a sip, glancing around her with a few quick turns, as if she expected the people at other tables to be eavesdropping on our conversation.

"Well, sometimes it does," she said, barely above a whisper. "Outweigh the good, I mean."

"Then what do you do? Keep taking more of the bad?"

Wanda rearranged her silverware again. Knife to the left of her plate. Fork and spoon to the right. She moved every piece as if she were following an invisible pattern on the table's surface.

"I don't understand you young people. Why do you think you

have to do something the minute you're unhappy for more than five minutes?"

"What if it's a lot longer than five minutes?"

"We're talking about you now, aren't we? Not me and Baxter."

Before I could answer, we were interrupted by our server, whose name, she announced enthusiastically, was Kimmy. She pointed to a plastic name badge that was pinned just above her left breast. She'd drawn a smiley face under her name and dotted the *i* with a heart.

"You just yell and I'll come running, ladies," said Kimmy, whose frizzy bleached hair exploded from a polka-dot hair clip perched at the very top of her head. "All you got to do is ask for me—Kimmy," and pointed to her name tag again.

She made a big production of bringing our sandwiches to the table, sashaying through the crowd with the plates held high above her head.

"Here we *go*, ladies. *Best* sandwiches in Glenville!"

Once the plates were in front of us, she stepped back and admired her handiwork. Before we'd taken a bite of our sandwiches, she started to chat in excruciating hard-sell detail about this or that item on the dessert menu. "I'm just saying you should live a little," she said. Kimmy's glossed pink lips slid into a smile, her free hand resting suggestively on the curve of her hip. It was a pose, and a philosophy of life, that I'm sure works more effectively on her male customers. "I mean, we've got a chocolate fudge torte that's to die for."

Mercifully, and without sharing with us any further advice on living and dying, she whirled around from the table and sauntered off in the direction of the bar, where a group of eight young men were gathered. All wearing suspenders and silk ties, they looked like the kind of men who might work for Turner's competitors on the local banking scene. Up-and-coming young MBAs who dream of the kind of life and luxury they've been groomed for—a big corner office and a reserved parking space. Men who want a life so successfully ordinary that they will blend in with every other successful, ordinary man of their generation.

It would be a good tip day, even for Kimmy. She was doing her desperate best to entertain the men. She was so full of high hopes that it broke my heart. Despite the fact that she was, by then, so caught up with entertaining the MBAs and hadn't visited our table to refill our iced teas, I decided I'd leave a big tip for her anyway. A good tip might just give her enough hope to keep dreaming.

"Yeah, we're talking about me," I said after Kimmy had finally moved a safe distance from the table. Over the previous few months, between the times Wanda was telling me about her own troubled marriage, I had wrongly confided in her, too, trying to explain the boredom I felt in my life, the ever-growing distance I felt from my own husband. I'd even told her about my miscarriage. She always listened patiently and, like any good therapist, offered no opinion either way about my situation.

Wanda blotted both corners of her lips with her napkin. "Sometimes the bad isn't as bad as you think it is," she said, leaving me to wonder how bad it was supposed to get before the pain I was feeling was real enough to be justified.

"Sometimes I wake up in the morning and I think to myself, 'Is this all there is to life?' "

"So what?" Wanda said as she nibbled a french fry. "You think that makes you special?"

"I'm miserable, that's what. I'm not sure if I even love my husband anymore. Oh, and to top it all off, I'll be forty soon."

Kimmy was seated on a bar stool, her crossed legs tapping out

the rhythm to the song on the radio, her right foot perched provocatively on a rung of the nearest MBA's bar stool.

*Come talk to me in twenty years, Kimmy. Then we'll see if you're
still drawing smiley faces.*

"Blah, blah, blah," Wanda snapped. "Most people feel that way.
Life isn't one big party, Jessie." She looked like she wanted to slap me.

"Thanks a lot. That's very comforting."

"You're not going to sit there and feel sorry for yourself, are
you?" she asked.

What kind of reaction had I really expected from Wanda? Did I
think she'd nod her head and, in a mimic of my own behavior with
my patients, tell me she understood, that she empathized with what
I was going through? After the damage she'd suffered in her own life,
is that what I expected? Unchallenged and automatic sympathy for
my predicament?

"I know you think I'm being hard on you." She lifted her napkin
from her lap and folded it next to her plate.

I tried to act like I wasn't bothered by her reaction at all, that it
didn't matter to me one way or the other what she thought. What I
need, I thought, is what Mary Chapin Carpenter was singing about
on the radio. Passionate kisses. Lots of them. The MBAs at the bar
were beginning to look like tempting prospects for helping me assuage my middle-age angst, providing I could somehow get Kimmy
and her youthful enthusiasm back into the kitchen and have them all
to myself.

"You probably think I can't understand what you're going
through."

"You're been through a lot, Wanda. My problems can't compare
with yours." I felt like I was eleven years old again, my mother and

Inez Sneed both trying to restore my self-confidence after a less than stunning performance at a piano recital.

Wanda reached over and patted my hand.

"Every woman goes through this, dear. It happens to us all."

That wasn't very comforting either. Are all the women I know tricking me into thinking they're happy when they're just as miserable? I looked across the bar at the group of women at the baby shower. Someone produced a dozen or more blue balloons. The mother-to-be, who looked to be in her early twenties, sat Buddha-like at the head of the long table, opening a gift and holding it up for inspection, which prompted a cascade of squeals from the other women at the table. Another young woman was seated close by, writing down each gift and who brought it, so all the proper thank-yous could be sent. Watching them, I felt lonely and small.

"So what do I do about it?"

"It's all hormones, honey," Wanda said. "I've seen my share of restless women, and I'd say you're definitely one of them."

"You think it's hormones? That that's all this is?"

"Don't make any sudden moves. That's the best advice I can give you."

TWENTY-FOUR

My sister and I are standing on the front porch, trying to decide what to do about Missy, who's still wrapped in a towel and resting in a cold and smelly lump on the kitchen floor. Two cars turn into my parents' long and dusty driveway. My mother is bringing home her Lincoln Town Car. My father's pickup follows close behind, partially obscured by a cloud of red dust. It's past five now, and the gray clouds are full of rain.

As they move closer, I realize that my father is driving the Lincoln, my mother wearing her seat belt but leaning as close as possible to him on the bench seat. They look like a couple of kids returning home from a date. As he rounds the last curve, he switches on the big car's windshield wipers. Cecil's the one driving our father's pickup. Justin sits far against the passenger-side door, his head barely visible over the dashboard, but I can see that he's laughing at something Cecil is saying. Justin is not a child who laughs often.

"Awwww shit," my sister spits. "He's the last person in the world I want to see right now," her voice trails off as she flees into the house with a flurry of door slamming.

They all tumble out of their respective vehicles. My mother unbuckles her seat belt and scoots over to sit behind the wheel of the Lincoln, hands poised in the correct 10-2 position.

"Just practicing," she calls to me and waves. "Your father's going to take me out for a driving lesson if the good Lord will let this rain hold off for a while." As soon as she slides out the driver's-side door a fat solitary raindrop hits her square in the forehead. She brushes it off as if it hasn't happened at all, then glances up at the darkening sky and closes her eyes, probably saying a silent prayer that Jesus will spare her enough time for a driving lesson.

"I still can't believe you never got your license," I say. I stand next to the Lincoln with them, peering into the open door at the leather interior and trying to look as if I think buying this car was the right thing to do.

"Yeah, Grandma," Justin chimes in, kicking up a swirl of gravel with the toe of his tennis shoe. Every time his foot hits the ground, the heel of his shoe lights up in electric blue. "Everybody drives. My friend Joey says his father lets him drive all the time, and he's only eight."

Cecil keeps a hand on Justin's shoulder but isn't listening to our conversation. He's scanning the exterior of the house, trying to find any clue as to Ellen's whereabouts.

"Well I'm going to learn now," my mother says, raising her nose to sniff the cool, wet air. "How hard can it be? I helped you girls study for your driver's tests, didn't I? I know all the rules already." She looks up at my father as if she expects him to defend her.

"She's been telling me how to drive all these years, that's for sure. I think it's about time I was the one giving the orders."

I feel compelled to make a few more appreciative comments about the Lincoln. My parents never bought a new car, one straight off the lot, as my father might say. This purchase, which my father already has deemed extravagant, is probably the closest they'll ever get.

"You know what the good thing about this car is?" asks my father.

"What's that?"

"This car," he continues, patting the hood, "is so big that whatever she hits will fold up like a tin can and she'll drive off without a scratch. Gas guzzlers. That's the only good thing about them."

Cecil looks like he'd like to laugh but has more important things to do. Head down, cap in his hands, he walks toward the house. Justin pulls a set of earphones from his shirt pocket and fidgets with the dials of a CD player hooked to the waistband of his jeans. Satisfied with the result, he scrambles to the edge of the driveway and starts kicking one of my mother's inflatable Easter bunnies. Soon, from inside the house, I can hear the sounds of bickering. I can't make out what they're saying, but it sounds like my sister is the one doing all the talking.

"So did you meet the one lady owner?"

It's my plan to keep everyone outdoors and away from Ellen and Cecil's brewing argument, even if I have to hold them at bay with one of my mother's inflatable Easter bunnies.

"Her son George was the one selling the car," my mother says.

"He's selling all her stuff, even the house. Lives in Charlotte, up there in North Carolina. Took a week off from work to take care of things here. An engineer, and such a sweet boy."

"Had his boyfriend with him at the house," my father adds, and makes a kissing sound. "Real sweet."

"You don't know any such thing, Carl Kilgore. That boy was wearing a little gold cross around his neck, and he wouldn't have been wearing one of those if he was, well, you know."

My father rolls his eyes. I feel three or four raindrops hit the back of my neck.

As we stand in the shadow of the Lincoln, my mother explains that the "lady owner" was seventy-eight-year-old Wilma Tibbetts, who, after suffering a severe stroke, is now living at the Sunset Springs Nursing Home with a ninety-four-year-old roommate. Her roommate, an Alzheimer's patient, is under the distinct impression that Mrs. Tibbetts is her third-grade teacher and spends most of each day asking Mrs. Tibbetts if today is the day for the geography quiz.

How my mother gleans these kinds of details from virtual strangers is beyond me. She can visit the Randolph Gap Swap Meet and learn that the man who sells pickled eggs wasn't there that day because he's recovering from prostate surgery. That the daughter of the woman who sells quilts paid $975 for a store-bought wedding dress though the marriage didn't last six weeks and the bride is already four months pregnant. That the minister of the Big Hurricane Church is suffering from bloody stools and the whole congregation has been praying about it. These are the types of things she reports to me in our telephone conversations. She considers it her duty in life to broadcast, like any good journalist, the private sufferings and embarrassing foibles of her neighbors.

My mother also reveals that George, the lady owner's son, is thinking of moving back to Randolph Gap so he can be closer to his mother and visit her more often. "What a sweet boy," she croons. "Trying to help his mother like that." She looks at me like she wants this message to sink in—like I've got a lot to learn about the responsibility that comes with being her daughter.

My father makes a spitting sound.

"What's that supposed to mean?" she says, and jumps back a little from my father's intended spitting destination.

"Not a thing, dear," he says. "I'm an equal-opportunity spitter."

❧

"God dammit, Cecil, I told you I'm not coming back."

That's the first thing we hear when we walk in the door, the voice coming from the room Ellen and I share.

"You know I don't like to hear that kind of language in my house," my mother says. One of my mother's latest projects has been to check out books from the Randolph Gap Public Library and scan them, permanent ink marker in hand, blacking out all words judged offensive and blasphemous.

She had to skim fourteen books until she found anything. Then she stumbled onto something that offended her moral sensibilities so dramatically that she fell to her knees, right there between the stacks, and prayed for the writer to see the light before it was too late. She nearly got away with it too, since the fiction section was quiet that day, until a group of well-intentioned sixth-graders roving the aisles for book report topics informed the circulation desk that "some lady's having a fit up there, like one of them epileptics." The library, smelling a lawsuit, called 911, and my mother's prayers were interrupted by paramedics who made her lie on the floor while they took her blood pressure and pried her mouth open to see if she'd bitten her tongue in half.

"I tried to tell them I wasn't sick, but they wouldn't hear of it. Had to check me all over to make sure. I said, 'Boys, haven't you ever seen anybody pray before?' And they said, 'No ma'am, not in no library.' I told them I wasn't going to the hospital, but they took me out in a wheelchair anyway." She slipped the offending book in her handbag before they wheeled her out.

"No decent Southerner would ever put pen to paper to write such trash. And you simply wouldn't believe how many women write this filth! I bet their mothers would just die if they knew what they were up to. If they were raised right, they shouldn't even be thinking such things."

In her zeal to edit every objectionable word from the Randolph Gap Public Library's collection, my mother convinced Inez Sneed to read the works of writers from the North. "Sister Inez has a cousin in West Virginia," she explained, "so she knows more about Yankees than I do." Now Sister Inez is beating my mother at her own game. They're actually keeping score. A total of 173 words censored by Sister Inez. Only 140 for my mother.

"Can't you do something about those two?" my mother asks me. "Go tell them to stop! You know I don't like hearing all this profanity."

The fact that my sister is in the process of leaving her husband doesn't concern my mother as much as the language Ellen's using. My mother starts circling the kitchen table, praying out loud, "Dear Lord, please let my children see the error of their ways, and let them have the common decency not to use this kind of language in my home."

My father and Justin make a break for it.

"Come on, boy, you can rack 'em for me," he says, and they go out the back door, headed for the pool table in the barn.

My sister doesn't let up.

She calls Cecil a loser.

And an asshole.

Then a loser and an asshole.

My mother is locked in a holding pattern. She circles the table and prays. Then, much to my alarm, she regains her composure and turns her attention to me.

"You and Turner don't fight like that, do you?" From the bedroom, I can hear the sound of someone crying. It doesn't sound like my sister.

"No mama, we don't." I don't have to lie about that. Fights like that require at least some passion.

"Well, I should hope not. Your father and I have never talked to each other like that."

"That's good." I don't know if it's good or not. Maybe it would be good if Turner and I could fight like that. Call each other names. Break a few things. Might do us a lot of good.

"The very idea," my mother wails. "I don't how Cecil puts up with it. What's got into her?"

"I don't think he'll be putting up with it for long."

"That child is willful, I tell you that. Always has been."

I can't argue with her on that one. Ellen has called me an asshole lots of times.

"I just don't understand it. Why can't people live together and just be happy?" She's still pacing around the table. From the general direction of the bedroom, we hear a door slam.

"People take things too seriously, that's what I think. They've got to have everything just so or they're not happy. Running off and getting divorced at the drop of a hat when they need to put their troubles in God's hands. God knows what to do." My mother and Wanda McNabb are in apparent agreement on this, though Wanda doesn't say God has anything to do with it.

Ellen storms through the kitchen door, nearly running into the table.

"You have no cause to use that kind of language in my house," my mother says, shaking a finger in Ellen's face. "No cause at all." Knowing my mother, her recent defeat at the hands of librarians has sent her sense of moral obligation to its boiling point. She has no alternative but to take it out on her family.

"Grow up, Mother. Adults talk like this," Ellen says. "Especially when they're pissed off."

"I've told you. Not in my house they don't."

"Ellen's going through a hard time now. Let her be." I can't believe I'm defending my sister, but there it is. It just slipped out.

At that, Ellen starts crying.

This stops my mother cold. No condition of the human spirit, however grim, justifies profanity in our mother's opinion, but Ellen's tears slow her down a little. Maybe she fears Ellen is on the verge of another nervous attack.

"But Cecil's such a nice boy," she says. "And he's good to Justin. Not many men would be to a boy that ain't theirs." Our mother doesn't refer to Justin's undetermined paternity often, and when she does, it's usually in the context of a compliment for Cecil. She respects the fact that he's willing to raise another man's child, even if she doesn't understand it. Ellen, she says, should be grateful she's landed such a husband.

"He's a loser," Ellen sobs, her head on the table.

"Why can't you two be happy? I just don't understand anything anymore."

Ellen knows when she's got the upper hand. She lifts her head off the table and sneers at both of us.

"Hey Jess, did you tell mama that smelly old dog of hers croaked?"

⅋

We bury Missy within the hour. I think my mother, once she recovered from the shock of seeing Missy wrapped in a towel on the kitchen floor, wanted to get it over with quick. She always liked a good funeral.

My father and Justin are summoned from the barn for the occasion. Cecil's still on the premises, but he must be hiding.

We all hike into the woods, where, in a flat section of ground just beyond the place where we always picked muscadines, my mother holds Missy in her arms while my father digs the grave. He digs a lot deeper than I thought he would. The site, according to our mother, was always a favorite of Missy's. She liked to chase squirrels there.

"That sure is a little dog for such a big hole," Ellen says.

"Coons," says our father, not looking up from his work with the shovel.

"Gross." This from Justin, who takes a few steps away from my mother, and from Missy. My mother says a short prayer, and we're done. She lowers Missy into the hole, towel and all.

⅋

We walk back to the house to find Cecil sitting on the front steps. Ellen looks off in the other direction and walks right past him and slams the door behind her, acting like he isn't there at all.

"I'll be heading out," he sniffles. "I'm just in the way here. Called a buddy of mine to come pick me up."

He runs a grease-stained hand through his thinning blond hair and folds his heavy legs close to his body, hugging his knees. He looks like someone sitting on the side of the road after an accident. Just sitting there shaking his head and wondering how he didn't see the other car weaving over the center lane; how he'll ever survive after this one blinding moment that has changed his life, and the lives of his family, forever.

"Okay, son," my father tells him. "Sure am sorry about all this, but thanks for taking a look at that car for me. I trust you more than anybody else when it comes to cars."

"Nothing to it," Cecil says.

Justin moves to sit beside his stepfather, puts an arm around his shoulder.

"You just need to give her a little time to calm down, that's all," my mother says. "She'll come around."

"I guess."

"You know so. Despite all her faults, I know she loves you."

"If you say so." He takes a handkerchief from his pocket and wipes his eyes.

"She does, Cecil," says my father, "even if she don't act like it sometimes."

TWENTY-FIVE

By six, we're all piled into the Lincoln Town Car and heading for the Randolph Gap Holy Rock Church parking lot. My father is driving, my mother pressed close beside him and watching his every move. My sister and I are in the backseat, Justin sprawled between us.

After Cecil left, my father surveyed the sky and, despite the thunder still rumbling in the distance, decided it was a good time for my mother's first driving lesson. At least it would keep us from having to sit around the house staring at each other.

"We've got a good hour before that storm hits," he says to my mother. "Let's go see if you can handle that car." Then, to Justin,

"Son, go tell your mama to come with us. With your grandma at the wheel, we're bound to have a real, once-in-a-lifetime family adventure."

He decides the parking lot of the Randolph Gap Holy Rock Church, relatively free of road hazards, will be a good place for the lesson. There's always a chance she might crash the Lincoln into a tree or jump the embankment to collide with a tombstone in the church cemetery, but this is the safest of all our options. Having her drive on an actual road is out of the question. My father doesn't care if my mother slams the car into a tree. Trees can't sue.

To get to the Randolph Gap Holy Rock Church, you take Rural Route 119 and head west, stopping just short of the Randolph County line. You won't find any signs marking the way. The only place it's called Rural Route 119 is on the most detailed of county maps. The locals call it Little Hurricane Creek Road. The road dead-ends in the church parking lot, so there's not much traffic except on Sundays and for midweek services, not counting revivals or funeral processions. Like the barn on my parents' property, it's the kind of spot frequently photographed by tourists looking for places off the beaten path.

Little Hurricane is the spring-fed creek that runs along the road leading to the church. Though barely waist deep in places, it runs clear and icy cold and is a favorite swimming spot for those in Randolph Gap not brave enough to tackle the Black Warrior River. The church-bound traffic crosses a small wooden bridge where the creek flows uninterrupted and winds its way along the east lawn of the church itself. On the lawn, makeshift sawhorse-and-plywood tables are left out year-round, weathered and buckled, and are used for church homecomings and other special events, many of which involve impromptu baptisms. To the west, running along a raised track maybe fifty feet high, is a railroad, as Randolph Gap was once home to a thriving coal mining village. Trains still pass by, though not as regularly as they once did.

When I was a child and attended this church with my mother, I counted an average of two trains for each Sunday morning sermon. If there was a revival going on, and we were there for night services, there were more. Sometimes, as many as six trains passed, whistles blowing. Every time it happened, the stained glass windows of the church shook violently and I cringed in my seat, waiting for a multicolored Jesus in the Garden of Gethsemane to come flying, piece by shiny piece, in my direction.

The Rev. Floyd Wheeling, who was pastor then, took full advantage of this proximity to the railroad. Whenever a train went by, he would, in a voice even louder than the train itself, yell to the congregation, "Jesus has your ticket! Are you ready to get on this train?" Or, in his best conductor's voice, "All aboooo-ard the train bound for glory!" It didn't matter when it happened. It could be during his sermon, or when the choir was singing. He always stopped whatever was happening to say some variation of these two lines, which usually proved effective. If only one train passed, turnout at altar call was slim. If three or more rattled the church windows, it was standing room only.

It wasn't until I was in the fourth grade that I realized not all church services were conducted in this manner.

"That church is one of those charismatics," my new best friend Melissa Tuck informed me, impressing me with her pronunciation of a word I'd never heard before, not even in spelling bees. "I bet you all dance around and speak in tongues. That's what my mama says you do down there."

Melissa and her family lived on a farm where they milked their own cows, but they considered themselves a higher class of Christian because they were Methodists.

"My mama says you holy rollers are plumb crazy if you handle all them snakes," she told me.

I tried to tell Melissa I'd never seen a snake at the Randolph Gap Holy Rock Church, much less ever handled one, but I couldn't convince her.

I'd grown up in that church and had never been embarrassed about it before. Melissa, though, had her mind made up already. "If you want to handle snakes that's your business," she said. That's when I knew Melissa was my new best friend. She didn't care what anybody did, as long as they realized she was above such outrageous behavior. Melissa Tuck, I told myself, was sophisticated.

The only time Turner visited the Randolph Gap Holy Rock Church with me, the whole experience took him completely by surprise.

"Where are the books?" he whispered to me as we took our places on the hard pine pews.

"What books?"

"The prayer books."

I had to stifle a laugh. "They don't use prayer books here, Turner."

"How am I going to know what to say?" asked my new husband, who had never attended any church other than All Saints. He looked genuinely concerned. As he scanned the pew in front of us, I could tell he was worried he'd end up kneeling on the hardwood floor. The velvet-covered prayer bench he was accustomed to was nowhere in sight.

"You don't have to say anything, and you don't have to kneel.

Just follow me and you'll do fine," I said, feeling a little guilty that I hadn't briefed him in advance on the charismatic practices of my mother's church. Only two or three women spoke in tongues that day, but by the time we left the church my husband's face was pasty white and he kept his shaking hands hidden in his pockets.

Directly behind the church, to the south, lies the Randolph Gap Holy Rock Church Cemetery, a three-acre plot of flat red clay covered by sparse yellowing grass. Since it is on a dead-end road, behind a church with ever dwindling attendance, it's a peaceful place as cemeteries go, the gravesites disrupted only by the protruding roots of magnolia trees. The trees are planted throughout the cemetery, and when they push their way up through the clay they threaten to topple even the heaviest of headstones, giving these monuments the appearance, from a distance, of being cut uneven on purpose, all triangles and trapezoids. The trees do improve the landscape, and provide some shade during the hot summers, but all things considered, they're a nuisance. After the flowers bloom, the graves are covered with rotting petals and seed cones. I imagine most of the coffins were long ago invaded by the thick and twisting roots.

The first grave here was dug in 1884. There are more than three hundred grave sites crowded into this small space now, some even dug close to the edge where the grass ends and the woods begin. Those who are buried there, on the outskirts of the civilized cemetery, find their tombstones regularly attacked by creeping vines and other infringements of the forest. From their less than prestigious location, I always assumed them to be thieves or murderers who were cast to the fringes of this sacred ground, though the simple truth is that the cemetery is quickly running out of space. Every time I visit, I expect a section of the surrounding forest to be clear-cut, a busy band of loggers pulling away tree stumps and vines, preparing to dig more graves and plant more magnolias. My grandparents, on both sides of the family, are buried in this cemetery. So are one set of great-grandparents and numerous uncles, aunts, and cousins.

My parents will be buried here one day, too, in adjoining lots they've selected. In an effort to discourage anyone else from digging up their spot, their tombstone is already there. A big chunk of granite with two intertwined hearts. Carl Jesse Kilgore, b. May 14, 1927. Lucy Elizabeth Kilgore, b. Oct. 2, 1932. Just waiting for them to arrive, their d. dates to be inscribed.

As my father once told me, "Your mama's got everything planned in advance. Long as she doesn't pick the date, I don't care where she plants me."

I hear Andy Leonard is buried here too. I've never visited his grave.

❧

My father starts the driving lesson the moment we're in the car, the big Lincoln still parked in the driveway. I almost gag when I crawl into the backseat. It smells like someone has sprayed an entire can of air freshener into it, but even that does little to mask a lingering, more objectionable odor. I roll down my window a few inches to keep from choking.

"Okay, the car is in park. I'm starting the ignition."

My mother watches all this and nods thoughtfully. "Dear Lord, please let us have a safe driving lesson and return home before it starts raining," she says out loud, hands in the air.

"Dear Lord, don't let Lucretia here forget to buckle her seat belt," says my father as the car grumbles and sputters to life.

"My seat belt's buckled, Carl. And I'll thank you not to take the Lord's name in vain like you did."

"Grandpa didn't cuss or nothin'," says Justin, who has removed his headphones and sits with both arms propped on the front seat, suddenly interested in what's going on in the front seat.

My mother whips her head around, coming almost nose to nose with her grandson. "No son, but he did it just the same." She looks at my father, and at Justin, like they're both in need of a lecture on the subject but she's not about to interrupt her first driving lesson to administer it.

"But—"

"But nothing. The Bible says—"

"The Bible doesn't have anything against having a little fun," says my father, who leans over anyway to make sure my mother's seat belt is properly attached. My mother flinches when he gives it a tug. "We'll have a safe driving lesson if you pay more attention to what I'm trying to teach you instead of praying."

"Hmmmph," she says, but lets it drop.

"Okay, I'm applying the brakes."

Seconds later, "I'm flipping on the right turn signal." He keeps this up for the entire drive.

From the moment she entered the car, my sister has sat slumped in the backseat, chewing her nails. At times it looks like she has her whole fist in her mouth. She's slipped into the familiar role of childhood: ignoring everything and everyone around her.

"I'm turning on the windshield wipers."

"It's not raining now, Grandpa," Justin corrects.

"I know that, boy. I'm just showing your grandmother how they work."

"For goodness' sake, Carl, I may not have a driver's license, but

I'm not a child," my mother says. Yanking on her seat belt like it's cutting her in half, she moves closer to her side of the car and stares out the window at the passing scenery. "And I'll thank you not to insult me for praying. It's something you should do more of yourself."

At this, my sister lets out an exasperated sigh.

We ride in silence for a few minutes, hearing only the thump, thump, ker-thump of the Lincoln's wheels over the pavement.

Then it begins.

"That's where you girls went to school," announces my mother, wide-eyed, as we pass the Randolph Gap Elementary School. "I wonder if that sweet Mrs. Emerson ever retired." She turns to look at Ellen and me, expecting this reminiscence to trigger a similar excited reaction.

"Uh huh," Ellen says, her fingers still in her mouth.

My mother does this every time I visit Randolph Gap.

"There's the place where we used to get ice cream," she'll say.

"Your friend from third grade used to live in that house. Remember? Her name was Debbie and she hated licorice."

Or, "I used to take you trick-or-treating in this neighborhood. You both looked so cute! Remember, Jessie?"

This can go on for miles.

I'm convinced my mother thinks both Ellen and I are amnesia victims. She points out the same landmarks every time. You'd think we'd remember them by now.

When we make the turn onto Little Hurricane Creek Road, I notice something new. The Randolph Gap Holy Rock Church has stooped to advertising. They've put up a portable message board with a big neon arrow pointing the way down the dead-end road to their door. The sign reads:

If God seems far away . . .
Guess who moved?
Rev. Floyd Wheeling Jr., Pastor
Join us Sunday!

In the growing dark of late afternoon, the sky full of black clouds, the sign's all lit up, though I can't figure out how, since it must be a good half-mile from the church itself. Maybe one of the reverends Wheeling figured out how to tap into the city's electrical supply.

"I'm coming to a full stop now," my father says as we pull under the canopy of towering oaks and arrive, at last, in the church parking lot. "I'm putting the car in park."

"Shut up, Carl," my mother snaps. "Just let me behind the wheel."

TWENTY-SIX

The three of us—my sister, Justin, and I—sit on the church steps and watch my mother give too much gas to the Lincoln, drive ten feet, and screech to an abrupt halt. She does this same thing maybe a dozen times until she gets it right. My father sits braced with both hands on the dashboard, like he's been strapped against his will into a vehicle at a demolition derby. His mouth is moving fast, spitting out a thousand directions at once, but the windows are up and we can't hear him. When his side of the car whips past us as my mother continues along her appointed circular path in the parking lot, my father shoots us a thumbs-up sign, but the look on his face tells us he'd be more comfortable wearing a helmet.

Ellen and I predict she'll aim straight for the big oak tree at the edge of the parking lot. Justin bets us a dollar the Lincoln will wind up in Little Hurricane Creek before this driving lesson is over.

"Come on kiddo," Ellen says to her son. "Let's go visit some dead relatives." She sticks a hand in her purse and pulls out two giant blocks of bubble gum, hands one to Justin, then unwraps the other one and pops a piece in her mouth. My sensitive and well-mannered little sister leads the way toward the church cemetery.

There are no paid grave diggers at the Randolph Gap Holy Rock Church Cemetery. Members of the family do the work. Friends or neighbors sometimes help too. The men all go out to the graveyard on the morning of the funeral, pick a nice spot, and start digging. That's the way it was when we were children, and despite the regular use of backhoes and specialized grave-digging tools that make the job easier in other, professionally landscaped cemeteries, I can't imagine things at the Randolph Gap Holy Rock Church Cemetery have changed much. Backhoes cost money to rent, and besides, most of these graves are packed so tightly together that getting a backhoe in there between the tombstones would be next to impossible.

If you tried to dig somebody's grave in Glenville, you'd probably be arrested for violating some important but rarely cited county health ordinance. To my knowledge, there's only one rule in Randolph Gap. You can't leave a freshly dug grave open overnight, which is why the grave needs to be dug the morning of the funeral. Why this is I don't know. Maybe there are people wandering around the cemetery at night, there for the sole purpose of finding an open grave to fall into.

We stop first at the shared tombstone of our mother's parents. Thomas Stover, 1891–1962, and Sarah Stover, 1898–1967. I can't remember my grandfather at all. My grandmother always smelled of

Ivory soap and ginger snaps and menthol ointment, the latter of which she used as a cure for everything from the flu to hiccups to asthma attacks.

"These are your great-great-grandparents," Ellen announces, pointing out the tombstone to Justin. Then she puts a finger to her lips. "No. Wait a minute. Is that one great or two? I always forget."

We need our mother with us to make this a true educational tour of our family's roots. She knows a great-great from a great, a second cousin from a cousin once removed. She could tell Justin how every person in this cemetery died, how each of them was connected to us either by blood or by church attendance. Ellen and I went on countless such tours of this cemetery in our childhood, but like the amnesia victims we are, we don't remember any of this stuff.

From the church parking lot we can hear the sound of squealing tires.

"Wow. These guys were really short," shouts Justin, who skips over to a row of small graves and gets down on his knees to give a little tombstone lamb a pat on the head. In those graves are the infant children of Thomas and Sarah Stover. Pearlina Stover, Aug. 14, 1926–Aug. 20, 1927, and Ervin Stover, Sept. 11, 1933–Jan. 19, 1934. These children would have been my mother's sister and brother, my aunt and uncle.

"Those were babies, kiddo," my sister says, smacking her lips and shooting a sneering look in my direction. "Sometimes babies die." My sister knows full well that my Margaret didn't even live long enough to have a tombstone.

"Babies? Yuck," Justin says, and bolts backward from the narrow strip.

Justin, grown bored with our attempt at a genealogy lesson, makes his way through the cemetery like it's an obstacle course. He takes calculated leaps over the smaller markers, landing in somersaults on the other side. Every so often, he pops up from behind a tombstone and hurls a magnolia seed cone at an imaginary enemy. Those things always made the best ammunition. When Ellen and I were children, we had many magnolia battles.

We soon notice there's a new grave on the east side of the cemetery. The long mound of red clay is layered with flowers and partially shaded by a broad green funeral home tent.

"Let's go see who it is," says Ellen, who abandons her gum in favor of a cigarette she has trouble lighting in the strong wind. The sky is growing darker, and the whole cemetery smells like a damp, overripe garden. Ellen sticks her chewed-up wad of gum to the side of a tombstone marked LAUGHTON.

When we find ourselves standing over the new grave, Ellen, to my amazement, leans down and pulls aside a spray of flowers. The headstone isn't there yet. There's only a small plastic marker. *Linda Crider: In Loving Memory.*

"Do we know her?" asks my sister.

"I don't think so."

"Name sounds familiar."

I shrug, no idea who this could be. Most of the flowers are plastic, some of them separated from their molded containers. The ones that are real look like they're at least a week old. The funeral home tent has kept them looking this good, but runoff from last night's rain has cut long red clay gutters in the new earth, unsettling some of the arrangements.

Ellen, moving her cigarette to her left hand, bends over the mound of flowers and scans them for any sign of life. She plucks out one long-stemmed pink rose. Then another. Then two white carnations browning at the edges. She selects a few sprigs of limp greenery to complement her bouquet. She stands there, cigarette planted in a corner of her mouth, and admires her scavenging.

"I can't believe you're doing that."

"Oh, hush up. People do this all the time."

"You don't even know her. You said so yourself."

"I said the name sounded familiar. She might have been a friend of mine."

I think about this. Andy Leonard is buried somewhere in this cemetery. I wonder if every year, on the anniversary of his death, his widow brings flowers to his grave. If the flowers are stolen, one by one, day by day, by people like my sister, until there's nothing left but the most wilted of stems.

I'm just about to ask Ellen where Andy is buried, if she'll point out his grave to me, when we both jump at the sound of a loud crash. Justin's head shoots up, a groundhog among the tombstones. He's thinking he's won his bet after all.

&

Justin sprints out ahead of us, zigzagging around the headstones until we see him disappear past the corner of the church. We're sprinting too, just not as fast as he is.

What we find is Justin standing beside the Lincoln Town Car with his mouth open, the hood of the car crumpled against the church steps. One corner of the front bumper rests against the second step, and both front wheels are still spinning. My father's head is slumped against the dash. My mother sits rigid behind the wheel, her hands still in the correct 10-2 position. It's not a serious wreck as wrecks go, but it's done some damage.

"What the hell!" Ellen shrieks.

I run to the passenger side and try the door. Locked. I knock on the glass.

"Mama, unlock the doors." She sits facing forward, blinking repeatedly, but makes no move to unlock anything. It looks like she's under the impression she's still driving. The car's motor is still running. Maybe it was her plan to drive through the church's front doors, squeezing the car down the narrow aisle between the two rows of pews, all the way to the altar.

"Unlock the doors now, Mother."

My knocking on the glass has no effect on her, but it does rouse my father, who sits upright in his seat, massaging his temples. He reaches across her and, while she sits there shaking her head and blinking at him, he unlocks all four doors and switches off the ignition. I help him out of the car and hold him in front of me, a hand on either shoulder, trying to see if anything is broken.

"I'm okay now. I'm okay. Quit worrying with me and go see to your mother."

"Unbelievable," Ellen says. She's surveying the damage from the top of the church steps, looking like a bride ready to toss her fresh-from-the-grave bouquet at those of us huddled below.

"For God's sake, Ellen, do something to help me out here," I scream at her. "Don't just stand there." I run around the back of the car and reach my mother just as she's trying to slide out of the seat, one foot searching for the ground below.

"Oh no, I left my purse in the car," she says and whirls around to reach blindly on the car seat in search of it. "And don't bring God into this."

"Forget your purse, Mother. We're not exactly going anywhere right now."

She turns toward me, her face in a pout. Justin is standing between us, jumping up and shouting, "Grandma! Grandma!"

"What are you all yelling about?" says my mother, blinking like she's emerged from a cave and is seeing the sun for the first time. "What's going on?"

Justin waves his pale arms excitedly. "You wrecked the car, Grandma!"

"Well, I know that, dear, but you don't have to yell at me."

When my father slams the door on his side, the car groans ominously and we all take a few cautious steps backward. Once convinced the danger is over, he stoops down to look under the front wheels. On the bend back up, he wavers a bit, looking dizzy. I'm not sure the car will start again, or if we can even coax it back down the steps.

"We need to get you to a hospital," I tell him. "You could have a concussion."

"Yeah, Grandpa," Justin chimes in. "Your head could swell up to the size of a pumpkin. To the size of a beach ball!"

"Thank you, Justin," I say. "That's enough."

My father reaches down to rub his hand over the stubble of Justin's hair. "Nothing wrong with me, kiddo," he says. "I've been knocked in the head lots worse than this."

❧

Once we get my parents out of the car, I climb in behind the wheel of the Lincoln and try to crank her. She sputters a few times, threatens to stall, but finally starts purring, and I ease her backward, inch by inch, until the bumper frees itself from the church steps by snapping into two pieces. The front right tire wobbles, but it'll get us home.

"Guess you were right, Dad," says my sister, who continues to watch us from her perch in front of the church doors, her grave site bouquet still clutched in her right hand. "That big old car hit a building, but it did more damage to the building."

Justin picks up the loose piece of the bumper and waves it around like a sword.

"That pastor of yours is going to want those steps fixed," my father says as he helps my mother into the car—the backseat this time—and buckles her seat belt. "I'll give you one guess as to who he's going to call."

In the rearview mirror, I can see a tear rolling down my mother's cheek. She knows she's blown it. My father is sure not to let her forget this soon.

We all ride back to the house in silence, listening to the slippery rush of the wind around us and the rattle of the Town Car's front tire, which I fear will fly off if I go faster than thirty-five miles an hour. Justin sits in the backseat between my parents, the offending piece of bumper resting on his lap.

&

My father refuses to go to the emergency room. "Get away from me," he snaps when I put my hand to his forehead, trying, in my inept attempt at a medical examination, to determine whether he indeed suffered a concussion.

217

"This ain't nothing but a little bruise," he says. "I've got to run the store tonight, and I sure can't do that from the hospital."

My mother, her Lincoln Town Car parked in the driveway with half its front bumper missing and at least one tire in serious need of repair, stations herself in her bedroom and refuses to leave. This means she's sitting on her side of the bed, back to the door, waiting for my father to come in and make his amends. She's done this lots of times, sitting there alone and tearful, for hours if that's how long it took, until I'd open the door and sit down beside her and apologize for whatever I'd done. The tactic always worked too, leaving me with such a guilty conscience—*I'd made my own mother cry!*—that I usually apologized within minutes, hoping I could catch her before the torrent of tears began. Ellen, on the other hand, would let her sit there alone for hours. "She can cry her eyes out for all I care," Ellen would say. "She's like a big baby. Sitting there waiting for me to come in and kiss her boo-boo and make it all better."

Ellen, grateful to not find the long-suffering Cecil still sitting on the front steps when we arrive home, sticks her pilfered bouquet into a glass of water, heads straight for our bedroom and slams the door. Ellen's doing a lot of door slamming this weekend.

Justin carries the car's bumper into the living room, and placing it on the floor beside him as his personal memento of our family's afternoon adventure, returns to his Nintendo. This time the sound of the bloody battle is turned up full blast, which prompts a chorus of squawks from my sister's birds. *Clong! Zap! Splat!* and multiple heads roll across the screen and into their respective wicker baskets. My sister's birds are soon mesmerized by his performance, each of them staring at the TV screen and clucking with rapt avian attention.

Over the sounds of his battle, I listen for thunder. It seems closer now.

One hippopotamus, two hippopotamus, three hippopotamus.

Earlier this afternoon, it had taken six hippopotamuses to get to us. I still haven't heard a weather report to prove it, but I know the storm is moving closer.

I look out the window, scanning the horizon for funnel clouds. It's a few minutes past seven, but with the storm on its way, darkness is closing in fast. I picture myself spending the evening in my parents' living room, sitting at the center of a newly founded support group, one in which I'm counseled by my sister's birds. Maybe I could spill all my secrets to them and I'd be safe.

 *TWENTY-SEVEN*

If we say that we have no sin, we deceive ourselves, and the truth is not in us.
But if we confess our sins, God, who is faithful and just, will forgive our sins
and cleanse us from all unrighteousness.

1 JOHN 1:8,9

AS USED IN A PENITENTIAL ORDER: RITE TWO

THE BOOK OF COMMON PRAYER

On a cloud-streaked morning in late February, I accompanied Wanda McNabb to visit Baxter's grave. For her, it was a fact-finding mission, pure and simple. The only reason she wanted me along was to be a reliable witness. It would be the last time we'd see each other, although I didn't know that then.

It had been almost five months since Baxter's death, and according to Wanda, the monument company still hadn't engraved the date of his death on his tombstone. Since the company insisted that the date had been engraved as demanded, she planned this trip to get photographic proof of their negligence. It had taken nearly three months before the tombstone was placed at the grave site in the first place, so she'd withheld payment of the bill in protest.

I planned to meet her outside the clinic for her regular Monday appointment. I left my cubicle a few minutes early and sat alone on the solitary bench underneath the canopy of the clinic's entrance, waiting for Wanda to drive up in her dented Ford Escort. Sitting on that bench, holding my purse on my lap, I felt like a patient who was being discharged after a long but restful stay in the inpatient wing. One who was waiting for her mother to pick her up and take her home, both of us hoping some kind of normal life could resume.

When she arrived, Wanda and I embraced in the same kind of hesitant, watchful way we would have in those other circumstances. Mother and daughter reunited, both of us slightly unsure about the journey ahead. Wanda carried a Polaroid, slung over one shoulder on a long strap. She popped the camera open, shoved me to the bench again, and pressed her face close to mine. With her left hand, she held the camera at arm's length, and, without warning, pushed the little red button and the picture slid out.

"For luck," she said, and handed it to me.

She drove to Glenville Memory Gardens, the largest and most populated cemetery in Glenville. Located just outside the city limits, it is a rolling expanse of some thirty acres, which, in keeping with its image as a tranquil and well-manicured resting place, is dotted with small fountains whose seraphim and cherubim spew blue-tinted sprays of tap water. There are a number of judiciously placed park benches there, too, which give mourners a comfortable place to sit and remember their loved ones.

Inscribed across the top rungs of the park benches are messages intended to be inspirational. They say things about resting in peace, angels watching over us, earning one's crown in heaven. Some even have the line from the Bible about suffer the little children to come unto me, which most certainly wouldn't console me if my child were buried here.

Glenville Memory Gardens is surrounded on two sides by trees. Some years ago, much to the disapproval of the cemetery's management and no small number of family members, a six-lane bypass highway was built on the property's east border. There were the expected protests, and one woman even chained herself to one of the large oak trees in the path of a bulldozer, but in the end asphalt won out, and for the next six months funerals were conducted amid the roar and dust of grading equipment and the stench of hot tar.

Once the highway was built, the cemetery, in an effort to put the best positive spin on things, erected on the most prominent of its many hills one 125-foot-tall gleaming white cross flanked on either side by two 100-foot crosses. At night, the entire scene is lit with giant floodlights, making it visible for miles in either direction. During the Easter season, when most of the crosses outside Glenville's churches are draped with the traditional purple sash, the floodlights at Glenville Memory Gardens are covered with some special kind of transparent red paper. On moonlit nights, it casts a bloody glow on the shining crosses above.

I know a few people buried at Glenville Memory Gardens. Every time I take the bypass, I give a little wave across the passenger seat, telling myself I'm always too busy to stop this time. I wonder how many of Glenville's residents do the same. Drive-by memories for the modern world.

Wanda turned off the highway and into the entrance, slowed by three consecutive speed bumps at the guard's gate. She leaned over in her seat and waved to the guard, who stepped outside his small office and waved back.

"Phil there," Wanda said, pointing back to the guard, who stepped back inside and pushed the button opening the gate. "Phil knows what's what."

The cast-iron gate creaks importantly on its rusted hinges, giving the impression that visiting Glenville Memory Gardens is the most solemn of occasions. Two grim-faced angels in ornately carved robes are poised at either side, each holding the end of a banner that spells out the cemetery's name and the phrase *Where Your Memories Are Forever.*

We followed the narrow access road to the Gardenia section where Baxter is buried. In a marketing ploy that gives new meaning to the phrase "pushing up daisies," all the sections are given flower names. Chrysanthemum, Columbine, Crocus, Daffodil, Forget-Me-Not, Forsythia, Honeysuckle, Primrose, Rose, Tulip, Violet, and of course Gardenia. When they're in season, the appropriate flowers are planted in decorative urns marking the entrance to each section. When they're not blooming naturally, fancy silk replicas take their place.

Forget-Me-Not, as you might expect, is especially popular, and is the largest section of the cemetery, the closest to the giant crosses on the hill. The cemetery even sells maps that point out the exact location of your loved one so you won't get lost among the 23,000 or more "residents." The map shows everything depicted in full bloom, each section a color-coded rectangle with graves in perfect, symmetrical rows. Only $7.99, plus tax.

Baxter's grave is located in Gardenia, fourteenth row, tenth grave from the left. Wanda didn't need the map to show me the way.

Even though it was early spring, it was still Christmas for some of the dead in the Gardenia section of Glenville Memory Gardens. As we walked to Baxter's grave, Wanda holding a leopard-print scarf wrapped around her new strawberry hair, we passed more than a few tombstones still decorated with plastic poinsettia wreaths, stuffed Santa Clauses, and other holiday ornaments. At a grave marked SWANSON, a two-foot-tall Christmas tree was propped against the marble, the tree covered with droopy, rain-soaked tinsel.

There are some 1,700 graves in the Gardenia section alone. Wanda set out at a brisk pace, navigating the tombstones in a short-cut she had memorized, her sharp turns making her look like a majorette on a football field, leading her squad into a V formation.

"Can you believe this stuff? Tacky, that's what it is. I can't believe they won't even let me plant a simple azalea when they let people leave junk like this all over the place. It could all blow out over that highway and cause a wreck."

She pried open the Polaroid again and took more pictures. Of the disheveled Santas, the balloons, all of it, then fanned out the photos like a slick deck of cards and waved them in the air. When we reached Baxter's grave, she took three more photographs.

"Just like I said, right? No date." Baxter's birth date, April 27, 1942, was there all right, but the date of his death was clearly missing. Like my parents' tombstone, it was as if he hadn't died at all.

Wanda kneeled in front of the tombstone, took another picture—a close-up of the date, or lack thereof—and then placed the camera and all her developing photos on the grass beside her.

"I loved you, you old son of a bitch. Lord knows I don't know why, but I did." She touched Baxter's name on the headstone.

The grass smelled sweet and freshly mown, not a dandelion in sight.

"I need to tell you something."

Across the expanse of the cemetery, past the towering three-layer fountain at the center of the circular drive at the main entrance, I saw a woman walking between the tombstones, a small bouquet of pink carnations cradled in her arms. She was young, couldn't have been more than twenty, and, despite the cold and the wind, she wore a sleeveless summer dress. As she walked, the breeze lifted the sheer green fabric of her dress up and around her thighs and it hovered there briefly before settling back around her ankles. She looked as if she were walking out of the ocean, trying to free herself from a mermaid's skin.

A small blond boy of about four trailed after her, bending over again and again to try a cartwheel, flattening out both hands against the grass but succeeding only in raising his chubby legs a few inches off the ground. I wondered who they were visiting, if the grave she would kneel at was that of a husband or a parent. Maybe it was the grave of another child, one the toddler with her would remember only through pictures and by repeated trips with his mother to the grave.

"Jessie?"

"Hmmmm?"

"I said I need to tell you something."

"Oh. I'm sorry, Wanda."

"Patient to shrink, you know. Private."

"Sure. Okay."

"I loved my husband, I think you know that. It was a long time ago when I loved him, but I did love him once."

"I know that, Wanda."

"Well, I'm telling you that because I don't want you to get the wrong idea about what I'm going to say."

"I won't, Wanda. It's okay." A long pause. "Really."

She studied my face for a moment. "What I wanted to say, I mean, what I really want to tell you is this. If Baxter had walked into the house that night carrying a dozen roses and acted all sweet and proper, like I was the only woman in the world he ever loved and like he'd never done anything wrong to me in all his life, well, it wouldn't have mattered. Course I knew he wouldn't do any such thing. The point is, he was going to die."

I thought about all the stories she'd told me over the previous months, about all the damage she said she'd suffered. Did the rest of it really happen like she said it did? I wanted to remember Wanda as she first presented herself in my office, a battered woman who had killed her husband in a clear case of self-defense. That was a story I could understand, and I didn't want to hear more, even if it was the truth.

"I could always count on my boy," she said.

"What did you say?" I suddenly felt dizzy, as if the ground under my feet was opening up to swallow me.

"My boy, Baxter Junior," she told me. "He knew what had to be done."

"Your son?"

"I asked him to shoot his father and he did it. He'd wanted to for a long, long time, maybe even more than me."

"What do you—?"

"Don't," she said, and placed her hand over my mouth. "That's all I wanted to say. All I'm ever going to say about that night."

It occurred to me that I had, during all those months before, lived out some of my own terrible fantasies through Wanda. The idea of what she'd done on that October night had fueled my confidence somehow, her stories giving me some hint of the possibilities I might have. It wasn't until I stood in the cemetery, listening to Wanda tell me this version of her story, that all of it—all of what had been happening to me, and to her, during those previous months— became real to me. The truth was much colder, much more unsettling, and I wasn't ready for it.

"You have to keep that to yourself, right?" she said, letting her hand drop to my shoulder. "Because you're my shrink?"

"Yeah, well, something like that," I said.

"You deserve to hear the truth, and to hear it from me."

"Sure. Okay."

"And you can't tell anybody, right?"

"Those are the rules, Wanda." The fact is that I do have a legal obligation to report a murder, but I didn't want to think about that. I'd fallen too deep into Wanda's world and I didn't know how to get out.

"My life just didn't work out like I thought it would," she said, reaching up to wipe a tear that rolled down her cheek. "I kept thinking things would change. That he would change, or that I would. That I'd get stronger. That I could take the children and run as far away as I could to get away from him. But I couldn't. Even after the children were gone, I couldn't do it. I didn't know how."

"I think—"

"Baxter Junior got the worst of it when he was a boy. We . . . did the only thing we knew we could do."

I listened to the quiet rustling of leaves around us, all the trees rushing into spring bloom, felt the wind against my cheek. As I waited for her to say more, the sun broke through the clouds with a flash of blinding white. I searched through my purse and found my sunglasses. I didn't want Wanda to look at me eye-to-eye. She would have seen too much disappointment there.

"You once asked me what happens if the bad outweighs the good, right?"

"Yeah, I guess I did."

"Well honey, sometimes the bad wins, and there's not a damn thing you can do about it."

I was way out of my league here. To absolve a woman and son for shooting a man in cold blood, even if he had deserved it in some way, wasn't something I was even remotely qualified to do. She needed to say these things to someone other than me. To her minister. To the priest at All Saints.

I wondered if Wanda would ever remarry, if she would someday walk down the aisle with Husband Number Two. Somehow, I didn't think she would. If she attended All Saints with us, she would be gathered up into the welcoming arms of the widows' club. Would spend the rest of her days attending their garden parties and their group shopping excursions. Would be only too happy to help organize bake sales and clothing drives to benefit the homeless.

"You know," Wanda said, "it's really pretty funny how it all worked out."

The woman I'd seen walking across the cemetery was arranging her carnations in front of a small white tombstone. She spread her green skirt around her and knelt directly over the grave, where no grass was yet growing. She pulled her child to her and held him close.

"We watched him die there on the floor," Wanda said, "him looking up at me like he wanted his last words to be *You bitch. You finally got me, didn't you?* After I got Baxter Jr. out of the house, after I had to go to the funeral and deal with everybody there. After I had to see my girls and see the looks in their eyes. Looks that told me they knew, that they knew we might have done this godawful thing but weren't surprised because it was something they'd all thought about doing themselves. After I had to go through all that with the police, being in jail and everything else. Finally, after all of it was over, I thought I'd be relieved. I thought I'd be at peace with myself and what I'd done. That was the plan, right?"

A plan. *Their* plan. I watched the woman across the cemetery. The boy wiggled out of her tanned arms and ran away, seemingly determined to run straight toward us. He ran and ran and then, his body outrunning his feet, tumbled headfirst into the grass. It didn't look like he was hurt, but he started crying anyway, and the woman quickly got up from kneeling, her grief interrupted. She ran over to scoop him into her arms.

"I walked into my house that first day, after they let me out of jail, and that house was quiet, quiet, quiet," Wanda said. "Quieter than I ever remembered it being. I sat down and listened to the quiet. Enjoyed it at first. Well, the joke's on me. I sit in bed every night, all night, every light in the house on, missing his sorry ass. Missing every stupid and ignorant thing he ever did to me. What a dummy I turned out to be."

"You're not a dummy, Wanda."

"That's sure what it feels like," she said.

"You, you and Baxter Jr., did what you had to do, right? Isn't that what you said?"

"You think so? Well, then you're a bigger dummy than I am."

This time, I wanted a straight answer. "So why'd you do it? Why did you have to kill him?"

With one hand, Wanda gathered up the photographs she'd taken, and with the other, braced herself on Baxter's tombstone to boost herself to a standing position. The photograph of me and Wanda, our faces smiling into the sun and pressed together like girls at summer camp, was still in my coat pocket. Later that afternoon, I'd add it to the items in my chest in the attic. One more friendship locked away in the past.

"Does it really matter?" she said and turned away, lost from me forever, her leopard-print scarf wild and dancing against the clouds.

TWENTY-EIGHT

rastic action is in order. I walk down the hallway to the
bedroom my sister and I share. I find her wearing only a
pair of pink bikini panties, admiring a rippling image of
herself in the beveled glass mirror of the chifforobe. On the glass,
with its waves and swirls, she's bobbing up and down as if in an un-
derwater ballet. From her right hand hangs a red leather jacket with
two layers of leather fringe in front and back. In her left is a strapless
black blouse. When I open the door without knocking, she's the very
image of a bored fashion model ready to make her final trip down
the runway.

"I've got to get out of this dump," she announces. "And fast. So what do you think? The red or the black?" Across her bed, and mine, it looks like the entire contents of her two suitcases have exploded. An identical leather jacket, a black one, is spread out on top of my bed, ready for inspection. A pair of worn black jeans, fraying at the knees, is placed next to it.

"The black's nice."

"That settles it then. I'll wear the red." She squirms into the strapless blouse, which turns out to be not a blouse at all but a black lace bustier, which she pulls together with a series of eye-hook snaps, the vertical boning squeezing her thin frame tighter and tighter. She eases up a zipper covering the snaps, ties a thin black ribbon at the top of the zipper into a bow, then sticks both hands down the front to adjust her breasts into a near falling-out position. Despite my sporadic trips to Victoria's Secret to purchase a garment that will arouse some untapped well of passion in Turner, I'm surprised they even make things like this anymore, much less that any woman in her right mind would want to squeeze herself into one.

"Got this at one of those ladies-only parties my friend Sherrie had last month," Ellen informs me as she bends over and begins to tease the underside of her blondish hair. Froth, froth, froth, froth— all with such fury that I nearly expect the wire-tipped brush she's using will yank her hair out by the roots. "Every kind of lingerie and sex toy you could ever imagine, all laid out there on Sherrie's dining room table like she was giving a Tupperware party."

"You've got to be kidding." This, to be sure, is the most shocking thing I've heard from my sister in years. I've obviously been missing out on a lot.

So now my guard is up. I try not to act too surprised, try to give her the impression that these types of parties are events that happen every day in the big city of Glenville. That I, of course, know all about them and, over the years, have purchased an array of such items. I imagine a circle of women sitting around in Sherrie's living room, my sister among them, discussing not the abuse they're suffering but the carnal surprises they plan to unleash on their husbands after their party is over. If they're having parties like this in Randolph Gap, I can only imagine what might be happening in Glenville without my knowledge. Surely Donna Lindsey would know if groups of Glenville ladies were meeting to discuss the merits of this or that crotchless teddy, this or that vibrator.

"I swear it's true," Ellen tells me. "This lady hostess, who must have been in her fifties and as sweet as pie, just like that little Dr. Ruth on TV, pulls up in this van and unloaded it all. Lingerie, toys, lubricants in every flavor you'd ever want."

Her hair whipped up to her liking, Ellen flips her head back to its upright position and reaches around on the dresser for a large tortoiseshell hair clamp. She pulls the mass of teased hair into a ponytail.

"This lady travels all over the South too, booked solid all year long, six days a week. Two, sometimes three, parties a day. Said she does a lot of parties for sororities down at the university. I bought this little number and two bottles of massage oil that heats up when it hits your skin. Mint and cinnamon. That's all I could afford, but I would have bought the whole store if I could have."

As my sister continues dressing, she tells me in glowing detail about every item on sale and how the hostess even gave out "these cute little party favor suckers shaped like penises." The sexual revolution has hit Randolph Gap all right, and with the full force of a tornado, leaving no telling what kind of damage in its wake.

"So our hostess, she starts the party off with these little games, you know, like the kind they do at baby showers. The first thing we did was introduce ourselves, but we had to do it by using the first initial of our names to describe our man.

"Well, the first lady who started off says, all sweet and proper, 'Hi, my name is Angela, and my man is an angel.'

"We kept going around the room introducing ourselves—there were about thirty of us there altogether, friends and friends of friends—and the more we did it, the more we caught on to the idea, and the sillier we got. One lady said her name was Jackie and that her man was a 'jackhammer.' Another one with an *A* name said her name was April and that her man was an 'all-nighter.'

"My mind was blank, but when my turn came, I blurted out, 'Hi, my name is Ellen, and my man is eager.' Everyone laughed, but this other woman, who also had an *E* name, Evelyn, got a bigger laugh when she said her man was 'edible.'"

Ellen tells me all this while she pulls on her jeans, an engineering feat in itself since they're so tight. She tucks her bustier into the waistband and, taking a deep breath, zips them up. The red leather jacket goes on next. Then a pair of cherry-red four-inch heels, which she finds only by crawling halfway under her bed and, in the process, pulling out not only the shoes but a solitary black thigh-high stocking, a handful of Legos, and a dust bunny roughly the size of poor dead Missy. The shoes, naturally, are the strappy kind that wrap around and around her ankles and tie in a bow at the front. When she takes her first steps in them, she teeters.

"This lady's real brave to be doing this too, since these parties of hers are supposed to be illegal and all, in Alabama anyway," she tells me. "That's why they're invitation-only. You've got to trust who you're inviting or you're screwed."

My sister stands in front of the mirror, steps back a few feet to get the full view, dusts herself off, and admires herself again.

"Do men come to these parties?" I ask, laughing at the image of Turner attending such an event. The very idea of me presenting myself to Turner wearing a black bustier, a garter belt, and black stockings, and thus attired, offering to give him a cinnamon massage, is ludicrous.

"No way!" my sister shouts. "Our hostess explained right from the start how men have been having their fun for years on end and that it was about time us ladies got in on a little of it. She made a big point of saying that her parties are intended to make relationships better, that all of us ladies need to get more involved with what's going on in the bedroom. That we need to take charge. Show our partners what we really want." As if my sister ever had a problem with taking charge.

"Plus she said she had a party where some of the husbands showed up anyway and everything got way out of hand. The men started saying all sorts of crude and vulgar things, like they expected their wives to be dancing on the tables wearing only whipped cream. Men can't handle good, clean fun. That's exactly what she said."

I try to think of what my introduction at that party would have been.

Hello, my name is Jessie, and my husband is definitely not a jackhammer.

A jackass?

Jack Frost?

"So how did Cecil react to all this? I mean, when you showed him what you bought?"

"Well, let me tell you," my sister says, her mood souring at the mention of her husband's name. "It was all wasted on him. He wouldn't have a thing to do with it, even with me standing there in this black getup and offering to give him a massage. That just proves he's a loser. And an asshole. Doesn't know a good thing when it practically slaps him in the face. Men go crazy for this kind of stuff, that's what that lady said, but no siree, not my stupid husband. Casting pearls before swine, that's what that was."

It's obvious my sister is now dead set on putting her purchases to good use, and on someone other than Cecil.

"So where're you headed?"

"Why do you care?"

"I might join you."

"You? Ha."

"You think I've forgotten how to have fun?"

"This ain't a cocktail party, Jessie. Where I'm going they don't serve caviar and those fancy little finger sandwiches."

"Sounds good to me."

"Yeah, right." She bends closer to the mirror to apply a second coat of eyeliner. "You'll run home tomorrow and act all weepy and tell your husband all about how your little sister corrupted you. You can't handle my kind of fun."

"After the day we've had, I'm ready to start trying. Now help me pick out something to wear."

"Okay, but we're taking two cars. If you wimp out on me, I'm not getting stuck without a ride home."

❧

We decide to start our night at the Green Duck. Since my father's shift at the Stop 'n' Shoppe starts soon, I can drop him off at work, then step next door to have a few beers with my sister. He might refuse to go to the emergency room, but I don't want to take any chances.

"Come on, Dad, I'm driving you to work."

He looks at me like that's the most ridiculous thing he's ever heard. "I can drive my own self," he says. "I'm not the one who wrecked that new car your mother paid good money for. And I'm not a damn invalid."

"Ellen and I are going to the Duck anyway. After you get off work, you can buy me a beer."

He laughs at this, shrugs his shoulders, and saunters off to the bedroom to change clothes. If he says anything to my mother, who's probably still sitting on the bed waiting for him to apologize, I can't hear it. He's back within minutes, too soon for them to have had any real conversation. He's wearing his Stop 'n' Shoppe shirt and khaki pants, and in that uniform he becomes the anonymous clerk behind the counter, a face you forget by the time you get to your car. He stuffs a large ring of keys into his right pants pocket so he jingles with every step. I'm overcome with love for him.

"The two Kilgore girls, let loose on the innocent citizens of Randolph Gap," says my father, who surveys my sister's attire for the evening and then looks the other way in embarrassment. "Should I alert the police? Ellen here is enough of a hell-raiser by herself. No telling what kind of trouble the two of you will get into."

"We'll have an adventure then," I say, tugging at the hem of the short pink skirt my sister loaned me. She paired it with a thin white shirt with a plunging neckline, the fabric so sheer I was thankful she let me borrow her black leather coat as well. We could pass as sisters all right, though unlike her, I was instructed to wear my own flats and not a pair of high heels, my five-foot-nine-inch frame judged too tall for anything more.

"You'll be taller than every man there if you wear heels," my sister warned. She pronounced my outfit acceptable, given what she had to work with. At the last minute, she added a pair of loopy silver earrings that clinked with every step I took. The earrings are driving me crazy by the time I reach the front door. My father and I are both tagged for the night, like cats with bells attached to their collars, so their prey can hear them coming.

"Well, come on, then. Let's go if we're going," says Ellen, who pulls her jacket up over her head as an umbrella, hops into her Honda, and speeds out of the driveway, a flash of light leading the way in the rain.

My father is out the door ahead of me. When I turn to find my car keys on the kitchen counter, there's a shadow in the doorway. It's Justin, crouched in the half light. He is, I realize, a child who has spent much of his young life standing in doorways, watching his mother leave. I reach out to touch him and call his name, but he's already turned away from me.

By the time we reach the Stop 'n' Shoppe, my wipers are on high, the rain coming down in sheets. My father, slumped in the passenger seat, says little. For the first time in my adult life I feel like our roles are reversed, like I'm driving my teenage son to a job he took so he can buy a car and won't have to be seen riding around town with his mother.

I try to concentrate on the road, squinting into the haze of water.

"Really coming down, isn't it?" I say.

"Yep."

"Hope it doesn't rain all weekend."

"Uh huh."

There are two cars parked at the Stop 'n' Shoppe, four more outside the Green Duck next door, one of them my sister's Honda. Not very busy for a Saturday night, but it's still early.

When my father and I walk through the door of the Stop 'n' Shoppe, shaking ourselves off like dogs, we find Lamar Hamby sitting on a stool behind the shop's counter, reading a magazine. He stubs out a cigarette butt into an already overflowing ashtray, his eyes never leaving the page.

"Well, son of a gun, Carl, you finally got your ass here," says Lamar, who gazes at me sheepishly, folds the magazine in half, and stuffs it under the counter. "I was about to call the wife and tell her I'd have to pull a double shift."

"Long story, Lamar," my father tells him. "You don't want to get me started."

"Looks like you got knocked in the head with a cue ball," says Lamar. As a result of the driving-lesson accident, my father has a rising blue knot on his forehead. "You haven't been over at the Duck, have you?"

"Naw, Lamar. My fightin' days are over."

Lamar lets it drop, knowing he'll probably get the details later.

"Who's that you got behind you there, Carl? New girlfriend?"

Lamar has worked for my father at the Stop 'n' Shoppe for more than twenty years but hasn't seen me in more than a decade. He's reliable, as convenience store workers go, even though he spends at least three weeks every summer holed up in a fishing cabin, doing more drinking than fishing. But he always comes back, and my father, who fires him every time this happens, rehires him. The two of them, Lamar and my father, *are* the Stop 'n' Shoppe. Students at the Randolph Gap High School work here off and on during the summer, but they show up late, smoke pot on their breaks, and can't make the correct change using the 1960s vintage cash register my father won't trade for a newer model.

"This is my oldest, Jessie," my father says, putting a proprietary hand on my shoulder. "You remember her. The one who went off to college?"

"Oh yeah," says Lamar, who stands up, pulls a fresh pack of cigarettes from the rack above the store counter, unwraps the pack, and lights one. "I remember you now. The smart one. Your sister I see all the time, but gosh, I ain't seen you in ages." He says the word *smart* like it's left a bad taste in his mouth.

"Been a long time," I say. The last time I saw Lamar Hamby he had a slicked-back Elvis-style pompadour, weighed about forty pounds less, and once, when he cornered me in the refrigerator section of the Stop 'n' Shoppe, offered to take me to the Black Warrior River for a picnic.

"You sure look good, honey. Grown up in all the right places," he'd said, putting a hairy arm around my waist. His voice went all raspy, like he'd been practicing this line for days, picturing me sprawled across a picnic table in some kind of *Hee Haw*–style attire. "We could have us a real nice picnic, you and me." His breath, I remember, smelled like wet cigarettes and vinegar.

"Sure," I said, pulling away from him. "But only if your wife can come too. She makes the best fried chicken I've ever tasted."

Lamar looked at me for a minute, smiling and confused, like I might be suggesting some kind of wild ménage à trois on the picnic table of his dreams. As I turned to walk out the door, he narrowed his eyes at me.

"Little bitch." That's the last thing he ever said to me.

"Here to visit your old dad, huh?" he says, his voice full of twenty years of smoke and beer, his broad grin not revealing whether he remembers that incident or not. More than likely he doesn't.

"Yeah."

"Well, ya'll come join me at the Duck later if you want," says Lamar, anchoring a large brown cowboy hat to his head and pulling the collar of his uniform up around his neck.

"And hey, Carl? If my wife calls, tell her I got washed away in the big flood outside. I may be a while getting home."

TWENTY-NINE

s my father settles in behind the counter, I look around for signs that anything has changed in all the years since I've been away. There's a row of video poker machines I don't remember, but the big sliding-door ice cream freezers are still there. The racks of bubble gum and candy are there, too, but they're full of brands I no longer recognize.

The most dramatic change is what's behind the counter. There, in all their shrink-wrapped glory, are at least twenty different brands of adult magazines. The average customer can't get behind the counter to browse the selection, and a foot-tall sign that reads 21 AND OLDER: NO EXCEPTIONS makes it all too clear that there's more than *Playboy* in these racks. One presumably has to choose based on title, or past experience, since the images on the covers are wrapped up tight with a special kind of black plastic that blocks all the more titillating views.

Above the magazines there's a display of condoms in bright, consumer-friendly packaging. The juxtaposition of these items—one intended for solo pleasures, the other for sharing—is ironic, but I don't point this out to my father. It's obvious my mother hasn't visited the Stop 'n' Shoppe recently. If she were to see these items, she and the Rev. Wheeling would gather up the active members of the Randolph Gap Holy Rock Church and arrange a protest by the next morning.

I go behind the counter with my father and sit beside him on an identical stool.

"The pay's not very good here," he says. "You planning to work the late shift with me?"

"Thought I'd just sit here for a while."

He doesn't say anything. If he notices I've spotted the change in his behind-the-counter merchandise, he doesn't say anything either. The radio playing over the store's speakers is tuned to the same country music station my sister was listening to earlier in the afternoon. All the songs they're playing are by female artists who sound like they're belting out variations of the same tune. Lyrics that inform the men in their lives they're "fed up" with the way they've been treated and are running off in search of a man "who knows how to handle a good woman." My sister, no doubt, considers herself philosophically aligned with this message, and so does Donna Lindsey.

By the time my father does say something I'm getting into the mood of the music. It reminds me that I'm a little "fed up" myself and this, according to the plan, is my night to prowl Randolph Gap's cache of available men. The sound of his voice, for a moment, startles me.

"What's wrong, Jess? I don't mean to pry, but is everything all right with you and Turner?"

"Things are fine." I open a jar on the counter and pop a jawbreaker into my mouth.

"Not running away from home, are you? I mean, it's not like you visit here every weekend, or even stay the whole weekend when you do."

He has every right to say this, but it still hurts. My guilty conscience kicks in again. "You don't like my company?" I slur, the jawbreaker rolling around between my teeth.

"I know an unhappy woman when I see one. I've lived with your mother long enough to know that much."

I'm not sure how to respond. My mother isn't one to admit she's unhappy, though I have to agree with him that it's obvious when she is.

"So tell me. What's the secret? To a happy marriage, I mean?"

"Ain't no secret, honey."

"You two seem to have one."

My father thinks about this, as if he's trying to remember some cherished quote someone told him long ago, the kind of advice his father might have given him on his own wedding day.

"You do, don't you?"

"I wake up every morning and your mother is there, same as always. I can deal with that. Most days, I even like it." This is the kind of answer I might have expected from Wanda McNabb. An answer without an answer.

"Do you think Mom's okay? I mean, with the wreck and all?" I try to remember all my recent telephone conversations with her, if she's been forgetting things lately, if she's been acting any different than usual. Three of my neighbors are caring for parents now, redecorating to install in-law suites in their basements and hiring round-the-clock nurses, or, in the most desperate cases, paying the bills at country-club-style rest homes.

"We're both just getting older, that's all. I think that's why she wanted that damn car in the first place. So she could prove she could get by on her own. Practicing, just in case she wakes up one day and I'm not around."

About that time, a dark green station wagon with Ohio plates pulls under the canopy of the gas station. A man of about forty steps out of the driver's seat and, squinting into the blowing rain, moves to the rear of the car to unscrew the gas tank cover and pull the hose toward it. The top of the car is piled high with luggage and covered with a dark blue tarp.

My father pushes a button under the counter that starts the pump and the man leans against the rear of the station wagon and closes his eyes, as if he plans to recline there, undisturbed, until the storm blows over. His brown hair is streaked with rain. From that distance, he looks like David Lindsey, so much so that I half expect him to wave, expect to see Donna and the boys piled in the car ready for a road trip. I feel a sudden pang of homesickness, a longing for my own comfort zone in Heritage Knoll. I should be in my den, reading gardening tips that will keep my geraniums alive.

There's a blonde head resting against the passenger-side window. In the back seat, two girls, somewhere between the ages of eight and eleven, are arguing. One pinches the other, causing her to wail, and wail loudly, though not loudly enough to rouse the woman in the front seat.

When the man finishes at the pump, he shakes his head as if trying to undo some hypnotic spell induced by gasoline fumes. He stretches his arms over his head and massages his temples. As he moves toward the store, his two daughters stumble over themselves to unbuckle their seat belts and get out of the car to follow him. Inside the store, they run straight for the gum and candy counter and get into an argument over what they'll buy.

"One apiece," the man instructs. They both glare at their father, and one of them makes a sour face. "And don't forget to go to the bathroom. I'm not stopping again until we reach the hotel."

They must be on their way to Florida, maybe to Disney World, trying to make good time by driving day and night, even in a downpour, and stopping only when they have to. They probably saved for months to pay for the trip, thinking this might be one of the last times their daughters wouldn't be embarrassed to be seen getting their pictures taken with their parents and Mickey Mouse.

The two girls, fresh from the bathroom and with their candy purchases in hand (they grab four each and slap them on the counter so my dad can ring them up), make a mad dash for the car and fight over who'll get in first. After his own trip to the facilities, where it looks like he stuck his entire head under a running faucet and forgot to wipe his face, the man from Ohio pours himself a cup of black coffee in one of those big thirty-two-ounce, travel-size cups. He moves to the counter slow and flat-footed. Harried, with dark rings under his eyes. Graying at the temples. He pays for his family's purchases with a credit card. The very model of modern fatherhood. I wonder if that's what Turner would look like if we had children.

"Be careful out there," my father tells Mr. Ohio. "Storm warnings all night."

"Yep."

"Pull over if it gets too rough. You don't want to push it. These back roads flood real easy, water up high before you know it."

"He's right," I say, more to myself than to Mr. Ohio. "We got caught in a flood once. Creek overflowed all over the road and nearly washed us away."

"You remember that, Jessie? Why, you was just a little thing."

"I remember." I haven't thought about that night in years, but the memory comes back to me now.

Mr. Ohio stands at the counter and takes a sip of his coffee, wincing at the taste of it. In the car, his two daughters are munching on the first of their candy bars. His wife's head is still resting against the window. He slides his receipt into his wallet and nods warily to my father and then to me. It's the kind of patronizing look that says, *I knew it all along. The South is different.* He stares at us as if we're deformed in some way, like he's counting all our fingers and teeth. Like he expects me to be sitting behind the cash register strumming a banjo, singing a twangy song about the big flood that almost washed us all away.

"We're taking the interstate most of the way," he says, which I know is a lie since the Stop 'n' Shoppe was long ago bypassed by any interstate. "Hasn't been too bad so far." He says this in a measured, deliberate tone, as if engaging in even the briefest of conversations is the most tiring thing he's done in years.

"We got maps if you want 'em," my father says. "Depending on where you're headed, of course."

"Don't guess you've got something stronger I could put in this coffee?"

"Nope. Have to go next door for that."

Mr. Ohio turns to look across the parking lot at the neon sign of the Green Duck, which gives off an eerie mist in the pouring rain. To

Mr. Ohio, it must look like the last place on earth he'd want to visit. With his family in the car, that is.

"Pills. That's more what I had in mind."

Mr. Ohio shoots me a nervous grin, giving me the distinct impression that he wishes I wasn't here. Maybe he'd have purchased not only pills but a big stack of plastic-covered magazines if I hadn't been watching. As Dr. Richard Blumegarten, Ph.D., might say, men want love just like women. They just have different ways of expressing it.

"Well, we got those all right," my father says. "Kind truckers use. All flavors, all varieties. What kind you want?"

"Strongest you got."

My father reaches under the counter and hands the man a small bottle with a black label that looks like it's been hand lettered.

"Only eight in there, but they pack a wallop. $12.98. And hey, don't take more than one at a time. Keep you sailing for at least six hours."

Mr. Ohio pays for them in cash.

THIRTY

I walk into the Green Duck and find my sister at the jukebox, feeding it dollar after dollar and punching in her favorite tunes. She stands there swaying her hips as one of the songs starts, the fringe of her red leather jacket jiggling provocatively, her red shoes moving heel to toe, heel to toe, in some sort of dance step it looks like she's just invented.

Two men at the bar are watching her with every bit of drunken attentiveness they can muster, their eyes glassy and dull yet trying to focus on the leather fringe as it sways across the backside of my sister's jeans. One has a crew cut, the other is wild-haired and thickly mustached; both have beer bellies and sport an assortment of what look like homemade tattoos on their beefy arms. It's obvious they've already singled her out as a possible target for the night's festivities, and, in doing so, are all too happy to provide her with her jukebox money. My sister generally prefers Red's Tavern for her nighttime adventures, but she isn't a stranger at the Duck either. When I walk in, I don't think anyone even notices.

There are only five other patrons in the bar. There's a couple sitting close, but staring into their respective drinks, not speaking. Two men, who look like father and son, are at one of the pool tables, a stack of quarters signaling their intent to occupy the table for some time. Lamar Hamby is slumped in a chair against the wall, watching their game and guarding a half-empty pitcher of beer.

People who come to the Green Duck do so for two reasons. To drink and shoot pool. But mostly to drink, and to drink seriously. The Green Duck is not the kind of bar where businessmen come for cocktails and hot wings, so unless someone like my sister appears, very rarely does anyone make eye contact. You can buy liquor by the bottle here, too, if you know whom and how to ask. You'll pay at least a $10 markup over the liquor store a half-mile away, but most of the people who come to the Green Duck, by the time they've gotten around to buying it by the bottle, don't care what it costs.

It's the kind of bar that reeks of more than thirty years of spilled beer, cigarette smoke, and testosterone sweat. A few of the neon beer signs advertise brands that went out of business long ago, but since there are no windows, those neon signs, outdated and dust-covered though they may be, are the only reminder that life exists outside these four walls. Long as they're burning, things must be going on as usual.

From what I can see, the only modern convenience is the addition of compact discs to the jukebox. They're mostly country, but if you're patient enough to flip through the selections you'll find the Eagles, a few Elvis Presley tunes, and, of course, *Lynyrd Skynyrd's Greatest Hits*, where the song "Sweet Home Alabama" is a sort of anthem. It's a sure bet that song is played here at least once every night, and when the University of Alabama's football team—the revered Crimson Tide—is winning, it's on nonstop replay. The floor around the bar, as usual, is littered with broken peanut shells. Everyone knows your name here, just like on *Cheers*, but they're just as likely to slit your throat if you make a wrong move, then go back to their drinking.

There's a woman tending bar this Saturday night, not the bartender who told me he'd take me dancing. Even in the dim light, she looks like she's about sixty, maybe older. Her hair, a striking shade of orange, is growing out in the kind of ragged layers that often follow a bad haircut and a bad perm.

"Ellen told me her sister might be coming," she says as I sit on one of the stools a good distance away from anyone else. "You got to be her, 'cause you sure ain't a regular."

The darkly shellacked bar of the Green Duck wraps around in a U shape, maybe forty feet long altogether but only about five feet across from one side of the U to the other. The bartender works in this small space, turning to one side and then the other, usually pouring drinks without having to ask the customers what they want since she sees them week after week, some of them six nights a week. On Sunday, everybody sleeps. In deference to its Bible Belt heritage, you still can't buy beer, wine, or any kind of alcohol on Sundays in Randolph Gap.

"I'm Peggy," announces the bartender, a cigarette dangling from her mouth. "Your sis there already started a tab." That, I know, means the tab's on me.

A portable TV perched on top of a stack of magazines in one corner of the U-shaped bar is tuned to a professional wrestling match, but nobody seems to be watching. Music from the jukebox masks most of the sound, but I still can hear the occasional grunt when one wrestler body-slams his opponent to the mat.

"You make a good margarita?"

"Best this side of the river," says Peggy, propping her elbows on the bar and looking at me as if I've already insulted her somehow. "Frozen?"

"Nope. Just ice. Lots of salt."

"Hmmmph. You look like the frozen type to me. You know, daiquiris and the like. Least that's what your sister says." She grins at me mischievously, as if she knows much more about my personal life than I'd ever care for her to know. The inch-long tower of ash that's been balancing on the end of her cigarette topples to the bar.

"Yeah well, you never know about some people. I might even get you to open that bottle of Cuervo once I get started." I'm doing my best to act tough and ward off any further conversation with Peggy.

"Well, woooo-eee," cries Peggy much too loudly, momentarily attracting the attention of the bar's other patrons. "Maybe you and that sister of yours ain't so different after all."

Ellen, her jukebox selections made, spots me at the bar and sashays over, much to the disappointment of the two men whose eyes follow every swing of her hips. I pull out the pack of Virginia Slims I bought at the Stop 'n' Shoppe, unwrap the pack, and light one using a flip-top box of matches left at the edge of the bar.

Peggy mixes up two margaritas in glasses roughly the size of fish bowls. "Happy hour for ladies, hon, so drink up, party girl," she says as she places the drinks in front of me on the bar. "You just let me know when you need a refill."

"I see you made it," says my sister. Then, to Peggy, "Jessie here is the original party girl. Bring her another round in about five minutes."

Peggy laughs at this, like she and my sister are sharing an inside joke, and with a flash of orange fingernails lights another cigarette.

"Thanks," I say, my outlook for the evening growing more grim by the minute.

"Well, have fun," Ellen says, heading in the direction of her two admirers, who have already grown anxious with her absence. "I'm certainly going to."

I sit at the bar and try to blend in, staring into my drink. Despite my less than warm welcome, I like it here already.

Turner wouldn't be caught dead in a place like this.

&

"Hey, don't I know you?" comes a voice over my shoulder.

I turn around to find a woman standing next to me at the bar, her long brown hair permed into a mass of curls and whipped up by some fervent Saturday night teasing. She's wearing black tights, gold spike heels, and an oversized lime green T-shirt that's knotted at one side. Upon parking herself at the bar stool next to me, she tries to shake out a golf-size umbrella that looks like it's been turned inside out in the storm, at least two of its wooden stays snapped in half.

"C'mon, you really look familiar. You from here? I mean, originally?"

"Born and raised."

"Went to Randolph Gap High?"

"Yep."

Across the bar my sister is wedged between her two new escorts.

One of them drapes a tattooed arm around her shoulder, letting his hand drop to fondle a row of fringe that dangles from the jacket at breast level.

"That's where I know you, then," the woman beside me says, throwing her broken and dripping umbrella to the floor, where it lands with a explosion of peanut shells. "You're Judy, aren't you? No, wait. Jessie? Jessie Kilgore, am I right?"

I haven't been called by my maiden name in years, so for a moment, I don't realize she's still talking to me. "Jessie, yes. Maddox now."

"Well, you may not remember me, but I'm Sandi Leonard, Sandi with an *i*. Well, Sandi Moore back then," says the woman, who holds up two fingers to Peggy in what must be a well-rehearsed signal for what she wants to drink and how many. "I was a sophomore when you were a senior, so you probably don't remember me, but I remember you. I was on the junior varsity squad!"

I study the woman's face, looking for any kind of clue, however subtle, as to who she could be. From what she said, she's probably a few years younger than I, even though she looks like she could be well over forty. It's useless. Amnesiac that I am when it comes to Randolph Gap, I don't remember her at all.

Peggy brings Sandi's drinks, two tall glasses of a murky liquid that resembles iced tea, and Sandi fishes in her purse, finally digging out a $10 bill and throwing it on the bar. "Keep 'em coming long as that lasts."

"Sure thing. And watch out for that one," says Peggy, tilting her head in my direction. "She's trouble just waitin' to happen."

Thankfully, Sandi ignores this assault. "You don't live around here now, do you?" she says, turning again to face me, her hair nearly swatting me directly in the face. "You visiting your folks?"

"I live in Georgia now. Little town called Glenville."

"Hey, I've been there once. My husband and I drove through on our way to Gatlinburg, on our honeymoon. God, that was a long time ago. Seventeen years, to be exact. Come to think of it, that's where I remember you from."

"From your honeymoon?"

"No, silly. You used to date my husband, you know, way back in the dark ages. In high school. At least I think you did. You've got to be the one. You were in the drama club, right? You were in that play . . . oh damn, what was the name of that thing?"

"Ummmm, I don't—"

"Oh c'mon, it was something about windows. No, glass. Yeah, that's it. Glass. That's funny, isn't it? A play about glass. Or was it glasses? Hell, I can't remember anything anymore."

"You mean *The Glass Menagerie*?"

"Hey, yeah, that's the one. That glass thing." She doesn't say any of this with animosity. She's just stating the facts. "Weird play, but I kind of liked it. You were pretty good. I remember that."

"Thanks," I say, still confused as to who my newfound friend could be.

"What'd you say your name was again?"

"Sandi, you know, with an *i*. Sandi Leonard."

"You're Andy Leonard's sister?"

"Ha. No, I'm his wife. Or I was, anyway." She takes a sip of her drink through a straw. "You heard what happened?"

"Yeah, I heard." I remember how I sat at my kitchen table and read about Andy Leonard's death, remember how I cried for him, and for me, for reasons I didn't understand.

"It was real hard on the kids."

"I guess it would be."

"On me, too. But like I said, that was a long time ago."

"You never remarried?"

"Nope, not me. Me and the kids get by. I work at the Craft Barn out on Highway 48. Your mom shops there all the time." She also reports that when Andy's father died, he left them two hundred acres of overplowed and overworked farmland, land that, much to their surprise, was snapped up by the new electronics plant off the interstate, at nearly $3,000 an acre.

"Made over half a million. Just like that," she says, snapping her fingers. "After taxes, we got some of it. Paid for our house, and the rest I've got saved for the kids' education. I want them to make something of themselves. Do better than their old mom here."

Sandi talks about school reunions, about who still lives in Randolph Gap and who, like me, left for places unknown.

"You wouldn't believe how fat that Melody Reeves has gotten," she whispers. "We were best friends for years, Melody and me, but when I found out she was screwing around with Andy, and me pregnant with my youngest, I just went crazy. Threw Andy out of the house, called her up and told her what kind of slut I thought she was. Believe it or not, it was that very next week he got himself killed."

At this point, she pulls out pictures of her children. "Can you believe it? My babies are all grown up. Andy Jr. is seventeen, Steven is fifteen, and Judy, my youngest, is twelve going on thirty. The middle one there, Steven, looks just like his father, don't you think?"

One look at that boy, posed in front of an Olan Mills fence railing and a picturesque country background, was like looking into my past, a past I had long tried to forget. He's his father's child, all right, pimples and all. I drain half my margarita in one gulp.

While Sandi fans out all her pictures in a wide arc on the bar, all

I can think about was how it felt to be pinned under a teenage Andy Leonard on that leatherette sofa in his brother's trailer. My sister, I notice, is ordering a fresh round of drinks for herself and her two companions.

"Now Melody's married that Steve Studdard, who she was screwing too before his wife threw him out, and all she does all day is sit around watching TV on that big satellite dish of theirs, getting fatter and fatter. Good riddance is what I say."

I can't remember Melody Reeves either, fat or skinny. I can't remember any of them.

"Oh, and you remember Lisa Poe, that skinny little girl whose parents owned the laundry downtown?" Sandi asks as she reaches across the bar for a bowl of peanuts, using her fuchsia nails to pop one open. "Killed herself. Pills. About four years ago. She had two little children."

Sandi is not one to keep her opinions about her friends, past or present, to herself. Her confessions mystify me, considering she hasn't seen me in some twenty years and that it's obvious I don't remember her at all.

Peggy, the bartender, gives us a little wave and says, "C'mon, girls, drink up. In thirty minutes you'll have to pay full price."

THIRTY-ONE

S oon enough, Peggy plants two more drinks on the bar. In my newly inebriated state, Sandi Leonard and I fall into the sort of languid rhythm of bar conversations everywhere. I'm not accustomed to drinking so much, and so fast, so I try to hold my own without doing something that will brand me as conspicuously drunk. At one point, while reaching for my purse slumped at the foot of my bar stool, I nearly topple over in a fit of dizziness, but right myself before I think anybody notices.

"Woooo, girl, watch out there," Sandi says as she helps me sit upright again. "Those margaritas of Peggy's will get you every time. Believe me, I know what I'm talking about."

"Thanks."

"No problem, hon. You need to let your hair down now and then. Everybody does." Sandi, it seems, will forever consider herself a member of the junior varsity squad, cheering on the losing team despite bleachers full of less than enthusiastic fans, some of whom, namely me, are getting drunker by the minute. Still, her bubbly technique is starting to work. For reasons I don't understand, she somehow views me as a long-lost friend. The even bigger mystery is that I'm beginning to feel the same way. I feel better, safer somehow, just having her at my side. Luckily, she also seems not to notice that I'm not holding up my end of the conversation. She talks enough for us both, which is just fine by me. She reminds me of Donna Lindsey in this way.

"Can you believe how much time has gone by?"

"Hmmmm?" I'm watching Peggy the bartender. She's answered the phone at least a half-dozen times since we've been at the bar and every time launches into a conversation full of important whispering, as if she's saying *I told you not to be calling me here.* She must have lots of secret plans in the making. I think of yanking the phone away from Peggy and calling Donna Lindsey at the Bay Island Hotel to get a report on her condition. That's what a friend would do. But I don't feel up to it. If Donna started drinking by mid-afternoon the way she planned, she's probably deep in sleep by now and in no mood to expound further on her recent abandonment.

Sandi, who's eating a good supply of the bar's peanuts, is still talking.

"Sometimes I look back on those days, you know, and think, 'Wow, that seems like it happened just yesterday.' Other times, it seems like a million years ago."

Listen Sandi, I've got this friend who left her husband and two children and ran off for the weekend with a twenty-something shirt salesman, but he dumped her at the hotel and ran back home to his wife. You think you could call her and say something to cheer her up? C'mon, it'll only take a few minutes.

I look at my watch. It's 9 P.M., happy hour for ladies officially over, as Peggy loudly proclaims. It's up to us now, all four of us ladies present, to fend for ourselves one drink at a time. Maybe Sandi and I can coax the father-and-son duo at the pool table into buying us another round. I don't want Lamar Hamby buying me any drinks, no matter how desperate I may get.

"It's not that late."

"No, silly, I mean since we were all in high school together," Sandi says, twirling a curl of long brown hair around her index finger. "I know that sounds like, you know, a cliché, but it's the way I feel." Sandi pronounces the word *cliché* like "quiche." I feel an immediate and overpowering sisterly affection for her. A need to protect her from the world outside the Green Duck.

"Seems like a million years to me."

Sandi is quiet for a moment, then, stirring her drink, adds philosophically, "I guess it would. You moved away. You got a whole new life."

A whole new life. Is that what I have?

No doubt due to my last margarita, this strikes me as outrageously funny. I laugh out loud, which causes Sandi to waver a moment in her continuing monologue and look at me as if she's missed something important.

"But me?" Sandi says after a moment. "I see the same people here all the time. We all take our children to the mall and drop them off so they can walk around and watch each other walking around, all of them acting like they're not there to do any such thing. They don't want their parents around, of course, 'cause that would be just *way too* embarrassing." She pulls a makeup compact from her purse and holds it close to her face, running a finger over her eyelashes to wipe away a few flakes of mascara.

"Funny how things turn out," I say.

Sandi turns to look across the bar at my sister, who is herding her two male companions toward an empty pool table.

"Yeah. That's what I mean. I try to tell my kids to enjoy what they've got now, because pretty soon it'll all be over and they'll be wondering where all the time went. Like they listen to a damn word I say."

For me, each day of the past few years has seemed like an eternity.

At the pool table, Ellen's companions rack the balls at her request, the request itself being suggestive enough for them to jostle against each other and clink their beer bottles in a toast.

"Your sister looks like she's doing okay, though," Sandi says. "Looks, well, happy enough."

"She just left her husband."

"Ha. Maybe that's why."

Ellen takes her time as she chalks the tip of her stick, doing it smooth and easy, so deliberate, that I expect the men watching her will be drooling by the time she leans over the table to make her shot.

"So what do you think about husbands?" I ask Sandi, remembering the line Donna Lindsey has asked me so many times over the years.

"Who?"

"Husbands."

"They're okay, I guess. Mine was pretty decent most of the time." I wonder what kind of husband Andy Leonard had been to Sandi, if he had been a good father to their children.

"You really haven't thought about remarrying?"

"I go out on dates sometimes, just for fun. But no, I don't. Not a lot, anyway."

"Really?"

"Andy and I got married too young, probably wouldn't have if I hadn't been pregnant. So no, I don't think about getting married again. Least not anytime soon. I'm pretty happy now the way things are."

"That's good. Happy is good."

"Are you?"

"Am I what?"

"Happy."

I take a long sip of my margarita. "Sometimes."

"Only sometimes?"

"Yeah."

"Sometimes is better than never, huh?"

"I guess."

"So who'd you marry? Not someone from here, right?"

"No. Not from here."

"What's he do?"

"He's a banker."

"Ahhhh," Sandi sighs, and raises her glass in a mock toast. "So you married money. You go, girl."

"It's not like they let him take home bags of cash every day," I say, vaguely aware that I'm beginning to slur my words.

"Yeah, but still. That's more money than most. You don't live in a double-wide up there in Georgia, I'd bet on that. Am I right?"

"Well, yeah. We don't."

"See there. You married money, or at least what counts for money around here."

I consider this. I feel suddenly defensive, as if Sandi has attacked my choice of a husband, and my lifestyle. As if my cookie-cutter Georgian on Shadowwood Lane is a symbol of some terrible crime— that of escaping Randolph Gap in the first place.

"You have any kids?"

"No."

"Really?"

"Really." I hope I won't have to explain that one.

"Well, that's good sometimes," Sandi says, pausing to snap shut her compact and slide it back into her purse. "Kids sure can make a marriage last a lot longer than it should. You know, all that putting up with it for the kids' sake."

"I didn't marry him for money," I insist, twisting my diamond engagement ring to the underside of my finger.

"So what do you do with yourself during the day? I mean, do you work?"

"I'm a case manager, a social worker. At a mental health clinic."

"No shit? You're a shrink?"

"I work with patients, yeah."

"Wow. I don't think I've ever talked to a shrink before," says Sandi, who's beginning to look a little glassy-eyed. "Hey, you're not charging me here, are you?"

"Naaaah. We only charge the crazy ones."

"Ha!" Sandi exclaims, motioning for Peggy to bring us another round.

"Here, put this one on my tab," I tell Peggy, my suburban guilt turning me generous.

"So what's it like? Working with crazy people, I mean?"

"It's just a job. Like any other job."

"You gotta see some pretty strange stuff."

"There's lots of strange people out there, that's for sure. Not all of them are locked up."

"You got that right," she says and raises her empty glass in another toast. She swivels around to look at Lamar Hamby, who's still in his chair, a pitcher of beer cradled in his left arm.

"A patient did bite me the other day."

"No shit?"

I point to the bandage on my arm.

"Bit you, huh?"

We sit for a few minutes without talking, each of us sipping our drinks.

"So you fell in love, huh? With your banker, I mean?"

"Yeah."

"You sure about that?"

"What?"

"The falling-in-love part."

"Yeah, well, that's what it seemed like at the time." I must not sound very convincing.

"I know what that's like," Sandi says. "One day you're on your honeymoon in Gatlinburg and then you wake up and years have passed and you think, 'How in the hell did I get myself into this?' "

"Something like that."

"Am I right or what?" Sandi asks, but now she's talking not to me, but to Peggy, who's brought us another round of drinks.

"About what, hon?"

"Falling in love."

"Not all it's cracked up to be," says Peggy, who shuffles off toward the other end of her U shaped space, flat-footed and weary, to answer the telephone.

THIRTY-TWO

*A*t the pool table, my sister is making her move. Her opponent is ready to make his shot, so she leans back from her resting position against the corner of the table, tilts her head to shake out her spiky Chestnut Blonde ponytail, and off comes the red jacket, fringe flying. "I've got to get comfortable if I got a chance of winning another game from you boys," she says, a little too loudly.

As expected, all eyes in the bar are on her as the jacket slides off her shoulders. She lets it drop with all the confidence that someone will catch it before it hits the floor. Predictably, someone does. It's Lamar Hamby, who, upon seeing the jacket in his lap, clutches it with both hands like he's handling a live animal. When he thinks no one is looking, he brings the fabric to his face and inhales deeply.

Ellen's bustier is doing its job all right. With every breath, her breasts push and strain at the edge of the confining garment, only a quick tug of a zipper away from being released into the hopeful hands of her companions.

"You were right about one thing," says Sandi, who pivots around on her bar stool and faces me with a supercilious grin. "Your sister hasn't changed much, has she?"

"Still going strong. Got a little boy at home. Seven years old." I imagine Justin, at this hour, still planted in front of his Nintendo, his performance applauded only by squawking birds. I feel a pang of motherly affection for this lost child.

"She better watch out for those two if she knows what's good for her," Sandi adds. "With a show like that, they're not likely to take no for an answer."

"Ellen never knows what's good for her. And she ain't likely to say no." At that, I start laughing so hard I nearly spill my drink. The very idea of my saying the word *ain't* is what makes me laugh, not any speculation on my sister's after-hours plans. Every time I return from a trip home, Turner listens to me and shakes his head, as if to say the proverbial, *You can take the girl out of the country, but you can't take the country out of the girl.* Like I'm his pet project, his very own Eliza Doolittle below the Mason-Dixon line. Like I've reverted to some primitive form of life, *Homo redneckus,* and he's afraid to engage in conversation with me without a translator nearby. Life in Randolph Gap, to him, means we're all running around barefoot and hookwormed and sneaking out after Sunday dinner-on-the-ground to screw our cousins in the woods.

I lift a drink to you, my dear Turner Maddox, my affable and grammatically unchallenged husband. Sometimes you don't know shit.

Sandi, the perfect drinking companion, lifts her glass and clinks it against mine, thinking my toast is meant either for her or in honor of my sister's performance. We clink glasses again as if to prove our mutual hilarity, that we are, after all, just two women out for a night on the town, not a care in the world.

Needless to say, my sister's opponent misses his shot. It's her turn next. When she leans over the table, the stark black line of her bustier rubs against the rim of the pool table. Her admirer with the mustache, her opponent in this game, falls against the wall and clutches his heart.

My sister, her feminine wiles in full tilt, wiggles a little in her bent-over posture. She looks up at both men and then expertly, and with her eyes still on them, sends the eight ball cracking toward the upper left pocket to win the game. Crew Cut runs over and grabs Ellen around her corseted waist and lifts her up into the air, swinging her around in a victory dance. As her feet sail off the floor and she looks up at him, it reminds me of the day she married Cecil at the county fairgrounds, when he lifted her off the stage as soon as they said their "I do's."

As if triggered by some kind of remote control listening device that told him what was going on in the bar at that exact minute, Cecil himself walks through the door of the Green Duck. He's wearing a military green rain slicker with a hood, and, head down, drips his way toward the bar, hands deep in his pockets. He must have seen Ellen when he walked in, and she must have seen him. He takes off his raincoat and drapes the wilted thing over an empty bar stool. He sits on the stool next to me, to my left.

"Some night, huh?"

"Yep."

Sandi, ever oblivious, smiles across me at Cecil like he's the most eligible bachelor she's seen in years. "C'mon, introduce me to your friend here."

"Peggy," I call across the bar, "get Cecil here a drink. Looks like he could use one."

Cecil mumbles something Peggy evidently interprets as a drink order, and she shuffles off toward the other end of the bar.

"Cecil here," I whisper to Sandi, "is Ellen's husband. Or was. No, is."

"Your sister Ellen?" A dim but perceptible light dawns in Sandi's semi-drunken state. Then, wide-eyed, she finally gets it. "Ohhhh," she says all soft and all ladylike, as if she's just been introduced to a clearly unstable patient of mine. She says a wary hello to Cecil over the rim of her glass.

The jukebox is blasting out a guitar solo. On the TV in the corner, a new wrestler is making his entrance. Flanked by two blondes wearing orange string bikinis, he strides across the ring, all three-hundred-plus pounds of him stuffed one muscle at a time into a glittering orange jumpsuit.

I turn around to find my sister sitting on the lap of Crew Cut, her arm around his shoulder. The other man stands close by, his pool stick moving like a metronome between his open palms, keeping it moving so he can transform it into a weapon if the situation demands. Sandi and I look at each other in disbelief. Ellen is brazen, yes, but this is going too far. Even Peggy looks like she might be catching a case of the nervous jitters. She's bent over behind the bar, on the phone again whispering, but her eyes are all jumpy. She's surveying the situation, ready to hang up and dial 911 if she has to, but for a second her eyes take on a zealous shine, as if it's been far too long since she was witness to blood sports.

"See your dad's working the store tonight," says Cecil, who takes a crumpled, grease-stained bandanna from his back pocket and slicks down his still-wet hair.

"Yeah. Always on the late shift."

"Said he might close the place down and join us over here. Nobody coming in anyway with all this rain." My father has often said the advantage of running a convenience store off the beaten path is that you can close it whenever you want. When he does, he simply hangs a little hand-lettered sign in the window. NOBODY HOME & NOTHING WORTH STEALING. COME BACK LATER & WE MIGHT BE HERE.

I try to will myself out of my drunken state and apply my clinical skills, or what's left of them, to this situation. Cecil looks calm enough. In fact, he looks almost happy, or as close to happy as I've seen him. From the left pocket of his shirt he removes a pack of cigarettes and lights one. I realize then that I don't know enough about him to judge whether he's happy or not. Under the circumstances, I feel I've failed him in some way, and need to make amends. My sister certainly looks like she doesn't intend to offer him any comfort.

"Hey, Cecil, you remember that ugly old stuffed duck that used to be at the door here?" I ask.

"Seems like I do. Sure." His eyes are focused on the wrestler in the orange jumpsuit, who is moving ominously toward a heavily bearded thug of a man whose silver trunks are anchored in place by a wide rhinestone belt.

"I remember that old thing," Sandi says, perking up. "I wonder what ever happened to him. He was kinda cute."

"He's in retirement," I announce with the authority of a local tour guide. "In the storage room back there, gathering dust. Somebody beheaded him."

Cecil keeps staring at the TV, looking like he's wondering why on earth I'd be interested in the fate of a stuffed duck when he's in the middle of a domestic situation he doesn't know how to handle and is watching a wrestling match he isn't interested in watching. On the screen, Orange Jumpsuit grabs Silver Trunks by the beard and yanks him to the mat, beard first.

"Well, I loved that duck. I really did. He was probably the first thing I ever really loved."

Sandi looks at me as if I've lost my mind. "Cut her off, Peggy," she says. "I think our Jessie here has had enough."

&

The three of us sit at the bar and try to look like we're all big wrestling fans. We can hear Ellen's occasional high-pitched giggling above the sounds of the jukebox.

Finally, Ellen excuses herself and stumbles her way to the facilities, which, in the Green Duck, consist of one small unisex room at the end of a dark hallway in the rear of the bar. Clumsy predator that I am, I stumble after my prey. I figure I can trap my sister there, lock the door if I have to, and convince her to do something about the brewing situation. Specifically, to abandon her two companions and talk to her husband in a civilized way. I know I'm expecting too much by thinking that she might actually respond to such a suggestion, but it's worth a try.

"Back in a minute," I tell Sandi, who, seeing that I'm headed for the bathroom, already has her purse slung over her arm in an attempt to join me. I wave her off.

"Give me a minute. I need to talk some sense into my crazy sister."

Sandi sits down. She looks at me like I'm far braver than she is, like I'm a soldier going off to battle and she might never see me again.

I catch Ellen at the door. She wavers a bit as she tries to open it, nearly knocking me in the forehead when the door opens outward.

"Let me in, Ellen," I say over her shoulder, and push her in ahead of me. She nearly falls over on her red heels, but then rights herself and twists around to blink at me in the suddenly too bright light.

"Leave me alone. And I mean now." She starts unbuttoning her jeans and pulls them down fast, nearly losing her balance again.

"Just what do you think you're doing out there? That's all I want to know."

"None of your damn business."

"It damn sure is my business," I say, looking at a blurry vision of myself in the grimy bathroom mirror, which is nothing but a rectangular piece of unframed glass bolted to the wall. A long crack runs from the upper left corner to the lower right, splitting my image in half. "You're going to get yourself killed if you don't start behaving yourself."

"Says who?" She zips up her jeans and wobbles to a standing position. "Cecil's got no hold on me anymore."

"He's still your husband."

"Like you're some kind of expert in the happy marriage department?" She brushes against me with enough force to knock me flat against the wall, and heads for the sink. A stream of rusty water pours out of the faucet. Ellen holds her hands under it while she stares in the mirror, trying, it seems, to determine if the two sides of the face reflected there are hers. After a moment she turns around, flinging her wet hands in my direction, then rips a piece of brown paper towel from the rack on the wall.

"You're the same as always, Jess, trying to tell everybody how to run their lives when you can't even run your own." She steps between me and the mirror again, unclips her ponytail, and shakes out her hair. Slicks down her lips again. She fluffs and powders herself up to her satisfaction, then pulls from her purse a can of hair spray and the whole room fills with the sticky odor of it.

"Fine. But c'mon, Ellen. Cecil's sitting right there, for Christ's sake."

"I don't care where he sits or what he does. He can sit there on that bar stool all night for all I care. He can rot in—"

"But Ellen—"

"I told you," she says, brushing past me and slamming into the bathroom door, obviously not intending to continue this conversation. "I'm sick and tired of his ugly face. If you care so much about him, you can have him." With that, she prances out the door, down the dark hallway, and around the bar where Cecil sits nursing his drink. She's ready to present herself to her two admirers, a free and wild woman wearing two fresh coats of lipstick.

THIRTY-THREE

I t's nearly midnight when I decide to kidnap the green duck. I've already started ordering coffee in an effort to sober up for the drive home, but there's still enough margarita in me to make me believe pulling off this small, ridiculous crime is the one and only thing that will salvage the evening, maybe the entire weekend. I put a $100 bill on the bar, enough, but just barely, to cover all our drinks.

Taking Cecil's limp raincoat with me, I saunter off casually in the direction of the bar's storage room. Peggy, who groggily says something into the phone before slamming it into its cradle, isn't paying any attention anyway. Her craving for combat within the walls of the Green Duck unsatisfied, she now looks bored with the lot of us, not likely to care where I'm prowling. Ellen and her two companions are in a far corner of the bar, huddled together behind a table with one unsteady leg. With their every move, their various drinks slide around and bump into each other on the table's shifting surface.

Cecil doesn't seem to care what any of us does. He has six shots of tequila lined up on the bar in front of him. It's only fifteen minutes until last call, when, at the stroke of midnight, Sunday officially begins and it's illegal to sell liquor. Rules are rules, even at the Green Duck. The bar's liquor license could be revoked for breaking the rules, and that, at least for Peggy, is reason enough. She'd pour Cecil six or sixty straight shots of tequila before midnight, let him sit there as long as it took him to finish, but pouring a drink on Sunday is out of the question.

I open the door of the storage room and feel along the wall for the light. I have to pull hard on the door to get it to close again, which it finally does with a screech of metal hitting metal, leaving me wary that I may have trapped myself here, that the door won't open again from the inside. There are crates stacked high with liquor, cheap brands mostly, along with the dust-covered remnants of brighter, maybe happier Green Duck nights. In one corner are two stained glass lamps with pieces missing. In another, three neon signs are stacked against the wall, a malfunctioning electronic dartboard tilted to hold them in place.

The green duck himself is reclining on a bar stool that's propped against the dartboard. He's still missing his head, but someone has taken the time to cross his gangly green legs, so he sits on his stool like a well-bred gentleman of some bygone era.

I tiptoe across the small room, trying not to knock over anything that will cause a clatter and get me discovered. I push a few tufts of cotton back into the duck's scrawny neck opening, and wrap the body in Cecil's rain slicker. About four feet tall, most of the coat covers the duck, but he seems smaller than I'd remembered.

The duck's head is perched on top of one of the crates, his sequined eyes staring down at a stack of yellowing newspapers. He's about nine feet off the floor, yellow derby nearly touching the ceiling, where a dark brown watermark spreads out over his head. I push some of the heavier crates together so I can stack them, ladder fashion. They're surprisingly heavy. Wiping a ring of sweat from my forehead, I climb my way to him. I have to stand on my toes to pull him free, and I must say he doesn't look too happy about it. Here in the storage room, the duck's cold plastic eyes stare back at me as if I'm disturbing years of philosophical contemplation and am, in doing this, insulting retired bar mascots everywhere.

After two or three rough turns of the doorknob, I get the door open again and breathe a sigh of relief as I head for the bar. "Let's get out of here, guys. It's time for a road trip," I tell my companions. "Meet me outside in ten minutes."

&

I step outside the Green Duck and walk across the parking lot toward the Stop 'n' Shoppe, the holy relic of my childhood tucked under my arm. The rain has slowed to a drizzle, but I can still hear thunder somewhere off in the clouds, can see the occasional flash of light across the sky.

"Hey, Dad," I say, my entrance signaled by a bell on the door. My father's elbows are propped up on the counter, his eyes closed. A crooked smile lines his face, as if he's dreaming of that chance encounter with his bicycle-riding mademoiselle, a loaf of fresh bread in her bicycle basket, ready to share it, and herself, with an American GI like him.

"Hey, Dad, you awake?"

"Ummmm, yeah," he grumbles, then bolts upright on his stool, as if he expects to find another teenager come to rob the place, catching him asleep behind the cash register.

"Jesus, you nearly scared me half to death," he says, rubbing his bandaged forehead.

"Sorry, Dad. I just came in for a few things."

"What time is it, anyway? I was about to close up and join you for a drink."

"Then I can be your last customer," I say, and set off down one of the store's aisles in search for my gear for the evening.

"What are you doing, anyway?"

"Just some things I need. And don't wait up for me. I may not be back home till morning." It occurs to me that since I'd driven him to work, he won't have a ride home if I leave this way.

"Don't worry about me," he says, yawning. "Peggy can drop me off. It's on her way. If I get really desperate, I can always call your mother and tell her to come pick me up in her new Town Car." He yawns again. Behind him, a congregation of glossy arms beckons lustfully from the magazine racks.

"Is your sister going with you, or is she still raising hell over at the Duck?"

"She's still there."

He considers this, and all its implications. "What's she been up to over there?"

"You don't want to know." At just that moment, Sandi and Cecil stumble out the bar's entrance. Sandi's arm is around his shoulder, steering them both in our direction. She peers across the parking lot and gives us an enthusiastic little wave, and then, not sure if we've seen her, keeps on waving.

"We're going on a road trip," I say.

"Who's we?" asks my father, squinting at the two stumbling figures, trying to bring everything into focus. "Wait a minute. Is that Cecil you've got with you?"

"Yep."

"Who's that with him?"

"That's Sandi Leonard."

"That girl who married Andy?"

"She's appointed herself my new best friend, so I had to bring her along," I tell him.

My father looks at me, then at Sandi, and waves back. He seems a little unsure about the appropriateness of sneaking my drunken brother-in-law out in the middle of the night with another woman in tow, but he doesn't say anything.

"Don't worry, Dad. Cecil will be passed out by the time we get him in the car."

"That girl comes in here all the time," he says. "Her I like, but her oldest boy I'm not so sure about. Worked here for a few weeks. Couldn't prove it, but I was sure he was stealing from me."

Sandi waves at us again, grateful to have been noticed at last.

&

Poor Cecil looks genuinely confused, as if he's trying to figure out who he's with and why he's standing outside the bar instead of inside it. He is, in fact, having a good deal of trouble standing at all.

"What's going on?" Sandi says, and lets out something that sounds like a cross between a giggle and a hiccup. "Are we going somewhere?" At some point since I paid the bill and announced we were leaving, Sandi must have convinced Peggy to sell her a bottle of something, which she now carries in a grocery sack that's all wadded at the top.

"Yes ma'am. We've got official business here." I produce Cecil's raincoat, which bulges from what's hidden underneath.

"Official business!" Sandi squeals and executes a kicky little jump. "Road trip!" Perennial cheerleader that she is, I know Sandi will be game for this impromptu excursion, even if she doesn't have a clue what it's all about. "You should have seen the look on your sister's face when we left. Priceless."

Cecil stares at his raincoat, blinking. "Is that my coat?" he says, bending over to get a closer look. "I've got a coat just like that."

"Get it in gear, Cecil," Sandi says. "We're going on a road trip."

I take his other arm and, with him balanced between us, we help him walk to my Explorer. It takes both of us to get him into the back seat, but he finally makes it, his head slumped against the rear side window.

Sandi squeals again and does a little bunny hop around to the passenger-side door, chanting in a high-pitched scream, "Road trip! Road trip!"

I get behind the wheel, Peggy's last cup of coffee jolting me fully awake.

"Hey," says Sandi, studying me with unexpected solemnity. "This ain't going to be one of those *Thelma & Louise* type of things, is it? Not going to drive us off a cliff, are you?" She lets out a nervous little laugh. "I mean, I liked the movie and all, but I got kids at home."

"Naaaah," I say, trying to look as if I have nothing more in mind than a little midnight picnic. "We're just going to have a little fun."

Sandi studies me for a moment, trying to figure out if I'm on the level. In the backseat, Cecil starts snoring.

"Okay, then, prepare for takeoff," she chirps, buckling her seat belt, holding up her sacked bottle and waving it in the air. And off we go into the night.

THIRTY-FOUR

In an effort to keep myself fully awake, I roll down all the windows, crank open the sunroof, and, after a lot of button-pushing, find an agreeable radio station and turn up the volume as loud as I can stand it. Sandi sticks her head out her window and yells "Woooo-eeeee," her long hair blowing in the night sky. On her side of the windshield, which is fogging up quick from the inside, she amuses herself by drawing a series of hearts with arrows pierced through them.

The temperature gauge on my dashboard reads forty-nine degrees. I'm shivering by the time we've driven a mile, but it's a bracing, wake-up kind of cold, and I'm grateful for it. No chance of falling asleep now. I can see Cecil's head against the open rear window. Still knocked out cold. If I remember correctly, we have twenty miles or so to go.

Sandi tears open her paper bag and eyes it with blurred disappointment. "Damn," she mutters. "I told Peggy I wanted the good stuff." She tosses the bottle into the backseat, where it lands, soft and unbroken, on the soft and pliable body of the duck.

જી

I drive on, past the on-ramp to the brightly lit interstate, past the new electronics plant that financed Sandi's home and her children's education, across bridges where signs warn us of ice in winter. On either side of the long and flat back roads we're traveling, it's all red clay and scrub grass. We pass rusted trailers with big satellite dishes parked out front; ramshackle fruit, vegetable, and fireworks stands set up on the shoulder of the road; fields that must once have been plowed for corn or cotton but are now thick with abandoned auto parts. Even in the dark I know these roads well, though over the years I've tried to forget all of them, tried to make myself believe that my real home is the one I've made with Turner.

Down that road near the post office is where Mark Coley kissed me good-bye. He joined the Marine Corps after high school and was leaving for Parris Island the next morning.

Take that turn to the left and it will lead you to the boat ramp at the Black Warrior River, where I baked for countless summer days and lathered myself with Noxzema at night, trying to scorch some trace of pigment into my skin.

That house on the hill, just beyond the road that leads to the Ran-

dolph Gap Holy Rock Church, is where Andy Leonard and his family used to live.

Ten miles to the north, in the direction we're traveling, is the Randolph Gap Wildlife Preserve, where Andy Leonard died.

The memories come flooding back, like I'm trapped in a dream and can't wake up.

The first time I made this drive into the mountains was with Andy Leonard. We were young, and Andy was driving fast along these old country roads. The air was thick with the smell of my mother's borrowed perfume, the leafy dampness of wet pine, and the faint horse-barn odor of the farms we passed. With Andy's arm around me, we sat leg-to-leg while he steered with his left hand. My hair blew up and around my face and across his neck, and I remember wishing we could drive like that forever, never reaching our destination.

Now I can see us for what we really were. Desperate, hormone-crazed teenagers stuck out in the woods and trying our best to make sense of that time in our lives the only way we knew how. All we had was this frenzied scrambling toward one another. Back then, nothing more seemed even remotely possible.

Sandi, like a child in the front seat of a roller coaster, sticks her hands up and out of the sunroof and waves them around. I expect her to let out another "Woooo-eeeee," but she pulls her hands back into the car and stuffs them under her legs.

"Damn, it's getting cold out," she whimpers.

"Want me to roll up the windows?"

"Nope," she says, cheerful and agreeable camper that she is. "So what's the deal with your sister and her husband? Are they separated, or what?" She's snapping her fingers and swaying back and forth to the song playing on the radio.

"She left him. Says he's a loser. And an asshole. Says she can't stand to look at his ugly face one more day."

"I think he's kinda cute," Sandi says, then turns around to make sure Cecil's still asleep.

"My sister's gone crazy. Completely loony tunes."

"Loony tunes, huh?" she says. "You should know, right? If she really is loony tunes, that is."

"I don't think Ellen would be happy with anyone she's married to, no matter who he is. She's happy for a while, then she just gets restless."

"Happily ever after," Sandi says. "What a bunch of crap. Then the years go by and one little thing after another happens and before you know it your husband's off screwing somebody else and you're sitting at home, trying to figure out if you should sign up at the junior college to take some computer class so you can support yourself, and wondering where in the hell your life went." She lets out a long sigh.

"So okay, that's what happened to me," she adds. "But it happens, you know. It happens to more people than just me. Maybe that's what happened to your sister."

"Cecil wasn't off screwing somebody else," I say, though the minute I say it I realize I don't know if it's true or not. If he was, my sister certainly wouldn't have grounds for complaint. She's done enough of that on her own.

"Love makes us all crazy, right?" Poor Sandi. Here she is pouring her heart out to me and that's all I can offer her.

She sighs. "Hell, love's the easy part. It's the rest of it that gets you in real trouble."

❧

We ride for maybe five more miles without saying anything, just listening to the radio over the intermittent swell of Cecil's snoring. Every few minutes I have to flip on my windshield wipers, but I don't hear thunder anymore. We must be moving away from the storm.

"Where are we going, anyway?" asks Sandi.

"It's a surprise."

At that, the disc jockey interrupts, proclaiming that a fifty-minute no-commercial selection of "oldies-but-goodies" tunes is on its way to those of us still up at this hour. He starts with the Eagles.

It becomes one of those moments of pure emotion, the song lyrics bringing us closer somehow. Like we're strangers trapped in an elevator, humming along to the same piped-in tune and feeling as if some kind of essential connection—a connection with another person, a connection with everyone who has ever heard and loved that song—is established, however brief. At the chorus of "Peaceful, Easy Feeling," Cecil's head pops up from the backseat.

Cecil makes it through the whole song after that, the three of us singing off-key and missing the occasional word. Like the talented karaoke performers we believe ourselves to be, we don't care what we sound like. We're free and riding through the night, the wind and rain in our faces, and we are, for those few minutes, just happy to be singing.

When the song ends, Cecil flops back in his seat and sighs loudly, and the moment itself ends just as suddenly.

"You know," he mumbles, "life is pretty fucking complicated when you think about it." As if those were his dying words, his head resumes its thump-ker-thump rhythm out the rear window.

Sandi lets out an embarrassed giggle. "Don't think about it, then, hon," she says. "That's what's causing all your problems."

❦

By the time we reach the unpaved road high in the Randolph Gap Wildlife Preserve, Sandi, too, has been lulled toward her own dreams, her hair flattened out around her on the headrest. I cut the engine and sit in the moonlight. It's just after 2 A.M. The leaves of the trees around us are dripping with rain, and we're surrounded by the hum of a thousand croaking frogs. I can hear the faint cry of a whippoorwill from deep in the forest.

I light a cigarette and sit there in the driver's seat, leaning back and blowing smoke out the sunroof and listening to the sighs and snorts of my passed-out companions. I try to listen for any sound that will remind me of my night here with Andy Leonard, for any hint that the past twenty years hasn't happened at all.

When he had pulled his father's Oldsmobile to the shoulder of the road, near this very place, I had been a little afraid of being so far away from the lights of town, and I jumped in my seat as he moved closer to me. Was he planning, as my mother would put it, to "take advantage" of me? Since I'd already decided I'd lose my virginity to Andy by the end of that summer, this "taking advantage" issue was fine by me. All he had to do was ask. It was being here in the dark that scared me more.

"Here, put this on," he'd said that night, handing me his blue-and-gold letter jacket that had the big white *R* and *G* sewn on the back. I'd wondered, then, if he would let me keep the jacket. Some guys did. The jacket was the first step. Then the senior ring, which I could wear on a chain around my neck or wrap the band with tape so it would fit my ring finger. That's the way promises were made, and everybody knew the rules. If all went as planned, a wedding would take place soon after our high school graduation.

"Hey, wake up," I say, poking Sandi in the ribs with an index finger. "We're here."

Sandi squirms around and flails her arms. Cecil is still snoring loudly. No sense in waking either of them. I've got work to do. Probably better if I do it alone, anyway.

I leave the keys in the ignition, roll up all the windows, but leave the sunroof open, which I figure will give Sandi and Cecil a little fresh air. I lift Cecil's raincoat and start off down the side of the cliff. The river's down there somewhere, and I intend to find it.

THIRTY-FIVE

I have only the faintest recollection of where I'm headed, proof, no doubt, of how ridiculous, maybe even dangerous, what I have in mind really is.

I can see the headline now: GLENVILLE WOMAN GOES NATIVE. The accompanying story would explain how Jessie Maddox was found weeks after her disappearance. That she was, for reasons unexplained, carrying a headless stuffed duck. That she had been eating pine nuts and berries in an effort to survive and that she was, no doubt about it, suffering from what must be a severe case of amnesia. People would discuss me in hushed tones, making one pronouncement or another regarding my mental condition.

The reporter, of course, would eventually learn that the duck had been kidnapped from a popular Randolph Gap nightspot, but I, amnesiac that I was, wouldn't be of much help to explain my motives. Peggy the bartender would be interviewed, earning her fifteen minutes of fame by describing how "no one in her right mind would want to kidnap that duck," and that she "knew that lady was trouble from the minute I saw her."

Sandi and Cecil would wake up to find themselves in my Explorer, the keys still in it. Given their respective marital circumstances, they might consider their abandonment a stroke of fate, and drive off the mountain to make their escape. Turner, of course, would make little effort to find me, and I, in my recovery, would be in no shape to find him.

I amuse myself with these scenarios and then before I know it I'm sliding feet first down the hillside, scraping through piles of leaves and mud and briars and landing, finally, against the side of a tulip poplar. The tree proves remarkably resilient in breaking my fall. Bent by my weight, it whips back on itself to smack me across the right cheek. The canopy above opens up to pelt me with rainwater.

I sit there for a moment, bruised but not much more than that. When Andy and I had made this same trip so many years ago, we'd done the same thing, and both went sprawling through the underbrush. "Jack and Jill fell down the hill and lost their beer in the process," Andy had joked.

I flip on my flashlight, give it a good shake to get it going, and shine it around dizzily, seized by a sudden irrational fear that I've landed in a pit of rattlesnakes, or in a bear's den. I imagine there are dozens of pairs of eyes focused on me as a possible midnight snack. This is no Girl Scout hiking trip. It's the middle of the night and I'm making my way down the side of a cliff in a wildlife preserve, and not doing a very good job of it. In my fall, the duck catapulted from the crook of my arm and slid some ten feet past me, coming to rest against a large rock. With both hands around the offending poplar, I pull myself up, knees first. The tree and I do a little dance together until I regain my balance.

⁂

I navigate my way to the water like an animal. I'm crawling through a thicket of mountain laurel, my hands and knees deep in muck, and then I see it. A rushing waterfall that falls, cliff over rocky cliff, to form a pristine pool of cold mountain water that seems to reflect the entire forest on its silver surface. This waterfall, which springs out of the mountain clear and icy cold, becomes the river that branches out to form Little Hurricane Creek.

On that night so many years ago, Andy Leonard had led me to a flat, moss-covered rock at the edge of the pool. We were close enough that I could feel the fine mist of the water as it churned and splashed. Andy sat behind me, his warm arms wrapped around my waist, his legs resting on either side of mine. I leaned back into him and looked at the sky.

Maybe there's something about being sixteen years old and being led to a secret place like this in the middle of the night, but the stars and the moon shone more brightly that night than I'd ever remembered. To this day they've never looked quite as beautiful.

"Well, this is it," Andy had said, popping a beer from the six-pack he'd brought with us. "Ain't it beautiful?"

"Do other people know about this place?" I'd asked. "I mean, do you bring other people here?" "Other people," in the language of all teenagers, meant "other girls."

"No, I don't take other people here," he'd said, pinching me around the waist. "I come out here sometimes to be alone, to think about things."

"What do you think about when you come out here?" What Andy thought about mostly that spring was leaving Randolph Gap on a football scholarship. It was only a week later when a 240-pound linebacker sideswiped him on the football field during practice, shattering both his knee and his dreams for the future.

"I think about lots of things," he'd said. "How all this has been here, you know, for centuries, and how it will go on long after we're gone."

He gulped his beer until it was empty, crushed the can with one hand, and popped another. "I know that must sound pretty stupid," he'd said, "but that's what I think about. I like to think that no matter what happens in the world, no matter where we all go after high school, that this place will never change."

"Do you think about me when you come out here?" I'd asked. It was the kind of girlish thing I hated to hear myself saying, but I couldn't help it. I wanted to know.

"I picture you there," he'd said, pointing to the glimmering surface of the water. "I see you standing there, buck naked and beautiful."

So there in the moonlight, I'd let Andy Leonard pull the elastic neckline of my blouse over my shoulders, let him take my breasts in his hands and unsnap my bra. I let him pull down my shorts, my white cotton panties. When my clothing fell to the mossy rock below, it fell without a sound, and I'd waded into the cold and welcoming water, not looking back, waiting for him to follow.

⅋

This is the perfect place for the green duck to start his journey. I position his head roughly where I think it should be, and start to work. I picked up a cheap emergency sewing kit at the Stop 'n' Shoppe, but the green felt covering is thicker than I expected and I have to push the needle in hard, bruising my finger. My stitching is sloppy, but I don't care. Holding him close, squinting to get the needle in straight, the duck smells of spilled beer and stale cigarette smoke.

After I finish my sewing, I sit there on the rock and try to think of something important to say, something memorable to mark the occasion. Like I'm the queen of England preparing to christen a new ship. All I can think of is Cecil's slurred pronouncement from the backseat, about life being fucking complicated. Most people I know would agree, especially my clients at the Glenville Wellness Center, who, through no fault of their own, have endured more than their share of life's complications.

I hold the duck up to the moonlight, ready for inspection. He looks rather jaunty, wearing his yellow derby. His head is crooked and leaning a bit to the right, but at least it's attached to his body. It almost looks like he's smiling. Maxwell and Dylan, my sister's birds, would be proud of their waterfowl kin, going off at last to see the wide world beyond Randolph Gap.

We wade into the water together. I hold the duck by its neck, hoping the slight current won't rip his head off before he accomplishes his mission. My feet curl around the smooth rocks on the pool's bottom. The duck floats out in front of me like a malformed life jacket.

I say a little prayer, the kind of prayer one says only when drunk.

"God bless the green duck, my first and true love, who, for reasons I can't explain, makes everything seem possible again." Andy Leonard never made it out of Randolph Gap, but the green duck will, and he's sure to have extraordinary adventures.

And off he drifts, slowly at first in the still water, then faster and faster until he disappears into the darkness, making his way toward the river. With good weather and a steady current, he might be lounging on a beach at the Gulf of Mexico within weeks, a piña colada in each webbed foot.

&

I must have made my way out of the water and onto the riverbank, where I drifted off to sleep. When I wake at dawn, I'm shivering and naked and sore from the rock I slept on. My clothes, still on the rocks beside me, are cold and damp, and I pull them on quickly, embarrassed. With a groan, I search my bag for aspirin, and wash them down with handfuls of water. When I see my reflection in the water I'm startled by it. There's no nymph looking back at me, just a woman with smeared mascara and wet, stringy hair. A woman who spent the previous night saying a drunken prayer and letting loose a stuffed duck on a waterfall in the Randolph Gap Wildlife Preserve.

In the clear light of the new morning, I feel like a complete idiot.

I make my way up the muddy hillside, squinting toward the sun, hoping to find my two late-night companions still snoring away in my Explorer. I stomp around the rear of the vehicle, trying to get the mud off my shoes. I open the driver's-side door and fall inside, grateful to find myself in familiar surroundings.

In the rearview mirror I see Sandi and Cecil, their arms awkwardly around each other, huddled together like they've fallen asleep at a drive-in movie. I turn the ignition, trying to act as if nothing out of the ordinary is happening. I hear an immediate shuffling of clothing.

"Jessie, is that you?" Sandi asks, yawning.

"Yep."

"God, is it morning already?"

Cecil remains slumped against her breast.

"Sure is. You okay?"

"We're freezing back here."

"Yeah, I can see that."

"Hey, Cecil, wake up," Sandi says, trying to pry him from her breast. "We've been caught red-handed."

&

I drive them to Sandi's house, at her request. There are arrangements to be made for picking up their cars, some mention of breakfast. They're deep in whispers for most of the ride.

"Thanks, Jessie," Sandi says as she leads him out of the backseat. "I may regret this later, but thanks anyway."

Cecil stumbles out behind her, and with his first step misjudges the distance to the ground. He stands there and rubs the back of his neck, looking at me with a sheepish grin.

"Hey, what'd you do all night, anyway?" asks Sandi, who pushes Cecil in the direction of the house. He looks away from both of us. Someone at the front window pulls back the drapes.

"Just took a walk in the woods." I look down at my clothes, stained with the mud and leaves from my fall. I'm soaking wet.

Sandi looks at me like I've told her the stupidest, most unbelievable lie she ever could have imagined, which, of course, is what I've done.

"You went skinny dipping in that pool of Andy's, didn't you?"

I don't say anything. My head is still throbbing.

"Thought so. Hell, girl, every woman in Randolph Gap under the age of fifty has been to that waterfall. At least everyone Andy could get his hands on. And that's a lot. You can bet on that."

She studies my reaction. "Sorry to disappoint you, but it's true." She smiles a smile wise beyond her years, a smile that says she doesn't begrudge me this futile attempt to recapture my youth and the feelings stirred by my first love. As she leans through the still-open door to kiss me on the cheek, I think, with some apprehension, that this must be the kind of smile I give my clients. The kind that says, *Look, honey, we both know you're crazy, but you've got to deal with that on your own.*

"I didn't do anything last night," Sandi says. "With your brother-in-law, I mean."

"Look, I don't—"

"No, really," she says before I can finish. "I mean, I wanted to and he wanted to, but I just couldn't. I guess I'm just feeling old lately."

"Don't be silly. You're not old."

"Doing it with Cecil would have made me feel old. And not doing it with him made me feel old. So. Old. The least I can do now is make him some breakfast."

Cecil has made it to the front door, but he stands there a little dazed, like he thought he was heading for his own house but now everything looks unfamiliar.

"Turner and I lost a baby last year," I say, and the tears start falling.

"Oh honey, I'm so sorry," Sandi says, and throws her arms around me. "I knew there was a sadness in you somehow."

She pats my back and holds me fast and tells me everything is going to be all right, and in that moment, in her arms, I believe her.

"Good seeing you again, Jessie," she says. "Maybe you won't stay away so long next time."

I mumble my good-byes. *Maybe I won't,* I think. *Maybe I won't.*

THIRTY-SIX

I make the turn toward the Randolph Gap Holy Rock Church just before Sunday morning services are to begin. Someone's changed the message board on the big neon sign at the side of the road. This time it reads:

Where the mind goes
the flesh will follow.
Come hear Rev. Floyd
Wheeling, Jr. today!

I park underneath the big oak my mother somehow avoided hitting the day before. The tree is covered with golden tufts that, in the sunlight, hang from its branches like so many knots of untangled string. Clumps of them drift downward with a gentle rustling and land on the hood of my Explorer. After fifteen minutes, its surface has turned from green to gold.

A few churchgoers are already arriving, and I slump in my seat, hoping to go unnoticed. They all stop and survey the damage to the front steps, where a sizable chunk of the second step is missing. They'll find out soon enough how it happened.

I wait until I see my father's pickup rattling down the road toward the parking lot. He stops in front of the church and lets my mother out, even getting out of the truck and going over to her side to open the door. Justin, wedged between them on the seat, scoots over to the passenger side. My mother walks up the steps with her hair curled on top of her head and her head held high, her worn red leather Bible in the crook of her left arm, a small clutch bag held in her right.

My father gets back behind the wheel and eases his truck over to where I'm parked, pulling up beside me in the opposite direction so we can talk window to window. The engine rattles and clacks its gears before turning silent. Justin strikes one of his bored, aging rock star poses and ignores me altogether, as if the view from his window is far more interesting than anything I might have to say.

"I see you're still alive and kicking," my father says.

"Alive, but I don't know about the kicking part." I'm massaging my temples, trying to will the aspirin to take effect.

"Staying the rest of the day?"

"Not sure. I might drive by the house and pick up my things."

"Turner probably misses you, you know."

"I'm not so sure about that."

"Awwww now, you know he does. He's like Cecil. He just doesn't know how to say it. Doesn't know you need to hear it now and then." This is the first time I've ever heard my father speak up on Turner's behalf.

"I might just sit here for a while."

I'm tempted to tell my father about Cecil spending the night in the backseat of my Explorer with Andy Leonard's widow, but I think better of it. I owe Cecil at least that much.

"Do what you got to do then. You always have."

I have?

"I'll make up some story for your mama if I need to." He cranks up the truck again. It takes him three tries before the motor turns over.

"Did Ellen make it home last night?"

"She was asleep when we left for church," says my father. "She ended up giving me a ride home last night. Said she felt like turning in early for a change."

I watch as people make their way into the sanctuary. Most are the same faces from my childhood, grown older and grayer. If attendance has dwindled to these few, the Randolph Gap Holy Rock Church may find itself extinct unless it can proselytize a new generation.

Inez Sneed and her son Harvey pull up in a big yellow boat of a car. Sister Inez's hair has gone completely white, and she walks with a cane. Harvey squints in my direction, but doesn't seem to recognize me. I see the Rev. Wheeling Sr. and his son walking side by side, carrying identical oversized Bibles. A few other men escort their wives to the church door, but remain on the steps to take the last drags of their cigarettes. They huddle briefly around the spot where my mother crashed her Lincoln Town Car, looking as if each is offering a theory about how it could have happened. This holds their attention only as long as their cigarettes are still burning, and after a few minutes they too go inside, flipping the butts of their cigarettes into the shrubbery.

My father groans. Rev. Wheeling—the elder—is making his way toward us, Bible in hand. There's a determined look on his face, like he's going to ask my father to produce a check covering the damage to the church's front steps. When he's within ten feet of our two vehicles, he stops, as if he's afraid that his very presence among those not planning to attend church this morning will somehow pollute the pure thoughts he's worked so hard to maintain on this sunny Sunday. When he does speak to us, he's already half-turned in retreat.

"Good morning, Brother Kilgore," the Rev. Wheeling says, lifting his Bible over his head as if he's preparing to hurl it in our direction. "Why don't you and the boy join us this morning?" He does not, I notice, invite me.

"Not this time, brother," my father says cheerfully. "We've got fish waiting to be caught. Jesus might have been a fisher of men, but we're going to be fishers of fish."

Rev. Wheeling frowns and gives his Bible a ferocious shake. "These are the last days, brother."

"Last days for me maybe, but not for the boy here," says my father. On my father's face is a wide and genuine smile, one so full of friendship that the Rev. Wheeling can't help but smile, too. If he senses he's been insulted, he can't figure out exactly how. He eyes me suspiciously, as if he believes I'm responsible for my father's behavior, then turns on his heels and strides toward the church.

"Keep up the good work, brother," my father calls after him.

Then, to me, "That jackleg preacher has been trying to convert me for the last forty years. Your mother tried too, but after twenty years even she had the good sense to stop wasting her prayers on me."

I'm lost in my own thoughts again when my father reaches across the small space between our two vehicles.

"I love you, Jessie, but you know that already."

"I know, Daddy. I love you too."

"Come home any time you want. It ain't much, but it's your home."

"Thanks." Despite myself, I feel a tear roll down my cheek.

"Call us. Let us know you got there safe and sound."

"I will."

"Me and the boy here, we better get going if we're going to catch those fish."

"Yeah," Justin says. "Grandpa and me are going to catch some whoppers."

"I'm sure you will."

Justin looks at me as if I've doubted him somehow. "Well, we are," he insists, then turns his face away from me.

I want to pick up that child and hold him close to me, tell him he's much too young to know so much about the world's disappointments, promise him that he'll catch the biggest fish ever caught in Randolph Gap, maybe even in all of Alabama.

"Hey kiddo, did you get that motorcycle tattoo yet?"

Justin rolls up his sleeve and there it is. It's about two inches square, and looks more like a moped, but if Justin thinks it's a motorcycle that's what counts. The other tattoo, the skull and dagger, is still on his wrist, but its colors are soap-faded and swirled together.

"Now that's a tattoo," I say, and nod my head in appreciation.

Justin, ever unsure, doesn't know what to make of this. He bites his lip.

"You know something, Justin? I'd bet you're going to catch more fish today than your grandpa there."

"Whatever," he says.

"Off we go, then," my father says, taking hold of my hand. He puts the fingers of his other hand to his lips and then touches them to my palm, folds my fingers over the kiss. It's a familiar ritual of ours, our private way of saying good-bye.

"Wave good-bye to your aunt Jessie."

Justin waves at me like he's told. This time, I think I see a smile. Or at least the beginning of one.

&

As I circle the church, I hear what must be Harvey Sneed striking a chord on the piano, ready to lead the congregation in song, which signals both the start and end of the morning's services. It sounds like the key of G, if my memory of Sister Inez's piano lessons serves me right. Sister Inez taught piano in only two chords—C and G— and I can't imagine that Harvey would stoop to showmanship and outperform his mother. The minister starts singing, whether on key or not, and by the time the first stanza has ended, most everyone is singing.

After a pause, with me standing underneath a pair of stained glass windows on the east side of the building, waiting for the song to begin, Harvey hits the same chord again. He's tuning up, again giving the Rev. Wheeling his cue to begin. And then I hear it, one of those hymns from my youth. I know that my mother is inside, probably standing next to Inez Sneed. My mother can't carry a tune, but she doesn't know that or, if she does, she doesn't care.

> *Just a few more weary days and then,*
> *I'll fly a-way, fly a-way; fly a-way;*
> *To a land where joys shall never end,*
> *I'll fly a-way; fly a-way, fly a-way.*

I stand there, frozen in time. The windows over my head begin to vibrate. Harvey bangs away on the piano, hitting all the octaves with just the right trills and quavers on the highest notes. Then comes the chorus, the women singing soprano, the men's voices echoing in bass. Someone starts playing a tambourine.

> *I'll fly a-way, fly a-way O glory,*
> *I'll fly a-way fly a-way; in the morning*
> *When I die hallelujah by and by*
> *I'll fly a-way.*

I walk in search of Andy Leonard, ready to face him at last. On my way I pass the grave of Linda Crider, where Ellen pickpocketed her Saturday bouquet. I hope Linda, wherever she is, will forgive my sister for removing a few flowers from her gravesite.

I scan every name on every tombstone. I see more than a dozen marked with KILGORE, who must be some relation though I don't know how. The grave I'm searching for is in the shadow of a large magnolia whose fat white blooms are just beginning to bud.

Big bold letters on a marble stone. LEONARD. Then underneath, in script:

Steven Andrew Leonard
Beloved son, husband, and father.
Sept. 9, 1960—Nov. 3, 1995

It's a tribute to a husband, but Andy's is a single tombstone, no room there for Sandi. As foolish as it may seem, I start to weep. How could I have forgotten his first name was Steven? This small detail overwhelms me. I cry a long time, sitting there on the cool ground in my sister's borrowed T-shirt and flippy pink skirt.

I tell Andy about it all.

About all the years since I last saw him in his brother Freddy's trailer. About the time I spent at my "high and mighty" college, when my life in Randolph Gap was already starting to fade in my memory.

I tell him about my marriage to Turner and how, despite all the years we've been together, I'm left wondering if we really know each other at all; if we would, faced with the decision today, even choose to be together.

I tell him about Donna Lindsey and Wanda McNabb, whose confessions over the past year have left me bewildered, sometimes envious, but, in the end, uneasy and a little frightened that I might choose to follow either of their paths.

I tell him about my family here, and how I'm feeling myself drawn back to them in some fundamental way.

I tell him about my baby Margaret with her ten toes and ten fingerprints.

I tell him all the things that seem to matter to me most.

I make my full confession.

And I believe in my heart that I am, at last, heard. That in the telling of my story, I'm finally beginning to understand it myself.

I expect the people in my life to wind up dead on the highway.

I expect them to be taken up in the rapture.

I expect to be left alone in the end, but it's better if those I love are taken by force instead of through their own willpower.

My husband passed away this year sounds a heck of a lot better than *My husband left me.*

My family was swept up by Jesus, I could say. Not, *Sometimes I'd like to run as far away from them as I can and never look back.*

Maybe this is it. This is what I fear the most.

I'm guilty of not loving these people the way I should. And for that, I deserve to be punished. I know then that I'm not a coldhearted killer. That my obsessive dreams of my husband's death, sadly, are a symptom of a more gradual heartbreak. That my very real fears of losing him, of growing away from him and from our life together, have taken shape not with any newfound desire to shoot him through the heart or put poison in his meat loaf, but with his falling victim to chance.

If it happened like I've dreamed, I wouldn't have to summon the courage to say good-bye.

 *THIRTY-SEVEN*

I open my eyes to a shadow crawling toward me in the grass. There are no footsteps that I can hear. Overhead, the leaves of the magnolias crack against each other in what sounds like a thousand random messages in Morse code. The figure on the grass is wide in the middle and slightly stooped, head dropped below the shoulders like a giant turtle and braced against the wind. I fear one of the reverends Wheeling has sent one of the Randolph Gap Holy Rockers out here to get some report from me about why I'm making a spectacle of myself in the church cemetery. Yet the voice I hear is as familiar as the sound of my own, even more deep-rooted in my memory.

"I come out here sometimes myself. Peaceful place, don't you think?"

In the distance, I can still hear the music from the church, where my mother is supposed to be, belting out hymns with Inez Sneed at her side.

"What are you doing, Mama?" I'm hoping I can cover up the fact that I've been sitting here crying for the better part of the morning service, but the question comes out sounding harsh and agitated, not what I intended at all.

"Oh, honey, I've heard Floyd Junior's sermon a dozen times already. Does a fine job, don't get me wrong, but he's never going to be the kind of preacher his father was in his day." She starts fanning herself with her Bible, holding it by its thickly cracked spine, the well-thumbed pages fluttering in the strong breeze.

"Does that train still pass by here?" I ask, remembering the elder Rev. Wheeling's voice thundering out his alarm-inducing, altar-call message.

"Don't hardly run anymore these days. The mill closed down sometime around, oh, I guess it must have been 1983 or '84. Not much to deliver with the mill closed. Only thing we get now is airplanes. Airplanes and helicopters, this way and that all day long. I can't imagine what they're doing up there all the time." She holds a hand over her eyes while she searches the sky. Sure enough she finds one, but the plane's flying so high that all we can see is its vapor trail, inching above the clouds in a silent, steady line.

"Brought a lot of people to the Lord, that train." My mother grimaces in the direction of the tracks, as if there is a direct correlation between the train's absence and a noticeable drop in the number of souls saved during the past two decades.

"I don't want you to worry yourself, but I'm startin' to get those flashes," she announces, and starts fanning herself again. "It can be thirty degrees outside, but me, I'll be burning up inside. That's what happened when I was driving that new car. One minute I'm fine, the next, well, I just don't know what happens." With the Bible aloft, she pulls a crisp white handkerchief from a sleeve of her dress, where she's kept it tucked under her watchband. She shakes it open and wipes it across her flushed cheeks. It bears the fresh creases of an iron, and a heavy starching.

"It's okay, Mama. About the car."

"I hope you and Turner have somewhere nice picked out," she says, changing the subject. "Somewhere nice" means a nice double cemetery plot.

"We haven't given it much thought, Mama," I reply. That's not exactly true. The Maddox clan has a sizable family plot and crypt—in, of all places, the Forget-Me-Not section of Glenville Memory Gardens—but the thought of my being planted there for eternity beside all those Maddoxes fills me with an unspeakable dread. The thought of facing Turner over the breakfast table on Monday, his face shielded by a curtain of newspaper, is bad enough.

"There's room here if you want. I come out here sometimes to see where your father and I are going to be, just to look things over." Picking a suitable spot for burial is serious business in Randolph Gap. I wonder if my mother thinks regular visits to her grave site will take some of the surprise out of dying.

"Your father and I had planned to be buried in the old section, near my parents, but we changed our minds. It's quieter in our new place, and there's more shade. We'll be just over there, near that dog-wood." With her handkerchief, she points to a location a dozen or so rows to the right of Andy Leonard's. She sniffs the air deeply, as if confirming by scent or temperature that her chosen section of the cemetery clearly is the more desirable.

"You want to see it? We've got a real pretty tombstone." She lets the Bible drop to her side, then whips the handkerchief up her left sleeve. She does a little pirouette in the grass, expecting me to follow.

"Maybe in a little while."

"Well, all right," she says, and comes to a halt.

My refusal has insulted her. She goes from chatty to dispirited.

"I'm sorry, Mama. Can't we just sit here for a few minutes?"

"Sit wherever you want."

When I look up at her, the sun is almost directly behind the mass of curls piled on top of her head. She remains standing. There is, I realize, no proper place for her to sit, unless she wants to join me on the ground beside Andy's grave. She looks in the other direction, a hand pressed against the rear of her hair's updo. I can hear her sniffing the air again.

"I don't see why you don't want to work somewhere nice, like in a sweet little store. A school, maybe. Like where your friend Donna works? It's a nice store, isn't it?"

"I'm not sure she's going to be working there after this weekend."

"Why on earth not?"

"Let's not talk about this now. Okay?"

"Isn't it a nice store?"

"I guess so. I mean, yes. It is."

"Some place where they have security guards? Where people don't go around biting each other?"

"We've got security guards."

"Lot of good they do."

"They need me at the clinic, Mama." I can see Melvin Spivey's wide and drooling face when, after he bit me, he presented me with a handcrafted get-well card, the look of drugged intensity in his eyes when he told me all of his enemies were dead. He'd looked like a child awakened from a nightmare, eyes full of sleep, not yet believing that the dream was over, that monsters still lurked underneath the bed.

"Well, I can't see why. I don't see why you can't listen to your own mother. Why you won't act rational about—"

"Mother, please."

"—things when I'm just telling you for your own good. Turner thinks—"

"I don't care what Turner thinks."

"Well, you should. You should pay some attention to what he thinks. He's the only one in this entire family who's got a level head on his shoulders. He's been good to you this past year, with all the trouble you've had. He's trying the best he knows how."

"Can't you just let things be?"

"And here he is, the only one in this family who's made something of himself and you're trying to bring him down. You and Ellen are just alike. You don't know a good thing when you've got one." She lets out a monumental sigh, as if it's just occurred to her that her daughters are a terrible disappointment and that, despite her efforts, both of us are headed for certain ruin in the marriage department.

"I can see things coming, whether you believe it or not. I don't understand why you can't be happy. I don't understand why your sister does the things she does, when Cecil's been a good husband and a father to that boy. I don't—"

"Are we talking about me or Ellen?"

"All I've ever wanted is for you girls to be happy."

"I am happy, Mama."

"You think you'd be happier with Andy here? With a dead husband on your hands? With no family to come home to?"

"I don't have children to come home to now."

"I didn't mean it like that and you know it," she says. She removes her handkerchief from her sleeve again and starts twisting it in her hands, then using her palms to flatten it out against her dress like a limp scrap of cookie dough.

"You've got to get over this, Jessie. You and Turner should try right away to have another baby. Miracles can happen, you know." She stares down at Andy's grave. "I thought you two might get married, you and Andy, and stay here and have children, but then you left." She lets the sentence drop. My desire to leave Randolph Gap is yet another disappointment, one she can't bring herself to discuss. I look to the sky and there's another plane, this one laying down an identical white line in the opposite direction.

"Why don't you see one of those fertility doctors like we talked about?"

"We didn't talk about it, Mama. You talked about it."

"Well, still," she says. "It's an idea. You can't wait too much longer or—"

"Or what? I'll be too old?"

"I wasn't going to say that," she says. "I saw on TV the other day where a woman in her fifties had a baby. Can you imagine?"

"I don't want to see any more doctors right now."

"Well, then, you could adopt."

"Mama, please. I don't want to talk about this."

"Well, if you can't talk about it with your own mother, I don't know who you can talk to about it."

"I kidnapped the green duck last night," I announce.

"You what?"

"I just told you. That duck. I kidnapped him and set him free." I don't mention that I also spent the previous evening with Andy Leonard's widow, or that she and Cecil are probably having breakfast in her kitchen at this very minute.

"That's the most ridiculous thing I've ever heard."

"You remember that duck, don't you? Used to sit right inside the door? Somebody cut off his head and I had to sew it back on, but I did it and now he's free."

"If you ever thought I'd set foot in that place, you've got another thing coming. You ought to know better."

"I loved that duck."

She's silent for a moment.

"Somebody cut off his head?" she asks.

"But now he's free. He's probably floating in the Gulf of Mexico by now."

"Why would somebody cut off that duck's head? That's the most—"

"It made me happy, setting him free."

"—ridiculous thing."

"It's the first thing that's made me happy. First thing in a long, long time."

She looks at me as if this irrelevant confession has sent a shock through her body that's led her to another very real conclusion: that her definition of happiness is far different from mine, and always will be. She moves backward a step or two, as if pushed by some unknown force, spreads out her handkerchief on the edge of a tombstone marked WEAVER, and lets her weight fall onto it. *Thomas J. Weaver, Beloved Husband and Father, April 20, 1932–Oct. 29, 1988.* It's a sizable, sturdy stone, so maybe Mr. Weaver won't mind her sitting there.

Her handkerchief otherwise engaged, she uses a sleeve of her dress to blot the sweat beading on her forehead.

"Before I married your daddy," she says, "there was someone else. His name was Earl Pate. Your father always said Earl was an old fool, but he wasn't an old fool back then. He gave me a gold locket once, on my birthday. He was my first love."

She brushes a ringlet of graying hair from her cheek, where it has freed itself from the clump that circles her head. It is a small act, this brushing away of a loose curl, yet it softens her features somehow. In an instant it transforms her into a more vulnerable, more fragile creature—a girl who long ago chose to marry my father instead of Earl Pate. I remember a photograph of her at age seventeen, a girl with shining eyes and one chipped front tooth. A girl with long blond hair rolled upward in the latest Hollywood fashion, a tortoiseshell clip securing it above her right ear. In that photograph she was wearing a dress with an eyelet lace collar, and an engraved gold locket fell over the lace and into the hollow space at her neck.

"Your father doesn't know it either, but I went to Earl's funeral. Even visited his grave a few times after that, over at the city cemetery. Nice little section, even if it is near the highway."

I open my mouth to say something, but she holds up a hand in protest.

"Just let me say this, Jessie," she says. "I love your daddy, but he wouldn't understand me going to see Earl like I do." She looks at me as if to say Turner wouldn't understand it either, this need of mine to recapture a moment in my past by visiting Andy Leonard's grave.

"I talk to Earl sometimes too, but mostly I just sit in the cemetery and talk to myself. I keep expecting I'll cry for him, but I never can."

"I just wanted to see where Andy was buried. I just—" but I find myself unable to find the right words.

I want, then, to tell her everything. The countless lonely nights spent with my husband, the guilt and fear rising up from the dreams that wake me in the middle of the night, the anguish and despair I see every day in my patients' eyes and, these days, am beginning to recognize in my own.

I want to make it all up to her in the telling.

I want to ask her what I should do, to be reassured with advice that's both kind and firm, and filled with a wisdom I don't possess. I want to hide my face in her skirts like a child, for her to wipe away my tears with her crisp white handkerchief, for her to pat my hand and tell me everything's going to be okay.

But I can't speak, and the moment when it could have happened, when everything could have changed between us, passes too quickly. Through the windows of the church behind us, I can hear more music rumbling out of Harvey Sneed's piano, and the voices of the congregation again singing the same song.

> *Some glad morning when this life is o'er*
> *I'll fly a-way, fly a-way; fly a-way;*
> *To a home on God's celestial shore,*
> *I'll fly away, fly a-way; fly a-way.*

My mother hears it too. Her lips are moving, and I know she's singing the words to herself.

> *I'll fly a-way, fly a-way, O glory,*
> *I'll fly a-way, fly a-way in the morning*
> *When I die, hallelujah, by and by,*
> *I'll fly a-way.*

My mother hoists herself up the tombstone, folds her handkerchief again and palms it. She starts walking back to the church, clapping her hands, the sound muffled by the cloth against her fingers. She's anxious to rejoin the congregation. Inside that sanctuary she can be heard. She's at home among these people, much more comfortable there than with her daughter.

"You see the doctor, okay?" I say. "About your hot flashes."

She gives me a little wave I can't interpret.

> *When the shadows of this life have grown,*
> *I'll fly a-way, fly a-way; fly a-way;*
> *Like a bird from prison bars has flown,*
> *I'll fly a-way, fly a-way; fly a-way.*

"Promise?"

"I'll see the doctor as soon as you see one," she says, then waves again. She doesn't look back.

My mother has flown away from me again, or me from her. The way it happened depends on which one of us you ask.

 *THIRTY-EIGHT*

O Lord, support us all the day long, until the shadows lengthen, and the evening comes, and the busy world is hushed, and the fever of life is over, and our work is done. Then in thy mercy, grant us a safe lodging, and a holy rest, and peace at the last. Amen.

PRAYERS AND THANKSGIVINGS

THE BOOK OF COMMON PRAYER

I walk into a small rectangular lobby stuffed with wicker furnishings and glass lamps filled with seashells, the room itself no bigger than the back of Donna Lindsey's minivan. The air smells like it's been blasted with coconut oil, but it's not enough to mask the pungent odor of cigar smoke.

Along one wall is an unsteady wicker rack full of brochures, all about places no one ever plans to visit when they check in here. Rodeos and giant flea markets. Civil War museums and folk art galleries. Gun and knife shows. Everything in the rack is covered with a thick layer of dust and most of the flyers are stuck together like bricks, as if they've survived a flood and are now glued together by mud and mildew. In another corner is a small table with an odd array of tourist gifts. Drink koozies and ball caps bearing an assortment of slogans from the silly to the insulting. There's music coming from somewhere, music that must be intended to set some kind of exotic-holiday-toes-in-the-sand kind of mood, but it's so full of xylophone and bongos that it ends up sounding like someone punched Caribbean on an electronic keyboard and let it go at that.

On this misty Sunday evening with more rain in the forecast, I've landed like a sailor blown off course, at the Bay Island Hotel, just off Interstate 124, near enough to Glenville but far enough from home. Other, more respectable hotels surround it—big chains with big recognizable names and big recognizable billboards on the interstate, all offering "family friendly" discounts of one kind or another—but the Bay Island Hotel is the lone siren's song. In the midst of all this wholesomeness, it alone beckons restless travelers looking for vibrating beds, straying spouses planning libidinous afternoons, traveling salesmen anxious to provide such comfort. Out front there's a huge plastic sign shaped like a palm tree, the outline of which is bordered in neon. Lucky for me, Sunday must not be the most popular of days here. There are only four other cars in the parking lot, and Donna Lindsey's powder blue minivan isn't one of them. I'd thought I might find her still here, but she must be on her way home by now, to her own husband and family on Shadowwood Lane.

From behind a thick glass partition a dim bulb switches on and the proprietor, at last, decides to make an entrance, a half-eaten slice of pizza hanging between his thick lips. He slides an index card under a half-moon cutout in the glass, which is, I notice, several inches thick. Bulletproof. His clothes, a yellowing V-neck undershirt and gray sweatpants, are rumpled, as if my arrival this late in the afternoon has interrupted his eating pizza in bed and he's none too happy about it. His eyebrows point directly at me, almost perpendicular from the rest of his face, and when he rubs his eyes sleepily, a glob of pizza sauce gets stuck there in the wiry outgrowth.

"You gonna fill that out or what?"

"I need a room. A single."

"Is that right?" He could care less who I am, or what I need, as long as I'm quick about it.

"A single." I feel like I need to emphasize my arriving alone. Like this is a virtue he should respect.

"Water?"

"What?"

"A water bed, lady."

"No. A real bed is fine."

"Ones we got here are waveless. Top of the line. Won't rock and roll you around all night. Course, if that's what you're after—" He narrows his eyes and gives me a sidelong smirk.

"Just a regular bed. Please."

"Sure, sure. But you're missing out on a real treat. Be $59.99 plus tax. Your pay-per-view's extra. It's $59 'cause the only thing I have in a *regular bed* is a king. Most folks like our water beds here."

"Just for the night."

"Look, lady, your business is your business. Now, you want to sign?"

I fill in the index card and slide it back under the glass with a credit card. He lets the pizza slice drop to the counter in front of him and rings me up. He gives me a real metal key, not a plastic card like most places use these days. It dangles from a key ring that has a little plastic palm tree attached. For Donna Lindsey and Perry Ferguson, this was the key to happiness, however brief, however foolish.

"Got toothbrushes if you need one," he says, peering through the glass to find that I'm standing in his lobby without luggage of any kind. "Toothpaste too. Shampoo. Whatever a lady like you might need."

"I don't need anything."

"Didn't say you did. Just letting you know." He picks up his pizza again and resumes chewing.

When I step back from the glass, I'm startled to find that the Bay Island Hotel lobby has dedicated itself not only to the preservation of long-forgotten tourist attractions and memorabilia, but also to the conversion of the lost souls who come through its doors.

A bumper sticker pasted to the glass reads: JESUS IS MY COPILOT.

The slogan posted above a photograph of a blond surfer, arms outstretched as he tops the crest, is: Surfing the Wave of Living Waters.

Another one, also a bumper sticker, says: W.W.J.D.

And so on. There are more stuck to or around the glass and its seashells.

"What's this one mean?" I ask, pointing to the acronym I don't recognize, but he's busy with his pizza again, and doesn't seem to hear me. I have to rap on the glass to get his attention.

"W.W.J.D.? What's that mean?"

"That? Oh, that's one of them 'What Would Jesus Do?' things. Wife got religion about six months ago and puts them on everything. Stuck four on the bumpers of my brand-new Cadillac, two in front and two in back, which I could've darn near killed her for doing, ruining a good car like that. Even bought herself this fancy little silver bracelet that says that. Wears it all the time."

"You didn't get religion with her?"

"Naaaaw. She won't work the front desk for me no more either, but still keeps the books. I've got to where I don't pay much attention to what she does long as she keeps the books straight."

"What would Jesus do," I say, repeating the phrase to myself.

"Yeah, you know. Like, what would Jesus do if he was in this or that situation."

"Oh."

"I guess it's what you'd call one of those philly-sophical questions."

"You don't have those for sale, do you?"

"You want one?"

"I'd like to buy one, yes." I decide I'll send the sticker to my mother as a peace offering. She could put it on the front bumper of her Lincoln Town Car, provided she gets it replaced.

"Wife'd be more than happy to give you one, but like I said, she ain't here. Don't have any I can sell you."

"What would Jesus do? I mean, if he were here?" This is out of my mouth before I realize I've said it out loud. In the hazy glow of the dilapidated Bay Island Hotel lobby, the very idea smacks of blasphemy so severe that I catch myself trembling in my thin raincoat. I haven't bothered to change clothes, and underneath I'm still wearing my sister's white T-shirt and pink skirt from the night before.

"Look, lady, if I was you, I mean, if Jesus was you, I'd tell you to go on down to your room and get you some rest. Look a little jumpy, if you ask me."

"Well, I was just wondering."

As I walk down the long hallway, I pass a mural that must once have depicted a romantic moonlit beach. The paper's peeling and there's a smattering of graffiti scrawled across the beach where seashells should be.

"Hey lady," he calls after me. "There's a Bible in that room. It's one of them the Gideons give us, but it should do just fine."

&

I stretch out on the scratchy chintz bedspread in room 107 and stare at my reflection on the ceiling. I should have known. Even with a real bed I get a mirror. Not much of the evening sun filters through the drawn curtains, but what comes in has a bluish cast. A cheap tropical print is bolted above the headboard. There's beach grass in the foreground, the obligatory sunset, and footprints in the sand. Vintage 1970s stuff, and faded.

I find the Bible in the top drawer of the nightstand. Sure enough, the Gideons have left it here for me, a woman in need of comfort. When I open it, the binding makes a crackling sound, like it's being opened for the first time. The inside cover advises me that I can contact Gideons in my area by looking them up in the local telephone directory, and for a moment, I consider doing this. I've never met a Gideon in person and don't know anyone who has, so the idea of talking to an actual Gideon is strangely appealing. Do they have a secret handshake, like the Elks or the Masons? My mother might be a Gideon and I wouldn't even know it.

I flip through the pages until I come to Psalms, ready to dial up not one of the Gideons, but one of my mother's Emergency Phone Numbers. Psalm 27 is what I'm looking for, the one that's supposed to be the answer for depression and troubles with men.

The LORD is my light and my salvation; whom shall I fear?
The LORD is the strength of my life; of whom shall I be afraid?

When the wicked, even mine enemies and my foes, came upon
me to eat up my flesh, they stumbled and fell.

I can't quite figure out exactly how this applies either to depression or to men, but I keep reading. The answer must be in here somewhere.

*THIRTY-NINE*

I haven't seen Wanda McNabb since our trip to the cemetery, when she told me who pulled the trigger that awful night in her sewing room. She canceled her next appointment with me, and the one after that, and I know this means she won't be coming back to the Glenville Wellness Center, not to see me and not to bring cookies to the members of her support group. The confession she made that day was her way of saying good-bye.

I'd needed more than that; knew I couldn't let her go so easily. After I drove away from Randolph Gap this afternoon, I first headed not east toward Glenville, but south, toward Bessemer, Alabama.

I parked across the street from the house at 19 Oak Springs

Avenue. In a corner of the front lawn was a child's wading pool, an assortment of toys left bobbing in one sloping corner, where the night's rain had filled the pool to overflowing. In the driveway next to two cars were two children's bicycles and a basketball hoop mounted on a pole. An orange cat reclined, grooming a paw, on the small concrete porch, and the Sunday newspaper lay undisturbed there too, rolled in its plastic bag. Easter eggs were strung through a budding azalea bush near the door, their plastic surfaces glistening with the morning's rain, like strange ripe fruit. There was a stillness here, at this house and at all the houses on this small street. The only sounds were birds singing, and the rustling of the new leaves in the trees.

A woman answered the door.

"Mrs. McNabb?"

"Yes?" she said, smiling, then looked beyond me to my Explorer parked on her street. "You need help? Car break down?"

"No, ma'am," I said. "I'd like to speak with your husband, if I could."

"You from the school? I already explained to the principal why the twins were out last week." Through the open door I could see them, girls ten, maybe eleven years old, doing a puzzle on the coffee table in the front room.

"I'm not from the school," I said. "I'm sorry, but I really need to speak with Mr. McNabb. Privately if I could." Then after a moment, "Please."

"Baxter?" she called into the house. She stood with a hand on the open door, but did not invite me inside. I understood her uneasiness, but didn't know what else to do.

"My name is Jessie Maddox," I said when he met me at the door. I offered him my hand, but he didn't take it.

"Let's talk outside," he said. "You want a beer or something? Honey, get us a few beers, will you?" Wanda had shown me pictures of her children, and of Baxter. The son's resemblance to his father was strong. He had the same thin and muscular build, the angular line of jaw and heavy brows that made his eyes look deeply set, shielded from the direct gaze of others.

I followed him to the front lawn, where he unfolded two low-slung beach chairs beside the wading pool and offered me one. I apologized for having disturbed him on a Sunday afternoon. His wife, still wary and studying my every move, brought the beer—three long-neck Budweisers—and stood beside us, not saying a word.

"Thanks, hon," he said. "Go on inside with the girls now. Seems we've got a little something to discuss." She walked slowly toward the house, glancing back at us a few times, then disappeared.

He popped the tops of two of the bottles and held one out to me. After the night I'd had, I was in no mood for beer, especially not at that hour, but I took a few polite sips.

"My mother told me about you," he said. "So I know who you are and why you're here. I didn't think you'd actually come, but she said you might."

This disarmed and unsettled me. The boundary I'd crossed between counselor and client had dissolved completely.

"She trusts you," he said. "Told me I might as well talk to you because you weren't going to the police. If you were planning to do that you'd have done it by now."

"Your mother's been through a lot," I said. "I just want to know she'll be all right, that there'll be someone to take care of her."

"Why don't you tell me why you're really here," he said, draining his beer and reaching for the other. The briefest of leers formed around his eyes and his mouth and then vanished, leaving me to wonder if I'd misinterpreted what I'd seen.

"I'm trying to understand what really happened," I said, stumbling over my words.

"No you're not," he said. He said this with a certain finality and confidence, with the voice of a man who knew far more about my relationship with his mother than I would have dared to guess, far more about me, and my own problems, than I wanted him to know. It left me vulnerable, and a little scared. I stood, moving away from him, and walked around the other side of the wading pool, bent down to pick up a toy boat that had sailed over the edge and into the grass.

"Look lady, I don't plan on killing anybody else," he said. "If that's what you're after, you've got the wrong man."

"What?" My head was spinning. "How could you—"

"She told me *all* about you," he said, and again grinned at me in that leering way of his. "The way I figure it, you wouldn't lose any sleep if your own husband was the one shot dead."

"She told you that?"

"Told me enough."

"Well, she told you wrong," I said.

"Whatever," he said, and finished his second beer.

"Just tell me why you did it and I'll leave," I said.

"You came all the way out here to ask me that?" he said. "If you did, you're the one who's crazy, not me."

"Just tell me. Tell me how you could do it."

If this man had shot his father to avenge years of abuse Wanda had suffered, I could understand that. He must have suffered, too. That's what I still needed to believe, but I wasn't sure what was true anymore.

"You get your kicks this way?" he said, laughing at me. "You get your answer and you'll go off feeling all better, like you've cracked the case or something? You'll have us all figured out then, won't you. You can run off all pleased with yourself, ready to help some other poor son of a bitch with his problems."

"I don't think that," I said, and felt a tear on my cheek. "I don't know what to think anymore."

"He took the life out of her, don't you know that?" he said. "It was time somebody took his."

"And you did it?"

"Hell yeah, I'm the one who did it. Proudest day of my life."

I wanted to run across the lawn and get as far away from him as I could.

"Better take one last long look, lady," he said, laughing even harder. "Ain't every day you get to drink a beer with a cold-blooded murderer."

 *FORTY*

here on my bed in the Bay Island Hotel, my mind drifts again to my youth and home. I'm on the stage of the Randolph Gap High School auditorium, flubbing my lines. I'm sixteen years old, in rehearsal for *The Glass Menagerie*, my first and only starring role.

Andy Leonard sits in the empty auditorium, near the back, but he's making faces at me and I can't remember my lines. This is our last rehearsal before the big dress rehearsal the next day, and the production opens the day after that.

I'm playing Laura, and we're almost to the end, in the seventh scene, but I've had to keep calling for my lines. Calvin Thacker, a senior and a self-proclaimed "serious" student of the theater, plays the role of Jim. Every time I call for a line, he throws his hands in the air and says, "For Christ's sake!"

Opening night will be a disaster, I just know it. Nobody at Randolph Gap High School would even come to something like this, but all the English teachers say it's mandatory. I'll throw up onstage. People will throw tomatoes. Sandi Moore, who would become Sandi Leonard, will be in the audience that night, and I won't even know it. Won't know until years later, after all this should have been forgotten.

Calvin and I are at the part where Laura has just shown Jim the glass unicorn in her collection. The Randolph Gap High School marching band, less a few of its more boisterous instruments, tunes up. There's no orchestra pit, so they're backstage, just beyond the innermost curtain. Even at sixteen, I can't imagine Tennessee Williams would have approved of this version, so I get the giggles. Calvin tries to act like nothing's happened so he can get this whole rehearsal over with and get as far away from me as possible, but I know he's plenty mad.

Correct to the script, Calvin sweeps across the stage with his arms held out to me. I look across the auditorium at Andy and give him a wink, even though I know he probably can't see it from where he sits.

I'm supposed to act breathless here, and protest that I can't dance, but I can't help myself. I end up giggling again, this time uncontrollably. Tears are streaming down my cheeks.

Calvin's doing his best to stay in character, but he starts throwing nasty looks offstage, where our drama coach is stationed.

I have to call for my line. This gets me another nasty look from Calvin. When he takes me in his arms, his anger at me is obvious.

His arms around me are so tight I can hardly breathe. I'm trapped in his grip. I get through the next few lines, but just barely.

Calvin swings me into motion and we're dancing across the stage. We spin around and around, as clumsily and as jerkily as poodles. The drama coach says this is what we're supposed to be doing. "Make it clumsy, Jessie. Our Laura isn't exactly a showgirl."

From the back of the auditorium I can hear Andy Leonard laughing too, but it's a laugh sweet and bright, not at all rehearsed. Not a gentle ha-ha, but a real guffaw. Andy's not much for going to the theater. His thick legs are propped up on the seat in front of him and his hands are folded behind his head. Fresh from a shower after football practice.

What was he thinking in that auditorium, sitting in the back by himself, watching me stumble around onstage? That I was his girl? That he would, that summer, take me to his brother Freddy's trailer?

From my room in the Bay Island Hotel I can hear doors opening and closing in the narrow hallway. There's a shower going full blast in an adjacent room. There's the rush of cars and eighteen-wheelers on the interstate, where the asphalt is incandescent with rain and floodlights in the copper glow of the evening. There will be rain all night.

All around me everyone is rushing, rushing, rushing.

To be somewhere else.

With someone else.

Attacking their lives with itineraries and agendas and plans for tomorrow. Trying, maybe, to keep something of themselves alive.

I think of that day in the trailer, and Andy, breathless from the heat and our fumblings on the leatherette sofa. I can see how he looked at me when it was over, remember the deep emptiness and regret when I saw in his eyes that he could, maybe not that day or even a year later but on some day in the future, raise his fist to me. That one day he, too, could be capable of swinging a baseball bat at my head. That I could, in my desperation or uncertainty, ask someone to kill him for me, just as Wanda had asked her son, or kill him myself. That it would have happened, in some way just like that, if I'd stayed in Randolph Gap and become his wife, raised his children.

If I'd stayed, he'd have taken the life out of me too.

Mildred Collier, on this Sunday afternoon, was in another room—room 235 of the Glenville Medical Center, her husband Houston stiffly anchored to a Naugahyde chair by her bed. Four days after the EMTs took her away from Shadowwood Lane, she had a severe stroke, and the doctors told Houston it was "only a matter of time," that all they could do was keep her comfortable. The peace lily I sent them sat in her hospital window for several days, but wilted because nobody except Mildred would have remembered to water it.

Donna Lindsey eventually made her own way back to Shadowwood Lane, and on this Sunday afternoon sat watching a basketball game with her husband and sons, on their big-screen TV. She made popcorn for the boys, and as they sat there together, she tried not to think about Perry Ferguson, or why she left the Bay Island Hotel and came home instead of packing her bags for a new life in Montana. She was already making other plans, her thoughts turning to her department store's assistant manager, Lawrence Sparks. He might, she thinks, be more solicitous of her affections, certainly more polite about ending things when the time came. Married, mid-forties, three children. A good and safe candidate, to her way of thinking. If only people didn't call him Larry. A safe enough sounding name, but she can't imagine screwing someone named Larry.

Wanda McNabb was at Glenville's Senior Citizens Recreation Center, where she'd win first prize and a $25 gift certificate at the Winn-Dixie for her recipe for chocolate caramel cookies. I read about this later in the *Glenville News-Tribune* and clipped her cookie recipe to add to my files.

I've already called Teresa Floyd at the Glenville Wellness Center to request some personal time, and she's agreed. Client appointments will be canceled or assigned to other caseworkers in my absence.

"When will you be back?" she'd asked.

I had to tell her I didn't know, and couldn't explain. "I just need a little time. To work some things out," I'd told her. I have five weeks of unused vacation coming to me anyhow. I hope that will be enough.

"Sure you're okay? Do you need me to do anything for you?"

I said I was fine, that there wasn't anything she could do. Teresa seemed to understand.

I knew Wanda wouldn't be coming back, but I needed time away from all of it. I'd gotten too close, too fast. She'd told me too much, and I'd asked too much in return. I also knew, as her son had predicted, that I wouldn't be calling the police, that her secrets—and his—were safe with me. I knew I'd have to live with that. Live with the burden of my knowing, and, to no small extent, my own bad judgment in overstepping my role as her caseworker. Of all of this, the greatest challenge was my doing nothing.

By late afternoon, Cecil returned to my parents' house. This time, for reasons unknown to everyone, my sister chose to talk to him, and they sat together at the kitchen table holding hands and whispering. Not wanting to interrupt and feeling generous toward this reconciliation in his midst, my father changed the tire on my mother's Lincoln Town Car and took her and Justin for another driving lesson. Just down the road and back again.

I close my eyes and can see myself standing in front of the closet I've shared with Turner for these many years, my face pressed against a row of his starched and pressed shirts, where I've ripped a face-size opening in the plastic laundry bag that contains them.

"Jessie, what on earth are you doing?"

It's Turner's voice at the door. A voice that, on that spring day in the early years of our marriage, could do all those things that people tell you love, in all its surprising forms, is supposed to do.

"I just wanted you close. I just—"

I can't forget those moments, can't make myself believe there wasn't tenderness in his heart, that there wasn't something like love between us.

So on this night, let me feel only this.

The caress of his hand as he lifts my hair from my neck.

His kisses, which were, on that day and in all the times I remember, tentative and true.

There's a phone by the bed.

I could pick it up.

I could call.

There are things I need to say. Things I need to find the words to explain.

"Turner?"

"Hi, hon," he says, a bit groggy. Maybe I've caught him napping in his chair in front of the television.

"I'm staying a while longer."

There's a brief pause while he considers this. "Are your parents okay? Has something happened?"

"They're fine. I'm just tired."

"Stay as long as you want. You need some time away from that place." That place being the Glenville Wellness Center. "Maybe you need some time away from me, too?"

"Turner?"

"Yeah?" If he notices I haven't answered his last question, he doesn't say anything.

"Do you remember that time we were in the backyard and raked all the leaves in one giant pile and jumped into it together? You wanted to make love to me there, right there in those leaves, but I was afraid the neighbors would see us?"

He laughs at this. "We never would have done it. We could have been arrested."

"Well, I wish we could do that. I mean, I wish we'd done it."

"You want to do that?"

"Not now, Turner. I just wish we'd done it then."

"Jessie, are you all right?" he says. "Why are you asking about this? That happened when we were newlyweds."

"Because I need to, Turner. I need to remember. I've been thinking about things. About us."

"You want me to make love to you outdoors so we can get arrested for indecent exposure?"

I've stretched the telephone cord across the bed. I'm lying on the bed, staring up at my naked body. My breasts are sagging on either side, the nipples pale and dimpled. There's a fold of flesh that crosses my abdomen above my pubic hair, which, much to my alarm, seems to be thinning and turning prematurely gray. I lift my left arm and jiggle the flesh hanging near my armpit. I haven't shaved for days. It's hard for me to imagine anyone wanting to make love to this body in a pile of backyard leaves, or anywhere else for that matter.

"I miss Margaret," I say.

"Oh, God. Oh, honey, I know you do. So do I." I can hear ice clinking in a glass. He must be mixing a drink.

"We'll try again," he says. "You know that."

"I don't know what I know anymore," I say. "I still blame myself. For everything."

"It wasn't your fault. It wasn't anybody's fault."

"I know, but—"

"You *know* that, don't you? That it wasn't your fault?"

"I guess."

"We can go see the doctor again when you get home," he says. "In fact, we'll see a different doctor."

I'm not sure if I'm ready to see another doctor. I raise my legs off the bed and try to imagine how I must look in the doctor's stirrups.

"Turner?"

"Yes, hon?"

"What were you doing putting together Mrs. Farmer's desk the other day at work?"

"She told you about that?"

"Yeah, she did. She said you were humming."

"I don't know," he says. "I always used to help my father fix things around the house when I was a boy. He'd let me hold his tool-box, and when he asked for a tool I'd give it to him. I guess that's what I was thinking about. That was a happy time for me."

I think of all the things in our lives that need fixing. Maybe putting together Mrs. Farmer's desk was the one thing Turner could fix—the one thing he could look at and say, *I did that. I'm proud of that.*

"I miss you, Jessie. Come on home."

"You do?"

"Sure I do."

"It's raining here." I can hear the rain dripping from the hotel roof outside my window.

"Is it?" he asks. Then, "You sure you're okay?"

"Yeah, I'm fine. I'm, well, I'm trying."

"I love you, you know."

I don't say anything. I can see his face, mouthing those words as he's done a thousand times before. I try to remember that I love him in return.

"You know I do," he says.

"Yeah, I know," I say. As I put the phone in its cradle, I can almost believe there is a new beginning in store for us. That if we try hard enough, we can find a new and beautiful future.

For now, let me live now only in room 107 of the Bay Island Hotel, where I am safe from all my obligations and my guilt. I don't have a plan. I don't know how long I'll stay. I press my face into the pillows. Regular hotel pillows for a regular hotel bed. They're freshly laundered and white, sheets cool to the touch.

When I close my eyes again, I am waltzing. Not with Calvin Thacker, but with my husband. With the man who is waiting for me on Shadowwood Lane in his own quiet, uncomplicated way. He doesn't even realize I need to be forgiven, that I need to find my way home again, but he will be there, I know, and I will be grateful.

Around and around the room we spin. We're waltzing awkward and clumsy, but waltzing still, and in his welcoming and familiar arms, I fall into the trusted unknown, into a free and dreamless sleep.